THE FOURTH GIFT

By Elizabeth Borton de Treviño

THE FOURTH GIFT

WHERE THE HEART IS

THE GREEK OF TOLEDO

EVEN AS YOU LOVE

MY HEART LIES SOUTH

THE FOURTH GIFT

Elizabeth Borton de Treviño

1966

DOUBLEDAY & COMPANY, INC., GARDEN CITY, NEW YORK

This book is a work of fiction, and does not pretend to be a piece of history in any particular. None of the events related in this series of chronicles, against a general background of the Cristero uprising, is based on true happenings. None of the persons mentioned in the stories are real persons, either living or dead. Should names or characteristics resemble any real persons, living or dead, this is coincidence only. The towns mentioned in the stories are inventions of the author. While Guadalajara is the background of a few of the chronicles, none of the houses or places described as part of that city are real places.

TO MY MOTHER

HISTORICAL NOTE

In the long history of this troubled world, the recurrence of rebellions of citizens against the state is impressive down through the ages, whether the rebellions took place in organized form or as guerrilla warfare. Few nationalities exist today which did not fight against authority in one way or another; every history has its glorious pages of defiance. A great many rebellions have come into existence for the purpose of wrenching from governmental control rights believed to be inherent in, and sacred to, the individual. The most intensely felt of beliefs is the conviction that every man should be allowed to worship as he pleases, and if he pleases.

One of the most dramatic of recent struggles to reaffirm the right to worship in freedom took place in Mexico, officially in the years 1926 to 1929, though tension and fighting occupied more years than four.

In 1917 Mexican lawmakers, passionate defenders of freedom, sought to "free" the citizenry from their centuries-old devotion to the Catholic faith. In affirming the principle of separation of church and state, they went further, and made it clear that Mexico, ideally, should be completely nonreligious. No teaching of religion was to be permitted, and the Roman Catholic Church, to which 97 per cent of the Mexican people adhere, was deprived of all but a mere skeleton force of priests, quite unable to serve all the faithful.

Since the overwhelming majority of Mexicans are Catholics, of varying degrees of intensity of belief and practice, most national and local executives, despite the Constitution, refrained from enforcing it so vigorously as to eradicate religion from the life of the people. But the truce was an uneasy one: the people feared that some of the legal steps would cut them off from their faith; and the government, nonreligious in principle, held off for reasons of prudence.

In 1926 the Mexican President issued a series of decrees that rocked the citizenry. With the clear intent of the Constitution as his authority, and (some say) at the instigation of powerful figures in the country who were fanatically anti-church, he began a systematic attempt to root out religion effectively. Priests were expelled from the country, and all churches were ordered closed. Catholics found themselves deprived of the sacraments. As rebellion against the decrees became stiffer and more impassioned, the enforcement of the decrees was made more rigorous and more cruel. Resistance flared up everywhere.

It transpired once more, as has so often happened, that the best way to strengthen a faith is to persecute it, and the most effective means of uniting a people is to give them something to unite against.

Some sections of Mexico (notably Nuevo León) cannily fought the decrees with economic boycotts, and they had some measure of success, since governments are acutely sensitive to wounds in the income. Others simply went underground; private chapels functioned, and hundreds of priests were hidden and protected. In disguise and at the risk of their lives, they remained in the country to give the sacraments and to say Mass. A price was on the heads of many priests and bishops who remained amid, and sometimes part of, the struggle. Today great numbers of those same priests go quietly but openly about their priestly duties in a peaceful country.

It was in Jalisco and a few contiguous states that the rebellion grew fiercest and became a full-fledged guerrilla war, with armies, officers, raids, and battles. There were acts of cruelty and of sacrifice on both sides. In government circles the struggle was known as a rebellion; the people who fought against the government called themselves "Cristeros" and their movement a revolution. Their rallying cry was "¡Viva Cristo Rey!" (Long Live Christ the King!).

Eventually there was an amnesty and all who had fought with the Cristeros were pardoned. Officially, charges against them were dropped. The Catholic hierarchy urged the faithful to lay down their arms, and they were obeyed.

Any story of that time must of necessity be a story of Catholics and of the faith they were determined to defend.

CONTENTS

The Fourth Gift of the Holy Spirit is Fortitude.

PROLOGUE

Por la señal de la Santa Cruz, de nuestros enemigos líbranos, Señor, Dios nuestro. En el nombre del Padre, y del Hijo, y del Espíritu Santo, Amén.

Creo en un solo Dios, Padre Todopoderoso, creador del cielo y de la tierra, de todas las cosas visibles e invisibles. Y en un solo Señor Jesucristo, Hijo unigénito de Dios, y nacido del Padre antes de todos los siglos, Dios de Dios, luz de luz, Dios verdadero de Dios verdadero. Engendrado, no hecho; consubstancial al Padre, por quien todas las cosas fueron hechas. El cual por nosotros los hombres y por nuestra salvación bajó de los cielos. Y por obra del Espíritu Santo encarnó de María Virgen y se hizo hombre. Crucificado también por nosotros, bajo el poder de Poncio Pilato, padeció y fué sepultado. Y resucitó al tercer día, según las Escrituras. Y subió al cielo; está sentado a la diestra del Padre. Y ha de venir otra vez con gloria a juzgar a los vivos y a los muertos: y su reino no tendrá fin. Creo en el Espíritu Santo, Señor y vivificador, el cual procede del Padre y del Hijo, quien con el Padre y el Hijo juntamente es adorado y glorificado, el cual habló por los Profetas. Y creo en la Iglesia que es una, santa, católica y apostólica. Confieso un solo bautismo para perdón de los pecados. Y espero la resurrección de los muertos y la vida del siglo venidero. Amén.

PRAYER AND CREED AS PRAYED
BY ALL SPANISH-SPEAKING CATHOLICS.

I

"Ave María Purísima . . ."

I am Chela. You understand, this is my nickname, my affectionate diminutive. My baptismal name was María Graciela Manuela Valera y Garibay. Señorita Valera. Only now that I am as I am, do people call me "doña" . . . Doña Chela. And for a time I was called *"La Despiadada."* The Pitiless One. I was not pitiless. I was only just.

No, I never married, but I was not *dejada,* or passed over, or left because nobody asked me. I had many suitors, and one or two who were too shy to come courting, and one who . . . yes, there was one who asked too late.

I was twenty-five when the Troubles began, the Terrible Time. That is old for a girl in provincial Mexico, and my suitors had given me up and gone to serenade other girls and to marry them. I did not care. How can I explain why I did not want to have a *novio,* a sweetheart? I did not want to marry. But I wanted to love, yes, and I did love, and I saved my virginity for Him.

Now that I have seen so much of violence and passion, I know that it doesn't matter really what happens outside of anyone. The only important things happen inside, and purity is a quality of the spirit, not of the body, which begins to die the moment you are born.

I was a country child, a village girl. Our town was small, and my father had ranches outside, to which he rode out every day on his big black stallion. He was a beautiful rider, a true *charro,* and it always seemed to me that there

1

was nothing in the world as splendid as my father in his tight trousers of black- and red-striped homespun, and short leather jacket, his big, flaring sombrero on his head, mounted on Cuervo. I used to ride with him, even as a little girl of ten, my flounced cotton dress spread out over the horse's rump, and my own big felt sombrero on my head, held on by cords knotted just under the chin.

I knew animals and how they mated, I saw them many a time, and there were no secrets from me about how God had made male and female, and what for. My mother taught us all modesty, and everyone in our big, rambling, many-roomed house, behind its high walls and barred windows, was careful and courteous, taking pains never to embarrass the other by any vulgar exhibition of his person. But Mamacita had three babies after I was born, and I saw her grow round and smooth and shaped to the little body within, just as a pea pod fills with the peas, and I saw her flat and slim again after the baby had been born, as the pods are flat when the peas are slipped out.

I knew of the desperate amours of Porfiria, our cook, for she used to drink too much tequila sometimes and tell me all the things she was ashamed of. And I knew why my little cat Michi moaned and rubbed herself on the tiles and purred so frantically before she went out to call the male cats to come and love her.

Knowing all these things and more, in the matter-of-fact way of country children, it seems difficult to remember what my thoughts must have been when I decided that I would endure none of these rhythmic humiliations, these joinings and burgeonings and separations. I could avoid the whole pattern and also gain great merits in heaven too. I could dedicate myself to God.

I told this to my mother one day as we sat at our embroidery in the patio. The fountain made its little imitation of the sound of rain, and in my nostrils was the spicy scent of the potted carnations with which my mother had surrounded it. She was making a baby dress, and I remember that a frown wrinkled the cream of her forehead under the dark chestnut hair. She was not beautiful, but there was peace and tenderness in her face; I have never seen a woman's face as lovely as hers was to me. When I pray, I softly slip a mask of my mother's face over the oval of the Virgin's face, and pray to that dear remembered image. It is not wrong; the images can not really show us Our Lady.

"You must not be afraid of these things, *hijita*," she told me gently. "I have never wanted to frighten you, my only daughter. There is some pain, but it is soon forgotten, and it is little to pay for the joy."

"No," I insisted. "I shall never marry. I shall be a saint."

Dear Mamacita smiled, but she did not make fun of me.

"*Preciosa*," she said, "my own mother was as nearly a saint as anyone I ever knew, and she had fourteen children. All her life was devoted to love and duty. You must not despise the sweet obedience of the beasts who only follow their nature and do what God has commanded them to do. They have clocks in their bodies which tell them when it is time to mate and have their little ones. And you have seen your Michi, how she loves her tiny furry kittens, and sleeps with her arms around them."

I tried to explain. "I don't despise, Mamacita. It is only that . . . virginity is a jewel, isn't it? So you have told me. Then of course, it is the best thing to offer to God. Like a gift."

"That is so. But you must think about this very carefully, Chela. There must be a true vocation. There must be no pride. You must not feel yourself better than the others, who give themselves up to the natural life."

"But I *will* be better," I insisted hotly. I remember that I said that. Poor Mamacita must have prayed for me very much, for I was always proud and arrogant.

3

Those qualities are bad, I know. But I had another quality, even as a child, which I think is a rare one. I could keep my own council. It served me well, before the Troubles and after, and it shall serve me till I die. I pray God that may be soon.

I never mentioned any of these thoughts to Bibiana, for instance, though she told me everything, and consulted with me about everything, from what color ribbon to run through the embroidery on her nightdresses to what she ought to confess to Padre Melesio.

Bibiana was the daughter of the doctor in our town, which had always been called Santa Eulalia. The government didn't like religious names, and officially marked it Aguacatitlán de Juarez on the maps, but we never called it anything but Santa Eulalia, or Santa Lala. Bibi's father attended us all when we were ill, and she and I were like sisters. I was the only girl in a family of boys, and Bibi was the doctor's only child. His wife had lain in bed, unable to move for two years after Bibi's birth, and then had died.

Bibi was fat when we were going to school, and she had crooked teeth. I told her she was very ugly, which was true at the time, but she always seemed to think that she was not attractive, even long after she became quite lovely. By the time we were both fourteen and no longer had to go to classes, and were learning cooking and sewing and embroidery from my mother, she stopped being fat and her teeth seemed to find room in her mouth. She had beautiful hazel eyes and softly curling brown hair, but, inside, she was still pudgy, homely little Bibi, shy and apologetic, and frightfully cowardly. More than once I saw her faint dead away at the sight of blood. Mamacita soon stopped taking her with us when we made our rounds to the old and sick people in the town; she was of no use at all around them,

4

but could only tremble and cry. Funny, for she was a doctor's daughter.

I looked after Bibi in a carelessly protective way. I saw that she had partners at the Casino dances, and every now and then I made my beaux go and serenade her, when they had been at my window. I could make Bibi do anything I wanted, and she looked up to me for advice on everything. I even controlled the list of boys she might walk with at the plaza on Sunday evenings when we all strolled, to the music of the band, under the eyes of our parents. I rather despised Bibi in a way, but I loved her too. I enjoyed managing her life, and living it as well as my own. I was cruel, even then. But after all, I got her a husband, didn't I? And that was what she wanted.

Bibi was musical and her father bought her a piano. She took lessons from Señorita Valdivia and once in awhile, Señorita Valdivia's professor would come from Guadalajara and have all her pupils play for him. There was great crying and sobbing whenever this happened; he was never pleased with anybody. But afterward he would always give a concert at the Casino, and he could make the piano sound like legions of soldiers, or a little singing brook. He was a great musician, I think. People said so. They also said he was a *"fifi,"* and a fop and a lady-killer, and they made fun of his velvet coats and his long hair, and the perfumed creams he used to rub on his hands. But he was valiant, and the time came when he taught them all that there is no gift like fortitude. His name was Refugio Pereda Holtz; his father was of an old Guadalajara family, and his mother German. It was she who took Don Cuco to Germany to learn to play the piano there. He was famous and gave concerts everywhere before he came home to live in Guadalajara.

I was a beautiful girl; men rode in from ranches and towns many kilometers away to see me when there was a dance, and when I was seventeen or eighteen, suitors came

5

even from Guadalajara. They wrote poetry about me, and one even wrote a song which began, "Chela, your eyes have pierced me . . ."

I was rather tall for a woman, perhaps taller than is beautiful, but I was proud and I never stooped. I held my head high. My carriage gave me a figure. Actually I was rather small-breasted and slim-hipped, but the clothes we wore in those days in Santa Lala favored me. They had full pleated or gathered skirts, with a ruffle at the hem, and often a ruffle gathered around a high-necked yoke. Even our dancing dresses were made at home. It was a rare and adventurous young lady who appeared in a creation from a Guadalajara *modista*.

When I told my mother that I would never marry, and that I was determined to become a saint, I must have been about twelve. Dear Mamacita warned me about pride very often, but perhaps she was too busy to see some of the danger signs; she had so much to do. Every day she supervised her children, gave the cook and housemaid their orders and frequently helped them, prepared special dishes for my father, and sat at her sewing machine, or stood over the stove stirring and cooking and making preserves of all the fruits of our countryside. In the afternoons, after our main meal, the *comida,* she lay down for a little siesta, for if she did not rest with Papacito he would not take his. When he woke, she brought him a cup of orange-leaf tea, and after he had dressed and gone off to his duties in the *bodegas* where we stored and sold the produce of our ranches, she went about her multitudinous works of charity. Our ranch people came to her with all their troubles, and in Santa Lala, too, there were many families who depended on *la señora chica.* They called her this because my grandmother, who had died when I was six, had been *la señora grande,* and Mamacita inherited all Grandmother's indigent poor, and did the same offices for them.

6

Mamacita gave every new ranch baby a *moisés,* or a little basket cradle decorated with padded sheets and cushions and a drape of mosquito netting, and a whole set of baby clothes. Older children were always provided with warm jackets and trousers and flannel dresses against the cold winters, and every day Mamacita filled several big baskets with meat and vegetables and bread to take to the families of men who had been hurt or were sick and couldn't work, whether they were from our ranches or anywhere near.

Papacito had bought her the sewing machine, bringing it all the way from Guadalajara on muleback, and she sat at it every day for some hours, even by dim lamplight at night, making a great clatter and turning out clothes for all of us, from Papacito's pleated shirts and linen jackets and fine nightshirts to the boys' underwear and shirts and all my dresses and underwear, as well as her own. We Mexican women have a reputation for being lazy, but try as I may, I cannot remember ever having seen my mother idle.

I loved her dearly, but my temperament, despite my pious pronouncements and my firm intention of winning heaven and also avoiding all the bother of life and subjection to a husband, was more akin to my father's, as I was also like him in looks, being black-haired and rather narrow-faced, and with his large black eyes.

How I loved to ride out to our lands with him! He was severe, but he was just in all his dealings with his people, and there was a streak of vainglory in him that made him show off to them. He was a brilliant rider and a fine marksman; indeed he could do wonders with a pistol or rifle. I have seen him bring down a deer at almost a kilometer, and one of his pleasures was to fix a bright silver peso to a tree trunk, take thirty paces from it, then stop and, sighting with a mirror held over his shoulder, strike it with two or three pistol shots.

Papacito taught us to ride, to be fearless, straight in the

saddle, and afraid of nothing in the land. He taught us to shoot, too, and I was even better at this than José Luis, my older brother, whose eyes were not too good. When he went away to Guadalajara to school, Papacito had to have him fitted with glasses, and this made him so sad that he would not speak to anyone except Mamacita for a week.

This was my life, and these were my people. I inherited the feeling of the patron, and I do not think it strange that when the time came I defended my own, and fought for the life we lived.

Church was always a part of that life, from daily Mass to frequent communions. Mamacita recited the rosary with us all every evening after supper, and she was often at her *prie-dieu* if only for a few moments. I sometimes wonder whether I was truly religious. I know only that the devotions were as natural to me as the color of my skin, and that all the patterns of my faith were as much an unconscious part of me as the language I spoke.

But when I was in my teens I had no idea of the Troubles to come. I was all wrapped up in myself.

There was a rancher, Don Jacinto, who sold produce to my father for his *bodegas* in Santa Lala, and as I grew to be fifteen and then sixteen, he seemed to attach himself often to my father and me when we rode out into the country.

"Silly old Don Jacinto has his eye on me," I announced one night at supper, and I regretted this, for afterward my father did not invite me out to the ranches with him any more. I did not dare tease my father to let me go, for he was indulgent but stern, and I made up my mind then not to toss off any remarks that could later go against me. In the end it was good that I trained myself to hold my tongue.

My absence from our rides precipitated an incident that freed me, I thought, from Don Jacinto. Papacito had taken me with him for a short canter around Santa Lala to exercise my mare, and we left our mounts in the back patio to be walked until they cooled and then rubbed down by our *caballerango*, or groom, an impudent cross-eyed child we all called Bizco, in the rough cruelty of country people about physical defects. It was a sweet summer day and the house was full of the perfume of boiling strawberries. Mamacita had left Porfiria, our cook, stirring the preserves, and had gone out to visit her *viejitos*, but I knew she would be home in time to take me to rosary, so I went to wash and change my dress. There was a great knocking at the front door, and I heard the voice of Don Jacinto.

My bedroom, like all the rooms in our house, opened onto the terraza that enclosed our inner patio; my one window, giving onto the patio, was barred, and could be closed with great wooden shutters that kept out all the light. I opened my shutters a tiny bit to spy out, and I saw that Don Jacinto was being led into the *sala*. He had come dressed for a formal call, in his best Sunday suit of black wool with silver buttons, and a big black-felt *charro* hat. He was carrying the hat, holding it by its chin strap, and I realized, startled, that I had never seen him hatless before. He was a tall, well-set-up man of some thirty-six or -seven, weather-beaten, without an ounce of fat on him, and not bad-looking in a leathery way. But he was bald! I let out a peal of derisive laughter, and I am sure he heard it. I meant him to. I thought, "So he has come courting, the old fool!" and I laughed at him.

My father and Don Jacinto talked alone in the *sala*, and then the rancher went away. I saw him leave on his horse, but I could not tell what he was thinking. His face was impassive.

After *merienda* Mamacita and Papacito kissed and blessed the two little boys and sent them to bed, and then they invited me into the *sala*.

9

"Don Jacinto has come to ask for your hand," my father told me.

I burst out laughing again, in utter disdain. To my surprise, my father chided me.

"Don Jacinto is an honorable man, a well-to-do rancher. It is true, he is a widower, but there were no children. He is a good Christian gentleman. And you must remember, Chela, there are not too many marriageable men with a reasonable fortune hereabouts."

"You have not become interested in some other man?" asked Mamacita timidly.

"I do not want to marry, ever," I told them flatly.

My father looked startled but came straight to the point. "Do you want to go as a nun, then?"

"No. I just want to stay here. Do I *have* to marry? I loathe that old Don Jacinto."

"You are sixteen, Chela. It is a time for courting, for thinking of marriage," said my father. "You can't be a child forever."

"You need not accept attentions from Don Jacinto if you do not like him," said Mamacita quietly, and so the matter was settled for a time.

I went to church and prayed diligently, and it seemed to me that I would prefer Christ to any earthly lover. Don Jacinto and what he represented shocked me into a complete reversal of my coquetries; I would not go to the dances any more, and I could not be persuaded to accompany Bibi to the walks in the plaza. She coaxed me to tell her what had happened to make me so pale and silent, but I never told her a word. And it seemed as if my prayers were heard; I began to feel the buddings of a real love of Christ in my heart. Or perhaps it was my selfishness seeking the right role to play, so as to be free of the demands that any other life would make on me. I don't know now, I can't remember, I am too tired.

We heard distant thunder in those days, and if we had known how to tell the weather of the government as well as we could tell the weather of God's skies, we might have saved ourselves heartbreak later. The time of Trouble was drawing near.

But before that happened, before Jalisco rose in arms against tyranny, before I learned how to put the safety of any other person before my own, God allowed my pride to be broken. He brought me to the very dust.

I had other suitors as the years went by, despite my father's pessimistic outlook, and some of them would have been a good match. There was the young lawyer from Guadalajara who came home to spend a vacation in our house with my brother José Luis, and to go hunting with him. The young man's name was Fernando Leyva y Portugal, he was of a good family, with a fair fortune, and he would receive his title as *licenciado* to practice law at the same time as my brother. Besides, he was nice-looking, with gray eyes and light brown hair and a slender, athletic figure.

Bibi and her father, the doctor, were invited to dinner with us when José Luis and Fernando arrived. I ran to throw myself into my brother's arms; I always adored him. I knocked off his glasses, which fell in the dust, and his annoyance at this cooled his usually affectionate reception of me. I felt momentary hot tears in my eyes as he presented Don Fernando, and I pretended not to see his outstretched hand. I merely bowed. But Bibi blushed and put out her hand at once, and all during dinner she hung on his words, and scarcely took her eyes off him. I was ashamed of her, and it made me cold to her and to him also.

After the meal my mother suggested that we go to stroll in the plaza, my brother, Bibi, Fernando, and I. It was a Saturday, and the plaza was crowded with young people. The girls were wearing bright dresses, the benches were lined with mothers and aunts in sober black or dark blue, and the band was playing romantic songs like "Ojos Tapatios." Sleepy birds twittered in the trees around the outer edge of the plaza and from the center, around the bandstand, the orange trees filled the air with a sweet heavy scent of blossoms. We had eaten at three, and had sat talking in the *sala* afterward; then we had taken our siesta, Bibi in my room with me, and Fernando with José Luis. Now it was dusk, the sun had slipped away and a few stars were beginning to shine in the still light blue sky. It was a time for romance, but I reacted against it in my own violent way, and I spoke sharply to Bibi when she whispered a suggestion about planning a picnic at the lake one day soon, before Fernando went home.

"They are going hunting with Papacito, and will stay out at some of the ranches," I told her shortly. "They'll leave tomorrow after early Mass, and I don't know when they'll come back."

Poor Bibi drooped, noticeably. Fearing that she would want to talk endlessly about Fernando in the days when they were gone, I stayed close at home and feigned a headache. I don't know why I was so contrary and difficult. But Mamacita was expecting another baby, and was not well, and something very deep in me still struggled against the bonds and slavery imposed by human love. I tried to turn my heart toward the Son of God, but my prayers did not fill me with any peace. I surged with unnamed resentments and resistances. Perhaps I never really loved Him. I worry so about that, now.

The evening before we expected Papacito and the young men home from their hunting, I suddenly heard music in the street outside our *sala* window. Throwing on a dressing gown, I went to open the shutters a tiny bit to see who it might be. As I suspected, Fernando and José Luis had hurried back to Santa Lala before Papacito and had brought me a serenade. I enjoyed it; I love serenades. The music sounds innocent and sweet when played in the street, music that is oversentimental and silly indoors. But then I heard someone singing, too . . . and as the voice was Fernando's I banged the shutters closed and went back to bed. He was rather pale and looked hangdog when he and the others came home toward noon of the next day. They brought two deer, and poor Mamacita, rushing away to vomit now and then, because her pregnancies always made her delicate of the stomach, supervised Porfiria in cutting the meat into thin strips to dry with chile in the sun so that it would keep —all except a great haunch which they buried over hot coals in the back patio to make *barbacoa* for supper.

I tried to keep out of Fernando's way, but he cornered me as I came out of church in the late afternoon, where I had gone to hear rosary sung. Mamacita had not accompanied me; she was very unwell, and I had with me only my two smaller brothers . . . Eduardito and Carlitos. They were glad enough to run along home ahead of us and I let Fernando send them off, each with a sweet to suck, so that he could speak to me alone. I was willing; there is nothing more tiresome than an importunate suitor, if you do not want him.

So he declared himself as we walked back to my home, past the plaza, past the pharmacy, past Bibi's house, and the little offices on the corner where her father had his clinic and consultation rooms. Fernando spoke swiftly and insistently into my ear as we walked, though I kept my head averted. I let him say everything he carried on his heart, and at last I turned and looked at him.

"You are wasting your time with me," I told him. "I love someone else. But you might consider Bibi; I think she felt attracted to you. I cannot speak for her, but perhaps you might find some response in her, if you were to . . ."

He interrupted me, pale with anger. "Love is not just something you dispense, like rice or sugar," he stammered.

"If one customer doesn't want it, another may. What do you take me for?"

He stood stock still in the street, and looked at me almost with hatred. I liked him better so.

"I was only thinking you might turn your eyes elsewhere," I murmured, "since I am committed."

"To whom? Who is he?" he demanded, hot with jealousy, but I would not answer.

But, as I had known it would, this settled matters between us, and he looked at me no more with big, imploring eyes. Even now I cannot stand that look in anyone, that look of the stricken deer just before it falls.

He was vain, as most men are, and perhaps ashamed that my father and José Luis should see him so scorned, and he began to take *serenatas* to Bibi. She was beside herself with joy, and, before Fernando's stay with us was over, he had asked Bibi's father for permission to court her.

I had been a fool to call her to his attention; now, when he was gone, I heard nothing but her breathless praises of him. I had to listen to her reading his letters, and I had to go over and over and over everything he had ever said to her, helping her extract the ultimate in meanings from every casual word.

But I was free of him at least, and I continued my efforts to come closer to Him on the Cross. There were days when, as I knelt at my prayers, I would feel a soft darkness enclose me; I would seem to be lifted up and up and out, insensibly through the very roof of the church to where I floated among the lazy clouds in the sky, and then I felt eased, and amost as if I had been in communication with Him. But these moments were infrequent, though I longed for them.

Then we had a very troublous time, and when I needed Him most He receded from me. They told me that this often happens; it seems unnecessarily cruel.

Mamacita's time came near, and I feared for her, because during this pregnancy she had been ill almost all the time. The birthing was hard, and she cried aloud. I did not remember ever having heard her cry before, but then I had been younger, and perhaps in the deep sleep of a child I had not perceived any sounds. But this time, despite Dr. Gutiérrez's pills and encouragement, Mamacita suffered beyond her ability to control herself, and her screams rang through the house. In the kitchen Porfiria wept, and boiled teas for her, and as we wore into the second day of her torment Bizco came silently leading my father's saddled and bridled horse, and silently urged him to go out. My father did. He rode hard, and came home with his horse badly winded, but Mamacita was no better. Toward that evening she ceased to cry out, and only groaned helplessly, and early the next morning she died. Of exhaustion, I think, for the child was never born, and died within her.

It was an awful time. I took charge of the household, ordered the meals, dressed my little brothers and kept them entertained. We all attended the Mass, *de cuerpo presente,* and my father wept dry, racking sobs, but I could not shed one tear. And He hid himself from me. I had no one to console me, and my tears, unshed, burned inside me and poisoned me. I remember the weeks following Mamacita's death as a kind of hell, for one of the visiting priests who had given a mission in Santa Lala had described hell very clearly . . . a place of silence and cold, he had told us, where one was forever cut off from God's love.

Bibi was married that spring. I was to have been her bridesmaid, but that was impossible because of my mourning. In my black dress and opaque, dark, mourning veil, I sat in one of the back pews with my little brothers, both in their black suits, with black ties, and my father in his.

Bibi was very happy and looked radiant. A little crack in my heart opened to let in some joy for her. Fernando

was stern and pale walking down the aisle with his bride
on his arm, but that is how a bridegroom should look I
think. There was a big banquet and a dance afterward as
is the custom, but of course we did not go. While all the
guests were dancing the bridal couple slipped away to
Guadalajara, where they were to live.

My duties were not heavy. Porfiria, the cook, and Horten-
sia, her niece, kept our house clean and our clothes washed
and our table spread with the good plain food of the
country. I did not even have to be *ama de llaves*, or house-
keeper, for after Mamacita's death Papacito rode over to
Concepcion de Diaz and brought back to us his old-maid
sister Tía Rita, who was delighted to come to us. She had
been staying with a nephew, but the young man's wife's
mother had come to live with them, and she and Tía Rita
were not compatible. Tía Rita was quite deaf and she liked
to pretend that she was not; she used to make the strangest
replies to questions, and the oddest comments during general conversations. Her deafness and her general lack of
observation (she was not at all curious, a strange thing in
an elderly single woman) were of inestimable value to me
later. When the Federal soldiers came often to our house
to try to get proof against me, or to question everyone, Tía
Rita always left them mightily confused.

I went as often as I could to look after Dr. Gutiérrez,
who continued to live alone and to work in his little clinic,
and I attended to all Mamacita's poor, as she had always
done. My little brothers went to school, and in the afternoons they studied their catechism. My father, after a time
when he sat at home dully suffering, pulled himself together
and began to take up the routine of his life again, riding
out to the ranches, buying and storing the crops, selling
them, and financing his people on the land.

The years began going by and I did not take off my
mourning. It seemed simpler to stay in my plain black. I

became Doña Chela, the old maid. Bibi often invited me to go and visit her in Guadalajara, but I never accepted. I did not want to go. I was afraid I might be pitied, and that a parade of widowers and elderly mothers' boys might be led out and past me, as stallions are led past a fine mare. And besides, from what Bibi wrote, I thought her mother-in-law, Doña Paz, must be a dragon. So I remained at Santa Lala and helped my father, and he never pressed me to marry or to come out of my shell.

I think perhaps he was jealous of the idea of suitors any-how. He had got used to my carrying out many little duties for his comfort, as Mamacita had always done, and he relied on me to help him in his business. Besides, I was still young and beautiful. Fathers remember the joys of love when they look on a fair daughter, and envy the young men who come courting. But as I say, by the time I was twenty-three no more came courting. That is old for the provinces.

Little by little I persuaded my father to let me ride out with him again. Not in my bright, flounced calicos now, but in a black full-skirted dress, my hair tied back in a dark scarf. I became very useful to him. I learned how to judge the weight of a pig and call it almost to the ounce as it was hoisted by its hind legs and tied, squealing, to the scales, and I could estimate the number of burroloads of alfalfa in a field within two or three. I was a good buyer and a hard bargainer. I never made a mistake on a mule or a horse or a burro, and I began to take over much of the work of the warehouse and the inspection of the ranches, things my brother would have done if he had stayed at home. And I loved what I did and the life I led. I loved the country sun on my face, tanning my cheeks and brow, and the feel of a swift horse under me. I loved getting the better of the slow-witted ranchers and seeing through their lies. The life had great excitement and satisfactions for me.

In the year before the Troubles began in earnest, my

father awoke one night with a sudden cramp. Tía Rita and I did all we could for him, but to no avail, and when I heard my father bellowing with the pain I flew into my clothes and ran for Dr. Gutiérrez.

It was a terrible night. My father was passing a kidney stone, and the doctor had no morphine; we put Papacito into a boiling hot bath to try to get him through the worst while the doctor wired to Guadalajara for medicines. In the morning the doctor left, my father lying exhausted and bruised, but without the awful tearing pains now. The doctor said, "Pobre Don Manuel. He will not be able to do much for a while. But I will have morphine ready for the next attack."

"The next one!" I gasped, aghast.

"Unfortunately, these attacks tend to be repeated. He should not go too far from home at any time. And if he gets the beginning of the same pains, come for me at once. I am old and don't need much sleep. I will always be ready."

While my father was recovering there was work to do, and I did it. I rode around to the ranches, made advances to the men on their crops, and took them medicines and other things they needed. Usually one of my little brothers rode with me, but as people grew used to me I sometimes went alone or with Bizco for company. My father did not like me to go alone, and I seldom did so, but when it was necessary I went armed and this calmed him, for I was almost as good a shot as he.

I remember now a bright day in April when I intended to go to one of the more distant ranches. Bizco was sick, or so he said; he was always a liar. I decided to take Tranquilino, called Chatito, the cook's little boy with me, and I set him on Polo, a docile old horse, and he, with big, scared eyes, clung to the pommel. But he was proud, too, and wanted to accompany me. I had to go slowly with Chatito, but my mare Mariposa was frisky and wanted to run. She was impatient at being held in. To make things worse, heavy violet clouds began massing toward the north, and I could see that we were going to have rain. We had gone some way, and it seemed to me that we had better turn back, but the storm was coming closer and I thought we should take shelter somewhere and let it pass. We were not far from Don Jacinto's ranch, and he had been provident enough to build closed sheds where his grain could be stacked in a hurry. He hardly ever had any losses from not getting his grain cut in time, while other ranchers were constantly losing the farthest *hectarias* because they couldn't haul their sheaves to shelter in time.

I saw Don Jacinto riding toward us and I galloped to meet him, letting go of the rope by which I was leading Chatito on Polo. At that moment there was a shattering peal of thunder, one of the clouds was sliced with a great silver dagger, and the rain poured down. The old lead horse, supposedly as tame as a house cat, screamed, reared, turned, and, with tail streaming out straight behind, streaked for home. There was little Chato hanging on for dear life.

"Oh please go catch him!" I shrieked to Don Jacinto, without taking time for any salutation. "The child will be terrified and will fall off. I will go into this shed here to wait for you."

"Just heave on the door. It will open," he cried back, and was already spurring his mount after the vanishing Chato. He leaned forward, his big roan horse lengthened its stride, and I saw that he would soon catch up with the runaway. I dismounted, pushed Mariposa ahead of me through the door, and shut it behind us. The storm was roaring and howling around us, and we were both soaking wet and trembling.

It was warm and dry in there, and I sat down on a heap of straw. Mariposa shivered and sent ripples of movement along her velvety hide. I wrung out my *rebozo* and rubbed her down with it, and then I took off my skirt and wrung it out too. Then, over the sound of the rain drumming on the roof, I heard hoofbeats. There was something odd, something wrong about them. As I hurriedly put on the still wet skirt once more, I realized what it was. There was only one horse. In a moment Don Jacinto came into the shelter, and fastened the door behind him.

I did not have time to defend myself, and besides, there was nothing I could have done. He was stronger than I. I fought silently. Not a word was said as we strove; not a word would I say to him afterward, though he wept then and kissed my hands, and begged me to forgive him. He loved me too much, he said. He was overpowered by his feelings. He would ride into Santa Lala that very night to ask my father for my hand. He begged me to look at him, to speak. But I would not.

He helped me mount Mariposa, and I swung her round and rode home through the still falling rain, not looking back at him.

It was a long ride, and despite the rain I went slowly. I was thinking. I made plans. It would be hard to convince people, but I would do it. I would practice acting in front of my mirror. So resolved, I felt the beginning of comfort, but when I came near home and saw the towers of the church, and knew who waited there alone, so patiently, so lovingly, so hopefully for me, I broke down into a torrent of tears. I had been striving to be worthy of Him. But now all was lost. Everything would have to be different.

I waited until I could stop crying and compose my face. I found Chatito in the kitchen, and treacherous old Polo was contentedly munching oats in the *traspatio*. Chatito had clung to the pommel of the saddle all the way home. I don't know how he had managed to stay on, but he had. I comforted him and told him he was a good boy. In a moment, when Porfiria left the kitchen, I asked him what had happened. Don Jacinto had caught up, he told me, and had given Polo a great whack on the rear with his whip. Polo had not stopped until he tore into our back patio.

Chatito seemed to swell up like a little brown toad at my praise. "We won't tell anyone about all this," I said to him, and he promised. He was always very loyal to me.

I told Tía Rita the storm had driven me home and I would go another day. Papacito was sitting at his desk in a chair well padded with cushions. He was going through his accounts.

"I can do those for you, Papacito," I said, "as soon as I have changed."

"Let me do something to feel useful," he answered me gruffly, and I knew he was grieving that he could not ride out to the ranches as he had always done.

The storm flung itself off to the south, and the sky was clean and the sun shining when we reached our dessert, after a meal of rice, beef in *adobo* of various chiles, boiled *chayotes*, and beans. I remember everything about that day, everything. The sweet was a favorite of mine . . . candied limes filled with sweetened coconut. I recall the tablecloth, a blue one with a wide border in drawn work, and the dishes were plain country plates with a dark blue glaze. I remember the flowers; Tía Rita had thrust a branch of honeysuckle into a squat brown milk jug, and it sat in the very middle of the table.

I made myself eat normally, and I made the food stay down. Don Jacinto arrived before we had finished our boiled coffee. I saw my father frown and glance uneasily at me, but he went into the *sala* to receive the rancher alone. Tía Rita arranged a tray with coffee and a dish of the limes in their syrup to send in to the visitor.

I waited in my bedroom and before long my father came to knock. When I opened the door I felt sorry for him; he looked so worried and bewildered. He knew I despised Don Jacinto.

"Don Jacinto has come once more to ask for your hand," he told me. "He seems to think that this time you will accept him."

I rose, stood straight, and followed my father back to the *sala*. Tía Rita waited for me. They stood there in the *sala*, my aunt, my father, and Don Jacinto, silent, waiting for me to speak. Don Jacinto was pale and looked at me with desperate dark eyes.

"Señorita Chela, I have the honor to ask your hand," he said, "if you will accept me."

"I do accept," I answered softly, and then I turned and ran to my room once more. I had time only to see my father looking thunderstruck, Tía Rita tremulously happy, and Don Jacinto overjoyed.

The marriage date was set for three months from that day, and Tía Rita began, so happily, to gather in sewing women to make my trousseau. They cut linen and made tablecloths and towels, and they embroidered sheets and pillow cases and crocheted doilies. Don Jacinto, of course, would buy my wedding dress and veil and all my underclothes, plus a few shawls and *rebozos*, according to our custom.

Don Jacinto came to call every Sunday now, and I was persuaded to lay aside my black dresses and wear white and pink and pale yellow, as I had done before my mother's death. Don Jacinto never had much to say. He held my hand and fondled it, and pressed rings on my fingers . . . all those that had been his mother's, and when he brought my wedding dress and the other things they came in a fine old chest that had been his first wife's.

I took great care of myself, for I wanted to be a beautiful bride. I did not ride out in the sun, and I washed my arms and face and neck with lemon juice every day until I was very fair. I rubbed hot olive oil and rosemary tea into my hair until it was lustrous. I filed and shaped my nails carefully and polished them with chamois cloth. I bathed my eyes in tea made from roses of Castille to make them brilliant, and I rubbed castor oil into my eyelashes.

Also, I behaved myself very carefully, for it was important. I was so taken up with my secret thoughts and my plans that I scarcely heard the talk about how delicate the situation had become, with the government determined to break the power of the Church, and to make the priests stop "meddling," as they put it, with the people's minds. Our old cura, Don Melesio, came often to talk things over with my father. He was very sad and worried. The Terrible Time was very near. The year was 1926.

Don Jacinto brought me serenades, and there were parties for me, and also for him. Once I heard he had been made so drunk drinking toasts to his married bliss that he could not ride home, and had been put to bed on a sofa in the house of the notary, Don Eleazar.

The wedding day dawned warm and cloudless. I heard my family up and whispering, and there was an undercurrent of excitement; I heard them in the shower, and I heard the little boys running along the corridors. Then, all together, and not all in the same key at first (though they righted that), they sang me a *mañanitas*.

Tía Rita brought me hot water and scented soap. No one else was to see me until I emerged, in my bridal gown, from my bedroom at ten-thirty. I bathed and dressed; Tía Rita, with trembling fingers, arranged my hair and twined into my high-piled black braids the wreath of orange blossom that my mother had used at her wedding. I looked in the mirror and felt chilled as I saw myself wearing her wreath, for it reminded me of her and of what I was doing. It would have broken her heart.

"Your dear mother in heaven will be glad for you this

23

day," whispered Tía Rita, and for a moment I hesitated. Then I strengthened my will again. I would have to go on acting a little longer.

Then it was time to leave, and the automobile came for us. There were not many automobiles in Santa Lala then. This one belonged to Don Timoteo, the photographer, and he rented it for weddings. The seats were covered with white satin, and swatches of white crepe hung in the windows. In the vases attached above the upholstery of the back seat there were always fresh white flowers for the bride.

My father and my brothers came out; the little boys rode crowded into the front seat beside Don Timoteo. Tía Rita, my father, and I rode in back. It was only three blocks to the church, but we proceeded there in stately dignity, being followed by a crowd of urchins shouting and asking for their *bolo*. My father leaned out of the window and threw them some coins. When we arrived my father descended and handed me out, and we went to appear in the door of the church. I hadn't a single twinge of doubt now about what I was going to do. I told you, during the Troubles they called me La Despiadada.

The church was as familiar to me as our own *sala*. I had knelt there to pray so often, had heard mass so many hundreds of times. I had burned thousands of candles to Our Lady, and there, forever on His cross, hung the one I had tried so hard to love worthily.

The church was crowded, and everywhere I saw the faces of friends, happy for me, admiring me, glad that at last Doña Chela was to be married. Padre Melesio waited in his shabby but beautiful gold and white robes. The harmonium up in the loft began to play the wedding march, and I heard the sharp sweet sound of Don Timoteo's violin, for besides photographing brides and conveying them to the church, he also played during the Mass and later at the dance.

Don Melesio, now accompanied by Don Jacinto, came to meet my father and me in the center of the aisle, halfway to the altar. Here we would be married, after which we were to walk to the altar and kneel there on the white-satin *reclinatorios* to hear our first Mass together as man and wife. Behind Don Melesio walked a little boy I knew who often carried the doctor's satchel; now he was dressed as an acolyte, and carried the basin of holy water. Don Melesio stopped to dip the Asperges rod into it and then sprinkled the congregation three times before he met us.

Papacito stepped aside, and Don Jacinto took his place beside me. The ceremony began.

"Do you, Jacinto María Rincon y Prieto, take this woman for your wedded wife, to have and to hold, in sickness and in health . . ." I forget some of the words. Then came the moment I had been waiting for.

"Do you, María Graciela Manuela Valera y Garibay, take this man . . ."

"No!" I cried out in a loud clear voice. "No, no, *no*. Never!" And I picked up my skirts and turned and ran out of the church.

I ran through the streets, my veil streaming out behind me. I am a swift runner—I mean I was in those days. The train of my dress dragged on the cobblestones; I swept it up over my arm and ran on. My braids came unpinned and fell down my back. I felt immense elation, and heat, and reckless joy, like people who have drunk too much tequila. He had shamed me, Don Jacinto, when I had been unable to defend myself against him, and where there was no one to see. Now *he* was shamed, and publicly. He would eat bitterness; his liver would pour gall into his mouth and he would writhe with humiliation, for everyone would laugh at him.

I beat on the *zaguán* at home, and at last old Porfiria, who had been far in back, in the kitchen grinding up spices for *mole,* came to swing it open. I flew past her and into my room, where I tore off all the wedding finery. I undressed to the skin, and was in the shower soaping myself when my father came and knocked on the door and called me.

I came out, my hair all wet, wrapped in a big towel. "Dress yourself," he said to me sharply. I quickly put on the old black dress I had worn during our mourning.

"Everything is there," I told my father. "I will have the dress and everything cleaned and pressed to send back to him in his chest. There are his rings, and the bracelet and earrings. I will send it all back, on a mule."

My father felt for the edge of my bed and sat down. He was very pale. I had not bothered to think that he, as well as Don Jacinto, would be shamed and humiliated.

I could not have told him the truth; he would have made me marry Don Jacinto at once. I merely sank to my knees beside him and begged, "Forgive me, Papacito. Forgive me."

He put a hand on my hair, and then drew it back. "Dry yourself," he said. 'You will catch cold."

He said no more to me about it, that day or ever.

I heard Tía Rita and the little brothers come in. Tía Rita was in tears; she looked in on me, her face utterly bewildered, her eyes and nose all swollen. But when Carlitos began a high-pitched giggle, she took him by the ear and walked him to where she kept a peach switch especially used for chastisements. She didn't hurt him, really, but that was one more person shamed that day.

My father came after a little while and said, "I shall go to the Casino, and ask that all the guests eat and drink, as the banquet has been prepared. You, Chela, will not go out to the ranches any more. I will hire Esteban Callada to do that work for me. You are to help me in the office and in the warehouse. You will not go out anywhere, but remain at my side from now on."

I suppose he thought I was a little crazy. But I had

known this might happen, and I was prepared for it. I
would miss Mariposa and the sun and the wind in my hair,
but that couldn't be helped.

In the days that followed I was silent and obedient, and
I made myself useful. I could not pray, and I reproached
my guardian angel, who had not sent help to me that hateful day in the rain. I made penances and I longed to feel
cleansed and hopeful once more. But nothing happened. I
was all stopped up with bitterness and hatred.

But then the Troubles began in earnest, and I had something else on which to pour out my resentment and my
fury. The orders had been issued. All churches were closed
to worship. Priests were expelled. We were to be left without our temples, without our sacraments.

Padre Melesio came to my father and they were closeted
in his office for several hours. What they said I do not know,
but at midnight my father went out and he did not come
back home until just before dawn the next morning. I
waited for him, I opened the *zaguán* for him, but he would
not speak to me. However, he went to the table and slumped
down into his seat, so I hurried and brought him chocolate
and bread. He ate silently, and then he went to his room,
and slept there until noon.

I learned later that he and Dr. Gutiérrez and Don Melesio had stripped the church of all its treasures and had
buried them in a spot outside the town. They had left only
the cheapest candles and vases, the absolute, the poorest
essentials for the Mass.

And they were just in time, for a few days later a detachment of Federal troops (we called them *sardos*) was
marched into Santa Eulalia. They set up offices in the
vestry and boarded up the doors of the temple. The officer
in charge of this outrage was a certain Major Gonzalez, a
stocky Indian who had, they told me, worked his way up
from the ranks and by participation in the Revolution had

become an officer. He was rough and brusque and taciturn, and a remarkable marksman. He gave the people of Santa Lala demonstration of this by setting up targets against the church door and then walking back, putting bullet after bullet into the heart of them from more and more paces away. He set up targets in the plaza and had his men shoot at them all day. He was from the north, this major, and I suppose he, like many others, supposed that grace and good manners and a fondness for music, which characterized the Jalisco men, precluded courage and audacity. He was entirely wrong, and we had our first laugh at him by setting up our own targets; and all of us, men and women, took turns demonstrating that we were quite as good shots, man for man and woman for woman, as his soldiers. He silently ordered his targets taken down.

My father quietly and secretly organized all the ranchers round-about into a guerrilla band, of which he was the leader, and now they all plowed with a rifle lying handy in the furrow. At night they met, mounted, and made forays on the soldiers quartered in our town and on some of them in other towns nearby. All our men knew every inch of that countryside in the dark, and they could find cover anywhere within a few minutes. At first they confiscated only supplies and food. Later they took horses and ammunition. Then the fighting began in earnest.

It had always been our custom to salute each other in the country with the words, "*Ave María Purísima . . .*" to which, in return courtesy, one was always answered "*Sin pecado concebida. . . .*" And these words identified the guerrilla bands to each other when they met. Later on the *sardos* tried to use our passwords, but they couldn't say the whole Litany of the Virgin as we could, and we always caught them. I said "we," but I am getting ahead of myself. It was some time before I began riding out at night with the Cristeros.

At first, I think, each side wanted merely to frighten the other into acceptance. The Federals wanted to close our churches and stamp out our faith and move on. The men of our countryside wanted to drive out the soldiers, open the churches, and be left alone. But nothing ever stays the same, and this quarrel became a revolution.

There was no going back. The government quickly became more oppressive as it became clear that we would not accept the amputation of our faith from our lives, and our retaliations became more desperate.

The rallying cry began to sound all over the high plains of Jalisco . . . *"¡Viva Cristo Rey!"* And before long our red earth was soaked a deeper red with blood.

Now our life at home became a nightmare of anxieties. For a while we hid Don Melesio, our priest, in our home, and he said Mass for us daily at an improvised altar in our *sala.* Then the notice was posted that persons harboring priests would be summarily shot. Don Melesio refused to let us take this risk for him. My father arranged for a group of his own men to come at night with an extra horse for Don Melesio; their plan was to escort him far to the north where he could catch a train to take him out of Mexico.

I recall the night they left. There was a moon, but scudding clouds made it possible to hide in shadows under the shoulder of a hill or in a clump of trees. All the men who followed him knew the land as well as their own patios, and so my father deployed them in groups of two or three, scattered, but within rifle shot of each other so that their passage through the night would not be noticed.

I went into the back patio when they started. My father swung up into the saddle, and the leather creaked gently as it took his weight. His horse danced around in a circle and I had to spring back to avoid the front hoofs. My aunt stood by me, with tears streaming down her face, her rosary in her hands, the beads dropping slowly as she silently said her prayers. But I felt a start of excitement and wished that I were going with the men.

They mounted Don Melesio with some difficulty, Bizco heaving him up from the rear. He was not a good rider, poor Don Melesio, and he clasped the pommel of the saddle and clung, and could hardly be persuaded to let go and take the reins, and he swung in the wrong direction when the horse curvetted. But he had to ride this young and mettlesome horse, for they had a long way to go.

They left quietly, and Tía Rita and I went back into the house to wait and to pray.

I had to tell a long story to my little brothers, who had caught the atmosphere of conspiracy and were awake and waiting for me in my bedroom, wide-eyed and full of questions. They were both barefoot and in their little flannel nightshirts, so I bundled them into my bed and told them fairy tales until they fell asleep. I knew I would not be in my bed that night.

How long are the nights when one awaits, shivering with apprehension, some bad news. Tía Rita and I prayed, we drank coffee, we whispered together. It is better to be a man, I thought then, as I have thought so often since. Better to ride out into danger and fight than to sit at home and wait. Toward morning my father rode in, pale and weary. All was well, but I could see that this kind of thing would be his death. He staggered toward his bedroom like a man who has spent hours in the *cantina*. And I made a resolve:

The next time Papacito prepared to ride out at night, I was ready. On Mariposa, I went quietly at his side, wearing some old clothes of my brother's, and in a holster around my waist a pistol. He glanced at me once, and pulled up his horse and turned to speak to me, and then he sighed, shrugged slightly, and said nothing. We rode along together.

It has seemed to me since that Papacito realized, long in

advance of the others, that the danger would spread to us all in one way or another, and that I might as well fight then as later. And maybe he knew that before long the men would need me . . . when he was gone.

He was a good commander. He had a master plan and several alternate plans each time we rode. But he persuaded each man to take his own responsibility, and plans were flexible. He deployed us in small groups so that we would never be without some plausible excuse for being together, and for going where we were. Some groups were to draw attention away from the working groups; the workers were to seize rifles, horses, or ammunition; other groups were to cover their retreat. We reconnoitered continually to find what might be useful to us and a harassment to the enemy. That is all that was meant at first . . . harassment. We wanted to drive the *sardos* back to their capital. We wanted only to be left in peace.

I went with my father now on all his raids, and I followed his orders as meticulously as any of the men. They accepted me and they treated me fairly. There was never any necessity to take a stand and demand consideration. I would not have done so anyhow. But all that sobriety and courtesy was offered because we were only in the beginning of the Terrible Time, and because my father was a *patrón* and a *jefe*, a leader.

We rested between raids and my father, dressed like the Mexican country gentleman he was, then went about his usual duties. Sometimes Federal troops came to our house to question him . . . in fact, every time they sent in a new battalion and a new commander to Santa Lala. The questioning was always courteous but stubborn, and my father behaved as if he were receiving distinguished callers. The commanders of the battalions never failed to be confused by Tía Rita, and they often looked very suspiciously at me. But I was silent, with downcast eyes and without coquetries and graces. I did not want to draw attention to myself in any way. I was just an eccentric old maid.

There had been defiance in Guadalajara and in Encarnacion de Diaz and the government had begun to lose patience. Then a crack battalion was sent into Santa Lala, commanded by a martinet who was ruthless, intelligent, and ambitious. This man felt that he was fighting traitors, and he announced that there would be no quarter.

Papacito sat up late, working by lantern light, planning a coup that might rid us of all the hated *sardos*. They were all over Santa Lala, with orders to requisition food for their men, fodder for their horses, and housing for their officers, just as if they were in the field against a foreign invader. We had to turn over to them our stored oats and grain, our beans and rice and oil, even room in our patios and stables and places at our tables. It was bitter.

We were without a priest now, though I had heard from a Cristero who came bringing us ammunition that within a few weeks a young man was coming to us to hear confessions and bring the sacraments. He would be in disguise, but he would reveal himself to my father.

Tía Rita and I worked steadily making conserves of the fruits that were coming into harvest. We cooked and stirred all day, until the fruit and sugar were thick enough to cast into molds, or *cajetas*. We sent out dozens and dozens of these to our men hidden in the hills, for nothing gave energy and heat sooner than a square of thick guava or quince paste, with a chunk of salty goat's-milk cheese. When I commanded my own troop I always tried to get fruit paste rather than *pinole* or even jerky for the men to carry on campaign, for the paste was easily carried and satisfied the stomach at once.

At last Papacito made a final plan, and as he rode about to the ranches he left word to his men so that each one knew what he had to do. I was in his plan, I think perhaps because he feared my impetuous spirit and was afraid I might do something to spoil all his scheme. So I was given a dangerous mission. Dressed in my black skirts, I was to ride out toward the north carrying a little basket of food and medicines. I was to pretend that I was going to an aunt's to nurse her.

Toward dusk I set out, accompanied by Bizco. What a sloppy rider that boy was, looking as if he might slide down one side or other of his horse at any moment. But that was deceiving. He could mount a whirlwind and never lose his seat. He got a lot of fun out of pretending to be stupid; our people often do this, and it takes a wise man to see through the silly drooping lips, the blank eyes, the look of wavering interest, to the bright, sharp, observant intelligence behind the mask.

I was stopped by a soldier, an orderly of the new commander, as we rode past the barracks. He was a good soldier I could see, tough and obedient.

"My aunt is very ill and I am going to nurse her," I explained haughtily.

"Let me see what you have in that basket."

I showed it. Under an embroidered linen cover, I had eggs, quinine powder, herbs, and teas.

The soldier let me pass by, but his dark eyes were full of suspicion. I rode forward, spurring my horse so that the soldier had to leap aside. I was arrogant, and I was sure that our ruse had worked. My father was using me as a decoy, expecting that the commander would send a dozen of his men after me.

But he had calculated wrong. The commander had taken me at my word and let me go. He had my father and his men ambushed, and they were all captured.

We went next day, after we had the news, to find their bodies and bring them home. They had been hung to posts along the railroad right of way, and they had been tortured and humiliated, and their manhood mocked.

I could not weep when I looked upon what they had left of my father, and I have not been able to shed one tear since. All, all were dried up and became a poison inside me.

We cut them down, our dead. The horses reared and snorted and would not carry them. I had trouble even with the mules dragging the wagon I had taken. The bodies were stiff, the arms and legs in contorted positions. I covered them with sheets as we drove home, but just before we came to Santa Lala I took off the coverings and I drove through the streets slowly, so the townspeople could see what had been done and to what end had come my father, Don Lencho the lawyer, Don Timoteo, and their friends. Somewhere the funeral bells of a church sounded, and then were stilled.

From that moment the Federal battalion in Santa Lala was doomed; Santa Lala was with us to a man, to a woman, to a child, trembling with the same hatred that I felt. The *sardos* could never trust any of us from then on; we betrayed them at every opportunity, over and over again.

We buried our people, we said the prayers, and did what we could. Everyone in Santa Lala wore mourning, every *zaguán* was draped with black; every office and every shop closed. The town was silent except for the monotonous drilling of the *sardos*.

Up to then I had almost enjoyed our night riding. There was a satisfaction in it, in the night sounds and smells, the companionship, the feeling of being under orders, horses and men working together swiftly in the darkness.

But now everything was different. I simply took my father's place, and the men followed me unquestioningly. They feared me, too, for I was hard and stern and I gave no quarter. I did to the *sardos* what they had done to my father. I took no prisoners and I made no trades, as some of the other Cristeros did. I was in the fight to take revenge, and to slake my hatred. They called me the "pitiless one," even my own men, and I did not care. I rather gloried in it. I knew that I would roast in hell for what I was doing, and I was willing.

Don Jacinto came to join my band and I used him as I did the others. I wanted brave fellows, good shots.

I could not allow smoking; I knew that when we rested some of the men smoked their corn-shuck cigarettes hidden under serapes, and I pretended not to know. In all else I was adamant.

I could tell you now about some of my campaigns, but it would not be pleasant for your ears. You are used to courtesy and *noblesse oblige,* to clean sheets and baths with soap, and other niceties. We were sometimes many days and nights in our clothes without even taking off our boots. We stank. We were eaten alive with lice. And we killed. I myself saw to it that not one *sardo* was left on the field of battle. Bizco stripped them of arms, watches, anything of value. And I disfigured them.

It was war now. No longer just raids and night riding. We were battle troops, drawn up against each other. And the fights were frequent.

We were camped one time in a town called San Lorenzo; we had been fighting at night, mostly to keep the railway lines free, for we had many sympathizers who brought in ammunition by rail and tossed it off to us at spots along the line upon which we had agreed. The men were tired and hungry, and the good people of San Lorenzo, Cristeros all, took us in and hid us in their stables, their chicken yards, under haystacks, and brought us food at night. I wanted the men to have a taste of hot food, and perhaps some fresh eggs. And the horses were weary and needed some good fodder and a few days rest. There was always the danger

35

that the *sardos* would ride in and requisition the horses in
the village, and if they did they would get ours, too, for
we were assigned in groups of two or three to the houses,
and our horses stabled with those of the townspeople.

I was sick; the life I lived or perhaps the very poison of my
hatreds, had dried up my body's juices, and many of my func-
tions seemed to have been suspended. I lay in great misery
and pain on the straw in the stable of a woman who made
chorizo; my Mariposa stamped and munched by the side
of her bony old *tordillo,* a dappled-gray horse she hitched
up to a light cart when she went about distributing her
spicy sausages to neighboring villages. All day, as I
retched and vomited, I smelled the chile and cumin and
the hot melted pork fat, and to this day I cannot eat a mor-
sel of sausage, though it had always been a favorite dish.
It was late spring, and the countryside was very fair; if I
could have any regrets it would be that the Terrible Time
had made it impossible for me to ride about smelling the
sweet *huizaches* as they burst into bloom, and the feathery
golden mimosa. My only joys were the colors of sunset and
dawn. To comfort myself I lay and thought of them. Once
I saw a dawn all pale violet except for a streak of jewel
green just above the breasts of the brown hills. I have never
forgotten it, and I like to think of it even now.

The woman who made sausages was called Doña Ma-
gos; she had been named for the Magi kings. She was a
good creature, fat and bustling and hard-working. She had
a husband, but he lived in the country in a little ranch
house where he raised and butchered the hogs she used in
her packing business. They were simple souls, and very
generous with us.

On the third morning she came to bring me hot coffee
and fried eggs and told me that a stranger had ridden in
on a fine strong fresh horse, and that she had given him a
breakfast.

I sat up, alert. "A spy?"

"No, Coronela, (The village people called me Colonel.) I think he is a priest, but I am scared of the *sardos*, and I didn't ask for fear he was not. Also, it is better not to know, should the *sardos* come afterward, and torment us to make us tell."

"Bring him to me."

I got to my feet, buckled on my gun, and waited. The moment he came in, I knew. There was something in his face, so contained.

"*Ave María Purísima*," I said, and he answered at once, "*Sin pecado concebida*. Be seated, daughter," he said, "I am a priest. I want to join your band."

"We are rough and cruel, Padre."

"I will say Mass for you every morning, and I will ride with you and comfort the dying. I can be useful; before I took holy orders, I was a doctor."

The stable stank of the horses and their dung, and of me. But to those odors, to which I was accustomed, there came now the very faint fragrance of antiseptic, a smell doctors carry about with them in their clothes.

"What is your name?" I asked.

"You may call me Father García. That is not my name. But I do not want to get anyone into trouble for me."

He was a short man, thick-set and strong, with large hands and feet and slightly bowed legs. His hair was a grizzled gray, his grave eyes the same color. He had a big nose, and a thin-lipped mouth that could smile very sweetly when he wished. He wore simple trousers and a short jacket of homespun cotton, a big straw sombrero, and good boots, soft and easy on the foot but coming up well over the calf. (We were always hunting among the dead on the field of battle for good boots.) Around his waist were two wide ammunition belts full of cartridges, and he wore two pistols. He saw my eyes stray to them.

37

"I do not kill men," he told me, "but I was brought up to put a bullet into the head of a dying horse or a wounded dog."

That is what he told me, and it is true I never saw him draw his guns to use in a battle, though he went straight into the fights with us. But the men never called him Padre García either; they always called him Padre Pistolas, and I never learned his true name.

I had to depend on my instincts; I trusted him, and took him in at once. It was a good thing, for he was a wonder at helping me plan campaigns. He did this for me when we played chess. For he had, in his saddlebags, besides a chalice and the ciborium, a small chessboard and tiny men, and they had been ingeniously designed so that, when a game was interrupted, he could, by pressing a lever, clamp the men in place so that the game could be continued afterward. When I could, I played chess with him, and those contests kept my brain alert for strategy and scheming. And he dropped hints to me sometimes. What a general he would have made!

I could easily have lost my hold on the men. They had always followed me out of sheer confidence in my single-minded leadership, and because my pitiless attitude toward the *sardos* had defeminized me for them. But I knew that, had he wished to exert his force, Padre Pistolas could have taken over my battalion. He did not. He took care, I think, to remain in the background, and he left me the work I had started out to do.

He said Mass, making his altar out of anything at hand, but blessing it to God's use . . . a tree trunk, saddles piled upon each other and a board set across them, anything. He urged the men to confess and to receive communion. The wafer, so often, was nothing but dry tortilla which he cut into tiny squares with his knife, and then blessed. The wine was whatever we could steal for him to use . . . some-

times pulque, or even water colored red with the flower of
jamaica. But the men were much comforted to have him with
them, and they attended Mass and received communion
with great reverence. It was, after all, what we were fighting
for.

I would not confess, and so I could not draw near the
sacraments. This was an added thorn in my heart, and I
think now that Padre Pistolas rode near me always, on
his big *cuatroalba*, thinking that I would call him in the
hour of my death.

He was always around, quiet, near when he was needed.
Once an *alicante* bit Don Jacinto when he was sleeping on
the ground. It is a nasty silvery-gray snake; there are ugly
legends about it, for some say it will slip into the bed of a
nursing mother and rob the milk from her breasts. I only
know that, no matter how much I may have wanted to be
a man all my life, I am a daughter of Eve when it comes to
serpents, for they chill and frighten me, and take all the
heart out of me. I could not even pursue the snake to kill it
when Don Jacinto called out. But Padre Pistolas did. He
simply threw his knife at it and caught it in the neck, pin-
ning it to earth, where it writhed upon itself for many minutes before it died. He knew the lore of the country plants,
Padre Pistolas, and he bound the leaves of a weed on the
snakebite, and Don Jacinto was well enough to ride again
that very night.

We were not much troubled by the snakes, really. A
worse pest was the scorpion, and Padre Pistolas always carried about with him a small flask of alcohol with several
scorpions in it, and he put more into it when he could, patiently catching them when we bivouacked. The animal
excreted its poison into the alcohol and this, taken by
mouth, helped cure the body of the bite. I do not know how,
but it was effective.

And Padre Pistolas did much more. When we lost men

he buried them. He always carried a small shovel with a short handle behind him in his saddle roll. It made hard work of digging, but it was something, and he did not like to leave our men. When we had to, when the fighting was hot and we could not stay, he tried to go back at night to sign the Cross on their foreheads and pray, and to cover them in earth. I went with him sometimes.

If I had listened to him, I would not have lost our last battle.

I had then about forty men, and we were encamped in ranches near the railroad. There were three men with me besides Padre Pistolas. The others were deployed in small groups, and we were to meet that night, six kilometers beyond the bridge of Alamillo, to receive a box of ammunition from the train. One of the brakemen was a Cristero and we had received word that he would toss it off to us at that point.

It was hot, and thunderclouds had been piling up all day in the north, growing darker and heavier every hour.

"It will be a bad night," Padre Pistolas told me. "Better not. If the Federals know anything of this they will ambush us, and our horses will give us away, for if it lightens they will whinny. Let the ammunition be thrown off and toward dawn we can send a couple of men to get it. If it is really there."

But I was resentful, in my stupidity, of his advice, and I gave orders that all were to meet.

"We cannot be ambushed, I know the country," I told him shortly. "And the horses have been trained to stand quiet at a touch. We cannot let the *sardos* get that ammunition."

"We could buy it back from them two days hence," he commented ironically, and it is true that there were always traitors among them willing to come and sell us bullets. But I was stiff and unyielding.

Thunder was growling as we set out, and the clouds riding before the moon made the countryside seem strange to me. A little wind rose, too, and moaned in the eucalyptus trees which lined the way I had chosen. It is always best to ride where there is some shadow.

There was a thick stand of pecan trees over toward the place where we had our rendezvous, and only a short distance between the ranks of eucalyptus and the pecans. We were to cross in groups of two and three, my party leading, and as it was a black night (with only a fingernail sliver of new moon), I thought we would have cover enough. But it happened that as Padre Pistolas, Don Jacinto, and I rode out to cross over into the pecan grove, there was a great clap of thunder, and a streak of silver lightning that illumined the whole scene more sharply than in daylight, and from the pecans came a burst of rifle fire. Our horses screamed and rose on their hind legs, and we tried to turn them and run. We had almost reached the safety of the eucalyptus shade when there was another strong, sudden glow of lightning, and I felt a blow in my back. I do not know what happened after that except what I learned days later.

I had nightmares of horrible agonies and fears. I was in darkness, I prayed to the Crucified, but He turned His face aside from me. Rain poured upon my body, but it was a rain of fire, and there was no escape. Vaguely I recall seeing Tía Rita's worried face, and I felt Dr. Gutiérrez probing, probing, sometimes with fingers that I could not feel, sometimes with long wands of what seemed to be white-hot steel.

At last I awoke, and found myself in my own bed at home, and in a white nightgown. Outside it was a sweet summer day; birds were singing in their cages in the corridor and the doors were all wide open. I could see the hot sunlight on the orange tree, and on the roses; the lovely fragrances were wafted toward me, and my instinct was to rise and go out at once. I wanted to trail my hand in the fountain, to watch the humming birds hover at the blossoms of the climbing passion flower vine, to feel the warm sun on my cheek. But I could not move. I was as heavy in my bed as a length of lumber. I was immobile. I could not do more than turn my head.

"Ayyyyy!" I cried out, when I remembered everything. Tía Rita came running in. She was wearing the long white cotton apron she always put on to nurse anyone who was sick.

"What is the matter with me?" I screamed. But even the scream, though I meant it with all the force of my desperation, came out only a hoarse whisper.

She laid a finger across her lips, as if to silence me, and ran out of the room at once.

I lay willing myself to move . . . willing my feet, my legs. Nothing. Only a terrible heaviness. I willed my arms to lift themselves. Nothing. I willed a hand. A finger. Nothing. When Dr. Gutiérrez came in, I was gasping and groaning hoarsely, like a dying person. But alas, I did not die.

He sat down and looked at me. I knew that I was lost when he did not immediately make the expected, the traditional gesture of taking my wrist to count the pulse.

"Chela," he said gently, and then was silent.

"I want to know," I told him. "I must know."

"You were . . . injured. In the spine. Don Jacinto got you home, and we have cared for you. Nobody knows . . . people think that you have had typhoid. I gave it out that way. No one has come near. You need not fear . . . for the men."

Of course he had known; all Santa Lala knew.

"Was I shot?"

"Yes."

"Have they been here . . . the *sardos* . . . to spy . . . to find out . . ."

"Yes. They come, now and then."

"What about me?"

"You are paralyzed. But I think we can restore partial movement. You will have to help. When I can get you propped up, I think we will be able to count on regaining some movement."

"Of my whole body?"

"Of your arms, upper body. I think you will not ride or walk again, Chela. You are brave, brave as a man. You must accept this, and make the best of it."

In my heart I was crying aloud, I wish I had died! But I knew that I must not say this aloud. It was part of my punishment.

My despair was deep and black. I cannot describe my suffering. I felt no physical pain at all, and I submitted to all the tiresome ignominies of my helplessness. I was praying, praying, begging the Crucified to turn His face toward me once more, but always, when I envisioned Him, He turned aside. I asked for a large crucifix to be placed so that I could see it well, but around the head was a shadow, and He hid His face from me. I was in hell.

It came to me one day that, when at last He permitted the shadow to be dispersed, I could know that I was going to be pardoned, and it seemed to me that I must recall everything that had happened, and each thing I had done, and say acts of penitence for them. Having found this possible road back to His peace, I felt somewhat eased, and I was able to sleep more than the few snatches which had been part of my agonies for weeks. I dedicated my thoughts to reviewing my life, and I gave a day, sometimes many days, to penance for each sin. Ah, there were, there are, so many. But when I came to the beginning of all my sorrows, that day in the rain, I could not be penitent. I could only rage and hate, and my prayers dried up.

I have no idea of the passing of time in those days, except

43

that it seems to me now that when I saw Don Jacinto standing at the foot of my bed, his poor bald head shining in the soft lamplight, that it was a September evening. I must have lain in my living coffin for more than four months.

"Doña Chelita," he said, when he realized that I actually saw him. "Doña Chela, the doctor says tomorrow he intends to help you to sit erect. In the bed. Later, in a chair. I have brought you a chair."

He went out, his somewhat stiff horseman's legs creaking and bending a bit at the knee as he walked. I heard the soft sound of wheels. He had had it made somewhere . . . and it provoked my tenderness somehow. It was a lovely soft armchair, the kind ladies sit in to take tea at little marble-topped tables, the kind they sit in, with skirts spread wide, bending their heads over their sewing or embroidery. Only it had sturdy wheels at each leg.

"Thank you," I whispered.

I do not know why, but a little feeling of calm came over my spirit when I said those words to him. During the fighting, when I was leading the men, I had never directed one word toward him, except a command.

I seemed to drowse awhile in a soft ease. Then I asked, without opening my eyes, for I knew he was still there, I could hear him breathing, "What happened to Padre Pistolas?"

"He fell, that same night. We went to find him and buried him. And the others."

"Who commands now?"

"José Luis. He came, as soon as he had news of your . . . accident."

"José Luis?"

I came wide awake.

"He is a good leader. Better than I, though I tried. He brought a little book of army rules, and everything is very formal now. We call him 'Major.'"

44

I don't know whether a day or more went by, or whether I saw my brother that very night. I do remember that at some time I opened my eyes and saw him there. He was thin and fine-drawn, but very calm. He took off his glasses and passed his hands over his eyes, and then he looked at me with that slightly vacant gaze of the myopic.

"Chela," he said.

I started to answer "José Luis," but then I said, "Major."

"Ah well," he sighed. "Somebody had to take over."

He drew up a chair, and sat down by my side.

"I am sorry this happened to you, little sister. I should have been here."

"How are things now?" I whispered. "Are there Federal soldiers in the town?"

"Yes, a new battalion. Fresh troops."

"And you?"

"We are quiet. In hiding at the moment."

The picture fades then and I suppose I fell asleep.

I remember now the day they got me up to sit in the chair. I couldn't feel anything, but I was conscious of their struggles, Tía Rita's and José Luis's, and of being strapped into the chair. There was a broad strap just under my armpits, fastened in the back, and another one that went around my hips. A third one crossed above my knees and held my legs in position. They fastened these leather bands around me, as I sat in a heavy cotton nightgown.

"I shall open her clothes in the back, so as not to interfere with the straps," said Tía Rita, and some days later she gave me a blouse, split down the back, and a skirt, which was just a flounced cover, to hide my legs. Thus held in position, and covered with the semblance of a dress, I could pass, in a shadowy room, for a delicate lady sitting in an armchair. That is, I could do so for a while. At first I could manage to remain erect for only about ten minutes. Then twenty. Later, it was half an hour. When I wearied I would

45

slump and tip over, and I was in danger of falling, chair and all. Tía Rita set the little brothers, or Chato, to watching me if she had to leave my room.

Maddening as it was to be such a helpless husk, the mere fact of sitting in a chair, and wearing a dress, encouraged me to try to move a little. I found I could turn my head slightly, and I began to be able to send impulses down into my fingers and to move them. Oh, it was not easy. It was bitterly hard. I would concentrate with all my forces, gritting my teeth, till the sweat stood out on my forehead, and sometimes, only sometimes, I could make my fingers obey me. To learn to move my hands and my arms took me many months of suffering and prayer and striving.

One day they were preparing to get me up. Tía Rita had the straps and the chair ready by my bedside when there was a sharp knocking at our *zaguán*. Little Chato came running toward us, and I knew by his face that the *sardos* had sent someone to question us again.

"Quick, the straps. Hide them under the covers," I hissed, and we got them out of sight just in time. When the officer entered he found a sick woman in bed, her aunt sitting in an armchair at her side, with a bit of crocheting in her hands.

From my position flat in the bed I could not see much of the man except his uniform; he was a colonel. Later, as he walked about the room, I saw his face clearly. He was handsome, a gentleman. But his image was blurred by my hatred.

"I suppose the Señorita Chela has been ill like this, off and on, all her life?" he questioned.

"Ah yes," answered Tía Rita. "We grow a lot of roses in our back patio."

"Typhoid, the doctor told me," murmured the colonel. "But it has been several months now. Are you sure the doctor's diagnosis is correct?"

"We sometimes make rose-leaf jam, we have so many," answered Tía Rita. "It is an old Arab recipe. Perhaps a little oversweet, but delicious."

I closed my eyes. He then said something meant to prick my vanity.

"It might be mental," he said. "Shouldn't she be in an institution? I could help arrange it. The government you know . . . some of your people do not trust the government, but you are wrong. It wants the best for you. She would be well cared for."

I didn't even flutter my eyelids. And Tía Rita went on, "Though I always say the old-fashioned fruit jams and *ates* are the best. I am getting together a lot of quinces to make some very soon. The grinding is the hardest. For that I really wish I had some kind of a machine . . ."

He left, finally. But he kept sending back his orderlies at odd times, or dropping by himself. I worried at first, thinking it was I he suspected, but it was José Luis. I believe he never did make up his mind about me, but then I suppose it was easy for him to decide that I was harmless now, whatever I may have been before. I was greatly relieved when I heard that his battalion had been ordered to another post. After he had gone I tried again to learn to sit in my chair, and I had the satisfaction of being able to do so, erect and giving a reasonably good imitation of a healthy woman, the next time the *sardos* came into our house. But that was months later.

In between my days were devoted to my efforts to learn to achieve a little motion where I could, and to examining my life. I could make penitential prayers for every moment of disobedience to my parents, for anger and pride and vanity, but I always stuck at the same point—forgive those hateful wrongs done to my loved ones by the soldiers. . . . I could not.

Some compassionate angel had pity on me though, for,

as the doctor had promised, I began to be able to move my
fingers, and then, as if I had achieved dominion over some
new section of my brain that had not been used before, I
began to be able to move my arms, and my head too. It
came quickly at the last, as a child learns to walk. At first
he falls and tumbles and returns to creeping, and then, in
a week, he runs everywhere, upright.

And so now I can sit in my chair almost all day, and I do
not need straps any more. I can be dressed in everyday dark
blouses and skirts. I can do a little sewing and crocheting. I
can be wheeled to a table and do my accounts, and write
my letters and give orders. It is a great deal. It is more
than I deserve.

When I was better I wanted José Luis to tell me about
his campaigns, his victories, his problems. But he would
never tell me one word.

"It is for your own safety," he always insisted. He was
away for weeks at a time, even months. Occasionally, on
black nights, he would creep home to wash and burn his
vermin-ridden clothes, and to sleep for two or three days,
but we always had orders not to betray in any way that he
was with us. We always said he was away in Mexico City.

We were very poor in those times, as most of the men
rode with the Cristeros, working their land in snatches between raids. Crops were poor, and the *sardos* requisitioned
much of what we had. José Luis had taken all the men of
our *ranchos*.

Tía Rita and I were hard put to it to feed our household;
she gathered wild weeds and fruits when she could, and
all the people of Santa Lala shared. We simply ate less, all
of us. As for me, I did with as little as possible. I merely
acceded to my appetite in small ways, for I did not eat to
get strength. What for? My legs were withered sticks now,
and always would be, and I needed only to keep my eye-
sight, my hands, and perhaps my brain. I needed some-

thing to be useful with, and I put in afternoon hours teaching my small brothers.

Then God saw fit to impose upon me one last trial of the spirit. It came about in this way.

I sat in my chair at the table one late summer day. I had cut up all my old light-colored cotton dresses and was making shirts for my brothers and for other boys their age. I cut and basted, and Tía Rita did the seams on our sewing machine. We had not heard from José Luis in many days, but then as now, no news was good news. How we loved those empty days when nobody came to call, with horror-stricken eyes, or white and terrified of a rumor that had drifted in to us from another town.

Suddenly a shadow fell upon my work, and I looked up. There stood Don Jacinto. He was clean, shaved, thin and drawn, but decent. He looked like an ordinary rancher, and as such the new battalion of Federal soldiers had seen him when he rode in from the country I had no doubt.

"Please sit down," I told him, my heart contracting, for I was suddenly afraid. "José Luis . . . ?" I whispered.

"*Bien*. All is well. They are laboring in the fields near Alamillo, and are not suspected. José Luis is planning something. He wanted me to come to find out how you are. I brought some corn and sweet potatoes, a wagonload. You can give them out where you think it necessary. Some dried chiles, too, and several sacks of quinces. Be calm, Doña Chela. There is a small lull in the fighting, and the men are working."

"Thank you."

"I spoke to José Luis about you, and he gave me leave . . ."

"Leave to come here?"

"Yes. And leave to speak to you."

I looked at him, frowning.

"To ask you once more to marry me."

How can I tell you what I felt? There he stood, scorned and humiliated, homely, middle-aged, asking once more to be spat upon. Knowing that he would be. Thinking that he deserved it.

And I? A husk, I could not be wife to anyone, physically, and even my heart and spirit were dry and stiff. I could not answer, I could not say one word. Far inside me I felt the swelling, the discomfort that used to mean tears when I was a girl. . . . I awaited that stinging in the nose, the thickness in the throat, and then the blessed relief of the wetness spilling over, pouring down my cheeks. It did not come. Just the swelling, the pain inside me.

He waited patiently, humbly, hopefully for my answer, but I could not move my tongue.

After some time he shuffled his feet a little. I could not make a sound. Apologetically he said, "Not now, Doña Chela. You do not have to answer me now. I will come back again . . . in a few days. . . . I . . . I have always loved you . . . always . . . I always will."

I heard him go away. I heard Tía Rita twittering to him in the corridor. He went out through the kitchen.

I sat for hours, it seemed. Eduardito came in for his lesson, but I waved him away, and I heard him calling Tía Rita.

"Chela is sick, I think . . ." And Tía Rita came running. She needed only to hear my name and her deafness did not matter. Whatever had been said meant that I needed her.

I motioned to my bed, and she helped undress me and move me over to it. I fell back against the pillows and could not move again. She covered me and tiptoed away, thinking that pain had overcome me. And so it had.

My head whirled with confusion, with hurt. The most bitter part of it was that I believed him, at last. He had not spoken in pity.

Nowhere in the Holy Bible, I thought, had it been told how sinners felt when God pardoned them. This unutterable misery and sorrow . . . could this be heaven? Could this be the paradise we dream of? What else could it mean? If I felt so, to be pardoned and loved by such as Don Jacinto, how would I feel when at last my Saviour turned his face out of the shadow and looked forgivingly upon me? I would die of the pain of it.

But that day has not come. I cannot speak, I cannot ask forgiveness for myself. I am bound in this hideous shell of my own making . . . immobile, and dumb.

O God, help me! God help me!

What will become of me. . . . Turn toward me, I beg, my dear Lord . . . help me. . . . Help me.

II

"Sin pecado concebida . . ."

THE CHRONICLE OF TRANQUILINO, "EL CHATO"

"Mamá! Mamacita!" I called to her. But she wouldn't look at me, just kept on stirring the *mole* she was making for the Señorita Chela's saint's day dinner. When Mamacita frowns like that, and won't answer, it is because she is praying, and I knew I mustn't bother her until she finished. A good *mole* has to be stirred for the length of a whole rosary, after you put in the ground-up peanuts. I saw her lips moving. So I took my bones outside again. They were old bones that Lobo, my dog, had chewed clean and buried. But I found them, playing out in the vegetable patch, and I dug them up and wiped off the dirt that clung to them. When I hit one of them with the other it made a good sound. I would save them, even though Lobo sat, with his ears up, jealously watching me. I had lots of things to make music with in some old boxes that Don Manuel, the *patrón*, had given me. I had a whistle made out of wood that Señorita Chela had bought for me once at a fair, and another one made out of clay. This one had holes, and if you stopped one of the holes with your finger you got a different tone. And I had a wine glass with the stem broken off. The stem didn't matter. But if you wet your finger and moved it around the lip of the glass, you could make music, though it was sad music for Lobo. Whenever I played music on my glass, he first became nervous and scratched all over, first one hind leg and then another, and got into very strange positions trying to find what made him itch, and then, giving up, he would

52

put his nose in the air and howl. He didn't like the glass. But he liked some rocks I had, a brown and a blue. Round ones. When I played them, striking them together, he would get up and dance, turning circles, wagging his tail and smiling at me. They seemed to tell him that we would play together. So then I would throw one of the rocks, and he would run and get it and bring it back to me and throw it down, all wet with his slobber. I would roll it in the dust to dry it, and wipe it on my sleeve and throw it again.

One day Señorita Chela found me under a *huisache* tree playing my music, making all my sounds, and she took me into the kitchen. "Come along, Chato, I will show you how to make music with many different notes."

Mamacita was sick that day, I remember. Every now and then she got a bottle of tequila and drank it all up and the next day she was sick all day and couldn't move from her bed, and had a terrible headache. Those were the days Señorita Chela cooked. That was before she had her accident, of course.

This day she had made us a wonderful *comida* of stuffed squashes and sausages, and she had cleaned up the whole kitchen afterward, and scrubbed the tables, and everything was tidy.

"Sit there," she said, "and watch me." She took out seven of our big thick water glasses made of blue glass, and into each one she poured some water. The first glass had just an inch of water. The next one two inches, and so on, until the last glass was almost full. Then she took a fork and struck the glasses. Oh it was beautiful! The glasses played a scale just like the piano in the *sala* of the Señorita Gutiérrez! She let me play the glasses then, and all afternoon I had wonderful music. I could even make tunes! But I could only play music with the glasses when Mamá was sick. When she was well she wouldn't let me touch any of her glasses or dishes or cups.

53

Bizco, that was the stable boy that lived with us, made fun of my music.

"I know why you love music so much," he said, grinning. You could never tell who he was looking at, for one eye pointed into the house and the other out the window. "It is because your father was *muy músico*."

I didn't know why Mamá got so mad and hit him with a wet dishrag until much later. I found out one time from the *patrón*. He had gone to buy horses at a ranch in the north, and he came back with four beauties. One was black with three white feet, two were *alazánes*, golden brown, and the prettiest of all was a palomino, with silvery mane and tail.

"Oh," I cried, "the palomino is the king of them all!"

"No, Chato," said the *patrón*. "He is *muy músico*."

I knew a horse couldn't sing or make music, so I asked, "Why, *patrón*? Does he dance?"

"No. I mean he is a cheat. He is a pretender, he promises a lot, and then won't keep his promise. But he is very swift, and I shall teach him not to try to deceive me. I shall get rid of his music, you will see."

So I learned that my father had not been one of the men who play in the band on Sundays, or a blind man who makes music at weddings. He had been just a cheater, a deceiver. I suppose that was why Mamacita cried so often, and bought her tequila every month when they paid her.

Bizco was a mean boy. His father had been gored and trampled by a bull, and the *patrona*, Doña Leonor, had asked him about how it had happened. When Bizco told, he laughed, but Doña Leonor had cried.

I heard her say to the *patrón*, "You must send him away, Manuel. He is a devil, that young one. He will teach evil to our little boys. I don't like him."

"He is a little bit touched," answered the *patrón*, "but he is a wonder with horses. I'll see to it that he stays out of the house except for meals. And tell Eduardito and Carlitos to stay away from him."

Bizco teased Lobo, and tormented the cats, who soon learned to keep out of his way. Lobo was more of a fool, hating to believe that Bizco wasn't just playing. But before long, even Lobo preferred me, and began to let me know that he was my dog. He never showed his teeth to Bizco, but put his ears down and tried to act humble when Bizco came near him, but the minute Bizco passed by, old Lobo would lift his black lip and let his white teeth show.

But Bizco was wonderful with the horses. They minded him and they loved him, and whenever he went into the stable they all came and pressed close to him and shouldered him, nibbling on his hair, and they pulled off his hat and threw it down. He loved them, too, and petted them and said soft words to them. I guess he didn't love anyone or anything else, really, for often at meals in the kitchen he would make fun of the *patrón*, walking like him, or swing about, looking haughty, imitating Señorita Chela. The only person he seemed to admire was the young *patrón*, José Luis, whenever he came home from Guadalajara, where he was studying to be a lawyer. Bizco used to hang about and run errands for the young *patrón*, saddle his horse and bring it around at any hour without a word of complaint, though when he had to saddle up and ride with Señorita Chela he usually muttered to himself and said bad words.

He was young, not more than twelve years old I guess, but he made himself respected. Nobody mixed with him, or called him names (except Bizco, for cross-eyed), or started a fight with him. He carried a knife, and he could throw it too. I used to watch him practicing out in the back. He made a mark on the limb of a tree, and then stood farther and farther away, throwing his knife, and making it stick into the tree at the place he had marked.

55

It was fun to watch him ride. He leaned over on the horse and rode sideways, almost slipping off, or almost doubled over. But whenever he wanted to he would lie down along the horse's neck and whisper to it, and away they would go like a streak of lightning in the sky, and you couldn't even see Bizco he lay so close.

He could break the young colts, too, and he never hurt them or made them scared like some of the other *caballerangos* did. He was patient and gentle with them and they learned easily and accepted the bridle and the saddle from him.

I admired him because I was always afraid of horses. They seemed so big and I was so little. I was small even for six, when Señorita Chela took me with her one day to one of the big ranches toward the north, and the horse, old Polo, ran away with me. Don Jacinto smacked him on the rump with his whip, and that only made him run faster. I don't know how I ever held on, but I managed to, and Polo ran right into our own patio and stood there puffing and snorting. I slid off and ran into the kitchen, and Mamá slapped me for being a crybaby. But Señorita Chela, when she came home much later, said I had been a brave boy.

She didn't make me ride any more, though. Even she stopped going out so much, and later on, when she began again, she called me to come to her room and she told me a secret.

No, I will not tell what she said. I promised. I will never tell.

But it was nothing bad. It was a game, really. Like playing that the enemy is in his fort, and you are in yours, and then you send messages, and you have to send them in a disguised language so that only the right people know what you are saying, and many other things. Señorita Chela promised me a trumpet if I would play the game with her and, of course, never, never tell. Especially I must never tell

Mamá because when she drank her tequila and cried she
told all kinds of secrets.

I was eager to begin our game. The *sardos* who had been
in our town (ugh, I have to spit when I think of them and
what they did later on to our *patrón*), were marching out
next day. They had stolen all kinds of things from us . . .
carpets and chairs, and even dishes. But Señorita Chela had
told me something. Diamonds can cut diamonds, she said,
and if the *sardos* could steal from us, we could steal from
them. And she had a plan.

The *sardos* had a boy *corneta* who played on the trumpet; he played signals the soldiers followed . . . for getting
up, getting in line, marching and so on. Señorita Chela
knew where the *corneta* had been billeted and she intended
to go and steal his trumpet.

I went along with her, because after it was stolen someone was going to pass it to me, and I was to hide it under
my shirt and go home with it right away. I was given a
basket full of bread covered with a napkin to hold over my
arm, and if anybody stopped me, I was to say I had been
to the baker's, and show the bread.

We went out at about six; the sun was beginning to
drop down and make long shadows. Señorita Chela was all
dressed up in her yellow dress with the ruffles at the knee,
and she had a yellow ribbon in her hair. We walked along; I
followed behind as if I did not belong to her. I was not to
speak to her or seem to know her, she told me, and everything she did was to be a secret.

The *corneta* had been sleeping in a small room in Don
Timoteo's house, and he was standing outside, waiting.
Señorita Chela walked straight past him, paying him no
attention, but as she passed him somehow her sash came
untied, and it began to trail down.

"Señorita . . ." said the trumpeter, and he went after her,
holding up the end of her sash.

She turned on him like a tiger. "How dare you molest me!" she hissed at him. "Take me at once to your commander!"

"But, señorita!"

He was only about eighteen, and I might have liked him if he hadn't been one of those hated Federals. He tried to apologize to her and held out his hand a little, but she struck it down. And then suddenly, there was Bizco, leaning against the wall, and he put two fingers in his mouth and gave a shrill whistle. Two soldiers came running, and also several of our townsmen.

"That *sardo* tore off the Señorita Chela's sash, I saw him," shouted Bizco, "and now he won't apologize!"

Don Celso stepped up. He is an old man, and everybody respects him, and he said, "What has happened here?"

Everyone answered at once, and more and more people came and began to shout, and women to scream, and pretty soon the whole crowd of people were marched off to the commander, and Señorita Chela in the middle of them. I stayed where I was; she had told me to. And before ten minutes had gone by Bizco came out of Don Timoteo's house, swaggered over to me, and passed me the *clarín*. I put it through the top of the rope I tied my trousers on with and let my shirt hang over it, and carried the basket of bread so it hid the bulge. This was my part of the game, and I slowly walked home. I had to pass a couple of *sardos*, but I went right past them, munching on one of the buns. Then I waited.

Finally two *sardos* came stepping along, escorting Señorita Chela home, and they saluted smartly as she passed through our big *zaguán*, though she held her head high and would not look at either of them.

As soon as the door was closed, she ran like a deer to spy out through the window, hidden behind a chair, and she saw them go marching away. Then she exploded into giggles and rolled about on the chair, beside herself. She grabbed me and hugged me, and asked, "Did you get it, Chato?"

"It is hidden under my bed."

"Bizco is so clever; I declare, he is a thief and a liar, but how useful! Thanks be to God! Bring it to me, Chato, they may send out a search, and I must hide it where they will never find it. Good thing they are ordered out tomorrow; they won't have time to do much about it. Even"—and here she broke down into helpless laughter again—"maybe, even, that little *corneta* has had enough trouble today, and won't report the loss of his trumpet."

I went and got it and brought it to her, and she hid it someplace. I don't know where. But there were secret places in the house that only she and the *patrón* knew.

The next day I tried to play with my musical rocks and my bones, but they did not satisfy me. I wanted that *clarín*, and I could think of nothing else.

It was the day when Señorita Chela taught us our *catecismo*, and we were very quiet in her bedroom, sitting on the floor, while she read the part we had to learn and explained it to us. We were four . . . her brothers Eduardito and Carlitos, Bizco and I. We had to whisper and be very quiet because the *patrona* was going to have another baby, and she was sick and had to rest.

We were near the end of our *catecismo*, and would all receive our first communion (Señorita Chela had promised) as soon as we could find a priest. The Bad Time had begun and they had closed our churches, and Don Melesio, our *cura*, had to go away or be caught and shot. But once in a while a *charro* would come riding in, and after dark he would take a chalice and robes out of his saddlebags and say Mass for us secretly, in a closed room. Or a country fellow in dirty clothes, with a load of cabbages to sell, would come peddling them from house to house, and underneath the cabbages he would have his holy things ready.

There was a big fat dark man who came into our town with sausages. He fried them and made *tacos* on the corner of the plaza, and the *sardos* all bought his *tacos* from him, and it turned out he was a bishop. He suddenly disappeared one night, but we heard he had been hidden somewhere and that nothing bad had happened to him.

We finished by saying all our prayers, and then Señorita Chela told me I was to go with her out to the back patio. When we got there she took the *clarín* out from under her apron and showed it to me.

"Could you blow it, Chato?" she asked. "Try."

I took the pretty silvery thing in my hands. Oh how wonderful it felt. So balanced, so shining! I put the mouthpiece to my lips and blew. But there was no sound. I tried and tried, until tears streamed down my cheeks.

"Never mind, Chato," said Doña Chela. "Maybe you are too little."

"Let me try." Bizco was lounging in the stable door, and, as usual, we couldn't tell who he was looking at. But he was smiling in a nasty superior way.

"Well," said Doña Chela reluctantly. She passed him the *clarín*. He put it to his lips and blew a fine loud note. Then, laughing, he blew a reveille. . . . I threw myself down on the horse's straw, and sobbed. Now that horrible Bizco would get the *clarín* and I had wanted it so much.

"Where did you learn that?"

"I was *caballerango* for a *militar* for a couple of years before I came here," he told her. "He had one, and I stole it and learned how to play the bugle calls. There isn't much to it. You just have to have lots of strength in your chest."

Doña Chela looked at his chest and so did I. It didn't look strong. He always stood all curved over and round-shouldered, sloppy.

"Is it for me, Doña Chela?" asked Bizco in his insinuating way, smiling his nasty smile.

"No," she answered. "It is for Chato. Give it to me."

"I could teach him to blow."

"We will see."

Doña Chela never promised anything.

My sorrow was lessened; at least the *clarín* was not for Bizco. And I would grow bigger and stronger and learn to play it.

Then, I guess, Doña Chela forgot all about it, for that was when the *patrona* died, and with her the little baby that could not be born. It was a sad time for us. Mamá put on a black cotton dress and a black apron; so did Doña Chela. Eduardito and Carlitos and the *patrón* had to wear hot black suits, and black neckties. Mamá cried a lot and so did I as we went around the house turning all the pictures to the wall. Doña Chela locked the *sala,* the shutters in the front of the house, on the street, were closed tight, and we hung black bows of cloth on them, and on the *zaguán.* We even put one on the back *zaguán,* where the horses were cantered into the back patio. We and the whole house went into mourning.

Doña Chela was in the church a lot, with the other women of Santa Lala, even though we had no more Mass there, and all the fine candles and the holy images were gone. But still, it had been a house of prayer, and people loved it, and went there to say the rosary, and also, every morning early, many people went and read their Mass books out loud, even though we had no priest to make the holy sacrifice.

Then they marched another battalion of *sardos* into our town, and the new colonel made everybody get out of the church. He propped the doors open and set up his office there, and he posted announcements that if anybody bothered him there he would stable his horses in the church.

Soon things were happening in Santa Lala . . . secret things. Doña Chela told me I must never tell anybody, no matter what they did to me.

"What will they do to me if I tell?" I asked her. I was scared.

"They will hang you up and cut off the soles of your feet," she hissed into my ear. "As they did to Padre Coronado! Shall I show you a picture of him, after they got through with him, the dirty *sardos?*"

"No," I told her. "Don't show me the picture, Doña Chelita. *Por favor.*"

"And when they finish with you, I will do something else to you," she threatened me. "If you ever tell."

I don't know what she told Eduardito and Carlitos, but I guess she scared them too. Doña Rita, who had come to look after the house and help my Mamacita, was entirely deaf, and as she never heard anything right she never said anything right, either. So she didn't count.

That was when the *patrón* began to ride out at night with other men from our town, and with men from the ranches, and they made plans to fight the *sardos.*

One day Doña Chela and Mamá were peeling and seeding quinces in the kitchen; they were going to make *ates.* *Caray,* they were making *ates* for the whole town, I thought. There were mountains of golden quinces.

"Come here, Chato," she called me. "Get a knife and help me. You can take out the seeds while I peel."

I got a knife and started, but right away I cut my thumb, and I had to be washed with alcohol and bound up in a rag.

"Useless little fatty you are," Doña Chela muttered, tying the bandage too tight, with a jerk. "Even Bizco rides out to fight with the men."

"If you would let me practice the *clarín* . . ." I began.

"And what good would that do?"

"I could hide and blow the wrong signals for the *sardos*. Wouldn't that help?"

"Poor Chato. I thought of that when we stole the *clarín*. Bizco will do it. When the time is right."

"Well . . . maybe I could do something . . ."

I hated for Doña Chela to be mad at me. She was a severe woman, and sometimes irritable, but she was the one in the *patrón's* family that I loved the best. I don't know why. I just did. The way Bizco loved the meanest horse in the stable, the one that always tried to kick him or bite him. But Bizco talked to that horse with love words.

And then the horrible thing happened, and we were stunned. Nobody knew what to do or say.

The *patrón* had gone out at night, and the Señorita Chela had left in the afternoon. She came back very soon, but the *patrón* did not come home for two days. Or Bizco either. Then, late on the second afternoon, Bizco stumbled in through the back *zaguán*. He was so scared he couldn't talk, and he had not eaten for two days either; he had been hiding under some rocks, which looked like just ordinary boulders, but they had a shallow cave under them. The *sardos* didn't know this, and there Bizco had lain, quiet, and terrified of the snakes that might be there, for snakes make their homes under the rocks, as we all knew. He spoke to Señorita Chela, and he was crying; I had never seen him cry before. She went out and hitched up a mule to one of the wagons, her face like a stone, and she made Bizco go with her, riding on the *alazán*. He went, hunched in the saddle, still crying. It was about dusk when they returned, and do you know what Señorita Chela had in the wagon? The *patrón*, Don Lencho, and four others, all bloody and dirty and stiff and dead. Señorita Chela drove all through Santa Lala, showing our dead. Even the *sardos* stationed in our town were ashamed, and went inside where they were billeted and would not look.

The colonel was in the church, with his papers and his tables, but I was little, and he didn't see me when I sneaked past; he was looking out of the window at the angry crowds that were forming in the streets and following after Señorita Chela and the poor dead men. So I got past him and I went up into the bell tower and I tolled the funeral bell. They came and caught me, the *sardos*. The colonel sent a man up into the tower, but he was ashamed to hit me, and just took me by the ear and pulled me downstairs and put me in front of that colonel.

He was a nice straight man, very clean, with a white skin, and clear gray eyes.

"What is your name?"

"Tranquilino Ortega, to serve God and you," I answered, as I had been taught.

He frowned and looked down, but he did not chide me.

"You must not toll the bell any more," he said. "Promise me that you will stay on the ground and behave yourself."

I did not answer.

"Promise," he insisted.

"What?" I asked, pretending to be stupid. He was easily convinced. He looked sharply at me, then shrugged, and motioned to the soldier to take me away. The soldier raised his hand as if to slap me, but I knew what to do. I cowered and covered my head with my hands. Then they were ashamed and they let me go.

The next day we buried all our dead people and the whole town closed its doors and its shops, and everyone went to the funeral. The Señorita Chela stood like a statue, and did not make a sound. Dr. Gutiérrez read the service, and then he said, "We do not need a priest to bless the graves, or this earth. Our tortured and martyred friends have blessed it."

And from that day on, nobody spoke to the *sardos*, not for any reason, and everyone wore black. Not a single soldier was allowed to forget for a single day what some of their men had done to ours.

I tried to make my music sometimes, by myself, to comfort myself a little, but I was very sad and the stones and the bones, and the leaves that made sounds, and the branches that made music when you swished them through the air . . . they did not satisfy me. I longed for a violin, one of those little wooden ones the country people make and string up with dried gut from a baby goat, and play with bows made of a branch and real horsehair.

Bizco was gone almost all the time with Señorita Chela, and they were often away for days. We had to be very quiet and careful at home, and never let on that they weren't in the house. We had to buy the same amount of bread and meat and everything, but Doña Rita always secretly passed this along to some poor families. And besides, times were bad . . . often there wasn't any meat at all. Some days not even a little skinny chicken. We were lucky to get some hard cheese and strong sausage.

I tried to make myself a violin, but the wood was too thick and I was too shy to beg Señorita Chela for one of the *patrón's* old cigar boxes. I thought that might be just right. And imagine that nice tobacco smell always, when you laid your *violincito* under your chin and began to play. I thought I would wait until some day when she seemed a little happier, a little less hard and desperate and angry. But that never came.

Then one day Señorita Chela called me, and said, "Chato, come to my room."

I went, and there she sat, sewing. It seemed funny to see her sewing. For now she often wore men's clothes . . . a pair of old pants of José Luis's, the young *patrón* who was away in Guadalajara, and boots and a dark shirt, and she had cut off her hair and wore it like mine, with a fringe down to her eyebrows and whacked off in back. She still had her long braid hanging on a hook on the wall, and once in awhile, when she put on a dress, she wound it around her head and you would never know that she had cut it off.

She was sewing a sort of long, white, cartridge belt.

"It is for you, Chato."

I waited for her to tell me more.

"I am going to ask you to do something dangerous. But I trust you. I know you can."

"Of course I can, God willing, Señorita Chela. What must I do?"

"Come here."

She hung one cartridge belt around me, over my shoulder and down to my waist, where it fastened. The second one went over the other shoulder and fastened on the opposite side.

"I will fill these with bullets, and you are to take them over to the men who are waiting at the creek beyond Santiaguito. No one must know that you are carrying ammunition. It will be hidden under your shirt."

"I could carry my fishing pole, as if I were going to try for a few little trout in the big hole there."

"Good. And if anybody stops you . . ."

"That's easy, Señorita Chela. I tell lies."

"Not too many, Chato. Better just say, 'Good afternoon,' or something like that. Now, I will fill these pockets with bullets and let's see if you can manage. I don't want you to go so loaded that anyone can tell . . ."

She filled the belts with cartridges from a box she had hidden under a board in the floor, and when she hung them around my neck again they were very heavy. I could hardly walk.

"Only one, I think, at first," she said to herself reluctantly.

It was all right with one; I could walk easily enough,

and the whole thing was hidden under my big white shirt that hung down over the outside of my pants.

"Go along some of the back paths, but don't try to hide," she told me. "And . . . Chato. If anybody should catch you, and make you strip . . . you are to say only that a man gave you a peso to take them, and that you were to bury them over near a tree . . . the one that was struck by lightning last year. Say it over to me. You must get it straight and not forget."

I said it over, and I learned it. Then she told me to take my fishing pole, and also one of the little garden hand spades, the tiny one like a child's toy. This was to prove that I had to bury the ammunition, if anybody found me out. And she got me a peso.

It was about four o'clock when I started, and that was good, because the fish, when there were any, rose to feed as soon as the sun began to go down. Though very few fish had ever been taken from that little stream. Still it was fun to fish, and we often did.

I went along the back paths, switching at the weeds and grass with my fishing pole. And I was lucky, because nobody at all came along the path except Lobo, who had been out hunting gophers. When he saw me he wagged and leaped and put his paws on my chest and wanted to come with me, so we went along together.

I came to the little village we called Santiaguito, and trudged through it; there were only three or four cottages and a small store. No *sardos* were hanging about. Beyond, about half a kilometer, was the creek. Before I got there one of the ranchers I knew came riding slowly along on a tired horse. Both were drooping with weariness. But when he saw me, Don Jacinto swung down off his mount, and said, "Tranquilino? Chato, she calls you. *Ave María Purísima . . .*"

"*Sin pecado concebida*," I answered. "She said men, the Señorita Chela."

"There are men, but they are some distance away. Safe. I will take what you have brought."

I gave him the belt of ammunition; he hastily emptied it and gave it back. He had put the bullets away in his own saddlebags, and I, in a matter of moments, had put on the belt under my shirt again.

"Is there anybody at the creek?"

"Nobody. Go and fish if you have time. Little fellows should have fun while they can."

I did get to the creek and I did fish, but I didn't catch anything except a little turtle which I put into my pocket.

Almost home again, with the sun setting, a *sardo* out on patrol saw me and stopped me.

"You, *chamaco!*"

"Sí, señor?"

"Where have you been?"

"Fishing."

"Did you see anybody?"

"No. I caught a turtle," I told him, looking as stupid as possible. "Look, he is green."

"You can't eat turtles."

"I just want him to play with."

"Where do you live?" He stopped me, still somehow scenting something suspicious.

"Over there." I waved. "In Santa Lala."

"Where's your father? Is he out fighting against us?"

"I haven't got any father."

"What does your mother do?"

"She washes."

I thought it was better to say this, so that he could not attach me to a special house.

He touched his cap with one finger, abstractedly.

"Well, go along home, it's getting dark."

"Sí, señor."

I went quietly along, but I took care to go around and come into Santa Lala by another way. Then I crept home through some little back streets. I did not see the soldier again.

So every two or three days I went out with ammunition under my shirt, sometimes to one place and sometimes to another. It might be Don Jacinto who met me, on a horse or driving a hay wagon, or maybe I had to hide it in a furrow, and cover it with earth. Señorita Chela always gave me careful instructions, and made me say them back to her four or five times.

We were very careful, and I was never stopped or suspected—until the new *comandante* marched in, with new soldiers.

He was a dark, strong handsome man. Indio, with a hawk face. And he wore a golden earring. He was hated by the people of Santa Lala because he was very severe. It seemed that he loved the army, the way we loved our land and our churches. He couldn't understand us, and we couldn't understand him. He was just. He never kept people in jail all night, as some of the others did, and he punished his soldiers if they got drunk. This was something new. Many of the others who came in and out of our town often let the men get drunk on Saturday nights, and looked the other way if they knocked in shop windows or stole. But Comandante Torres Mina kept order like a lady keeping her house.

He put up a sign one day in the plaza that all children under fourteen years of age were to report to his office in the barracks. (He wouldn't set up his office in the church; instead he had boarded it up.) He worked in a big campaign tent in the main square.

We had to go, and we arrived at the tent, a large surly group, and very quiet. The *comandante* took names and addresses and ages. He didn't know, he couldn't, that we all gave wrong names and wrong addresses, just as a matter of course. He would probably be transferred away before he could check on all of us anyway.

The line was long and it was already afternoon, and I was hungry when they got to me.

"Name?"

I had made up my mind what to say.

"*Juan Músico,* to serve God."

"Just the name, thanks. Age?"

"Seven past."

"Address?"

"One-twenty Hidalgo."

That was not my address. The only things I said right were my age, and that I wished to serve God.

I didn't like it that the *comandante* took a long, keen look at me, though. Still, there were many children in Santa Lala like me, dressed like me, about my size.

And yet, walking slowly home, and by a roundabout way, I wondered if maybe I could look different. Señorita Chela had made herself very different, almost like a man. What could I do? And it came to me that I could dress as a girl. I didn't want to, though. Still . . .

Señorita Chela wasn't home. She had ridden out, secretly, with Bizco the day before, and had told us not to expect her for several days.

That night after our supper (times were bad, but at least we each had a good bowl of hot beans and a few tortillas), a soldier came and pounded on our door. Doña Rita went to open the little peek window at the top; we never opened doors after dark. The soldier said, "Who is home?"

"What?"

"Who is here? Whole family?"

"I can't hear a word you say. Speak up, don't mumble."

"Who is here?" the man shouted.

"I'm here. What do you want?"

"Open up."

"What?"

"Open the door."

"Never. I'll have nothing to do with drunken soldiers. Get along with you."

The soldier exploded into curses and went away.

We heard next day that the *comandante* was sending soldiers around to many of the houses of suspected Cristeros to make sure people were home. We could expect that they would come again, and so Señorita Chela, when she got home that next evening, worn out and weary, bathed and put on a dress and wound her braid around her head. She was just in time.

The knocking came at the front door.

Doña Rita went, but the soldier was prepared this time. He passed in a note, signed by the *comandante,* demanding that the door be opened and the family lined up.

Señorita Chela swept up to the door and swung it open. She looked very beautiful, even though her dress was plain black. She was worn out and ready to fall with weariness, but she held herself straight as a queen.

"What is the reason for this invasion of a private home?" she asked the soldier. "I am not obliged to open the door, but I do so because the *comandante* has requested it. I would like to know, however, why we are harassed in this way?"

The soldier saluted and then shuffled his feet.

"We have to see if everybody is at home."

"Isn't the curfew you have imposed enough to convince you of that?"

"People have been sneaking out . . . riding around . . . stealing our horses . . ."

"You are free to examine my stables."

"Well . . . I wasn't told to do that. The *comandante* will send another man to check all the stables tomorrow."

"What is it you want then?"

"Where are the men in this family?"

Señorita Chela said, "I will get them." And she called Bizco and me, and made us come in and stand by Carlitos and Eduardito.

"These kids?" asked the soldier, unhappily.

"My father is dead and my older brother is in Guadalajara."

"Who supports you then?"

"I do," snapped Señorita Chela. "I ride out and supervise some of our planting, and buy and sell grain and animals. And if sometime I am late, I hope the *comandante* will remember that somebody has to earn the bread for this household."

The soldier finally saluted and left, and the minute he was gone Chela hissed to Bizco:

"Run round to Don Mateo and to Don Camilo and tell them that stables will be inspected tomorrow, and to get the horses out into the country somewhere. Quick!"

She wouldn't go to rest until Bizco came back and told her that he had warned the men, and that everything would be taken care of.

For a while she didn't go out again, and she wouldn't let any of us do anything to help. It was late fall and the *tunas* (cactus fruits) were getting ripe. She took me and Bizco and we went out to pick many sacks full, and then, back in the kitchen, we peeled them, saving the husks for two pigs she was fattening. Afterward she and Doña Rita made quantities of *queso de tuna,* boiling the fruit with dark blocks of hard sugar, and when the mixture was all thick they poured it into wooden molds, and made solid chunks of *tuna* jam. When we got through we had eighty-two of the molds, and each mold would keep a man, even riding hard, for three days or more. You need only a bit of water now and then. Señorita Chela never wasted any time.

72

When the molds were hard she sent us out with them; sometimes Bizco, sometimes me. We carried them to various places, always some different house or ranch. We were to say that they were for sale, if anybody stopped us. And once, in the country, the *comandante* himself overtook me carrying a big basket of *tuna* cheese, and he demanded to see it.

"Where are you going with that?"

"To sell it, in San José del Monte."

"I will buy it."

"*Muy bien.* Ten pesos a mold."

"That is expensive."

"That is the price I have to get for it."

"Some of these Cristeros who ambush us eat it. I have found scraps of it where they waited for us."

"Everybody eats *queso de tuna*. And this is homemade."

"Well, I will buy the lot."

"One hundred pesos. No credit!"

"I could make you give it to me, do you know that?"

"I know it."

"What do you want more than anything else in the world? Come on, answer me."

I could not stop myself.

"A little violin," I said. "To play on."

"That shouldn't be so hard to acquire," he said, looking thoughtful. Then he spurred his horse and cantered away.

"Your *tuna!*" I screamed after him. "My one hundred pesos!"

But he made no answer and did not return, so I trudged on to the place near San José where one of Señorita Chela's friends was waiting.

I played along the way, going home. Señorita Chela was very nervous waiting for me.

"The *comandante* talked to me," I told her.

73

She was pale, and her eyes grew big and black, and the violet circles that shadowed them grew darker.

"What did he want?"

"He said he would buy my *queso de tuna,* but then he went away, without."

She sighed with relief.

"We must be so careful now," she said. "So careful. Don't forget, Chato."

For many days she didn't send me anywhere, and I played music with my bones and my rocks.

Then came the day when Señorita Chela said we were to make our first communion. But it would be in secret, and we would not be allowed to have armbands and candles, or any of the other things. A priest was coming, and Don Evaristo, who had some grain warehouses, was going to hide him.

I didn't see him come, but I heard Mamá in the kitchen tell Bizco that the priest had come into town secretly, and was now hidden and safe.

Señorita Chela sent us, Eduardito and Carlitos and me, to Don Evaristo's at lunch time. The priest was young and thin. He looked just like a picture of San Antonio that Mamá had on an *estampa* that she kept inside her dress in a silk envelope, and showed me sometimes. His name was Félix.

The family of Don Evaristo stayed in the dining room, eating lunch, looking ordinary as could be, with their old tablecloth with sauce stains on it, dishes of beans and corn, and a rabbit stew with chile. While they ate, a few of us followed Señorita Chela (who had gone there very early in the day) and we went quietly out to the kitchen. We passed through it and into a very big *despensa* that Don Evaristo had built onto the kitchen. It had no windows except a tiny little screened place near the top, because that was where he kept his oats and sacks of corn. This had been cleared out, and a small table was placed at one end and covered with a white cloth. On it were two candles. Before it stood the priest. He was dressed in a black soutane, and over it he wore a plain, white silk robe with a cross embroidered on the back.

We all knelt down. There were only about seven of us. In those times you couldn't trust many people. Señorita Chela had told me that often enough.

Inside, Don Evaristo had put a record on his gramophone, and it made loud scratchy music. The tune was "Zacatecas." I remember that he played it over and over, and all the while the young priest was saying the words of the Mass. He came to the part where he consecrates the host, and he held it up . . . a little square of white bread. His face seemed very holy to me, and when it came my turn, and I felt the crumb of bread in my mouth, I forgot to keep my eyes closed but looked straight into his face, so calm and tender, as he bent above me.

Afterward we had to go home one by one, and by different ways. A few ladies had come, and I saw them waiting quietly in the kitchen, on benches. They were going to confession and would then receive communion too.

"How long can you manage to stay, Father?" I heard one of them ask.

"As long as God lets me," he answered her.

I went out through the back, and went away into the fields awhile and picked sunflowers. Mamá liked them, and she dried the seeds and used them, ground up, in some of our dishes. There were some *quelites,* too, and I picked a big bunch. They would taste good, like spinach, fried with onion and a little lard. I had to give Eduardito and Carlitos time to get home, one by one, and also Señorita Chela. Later in the day, Mamá and Doña Rita went over there, Mamá by the back way, to hear Mass.

About three days later, while Padre Félix was confessing,

soldiers came and took him and marched him to the *co-mandante*. We never knew whether somebody betrayed us, or whether they had been spying on us.

One afternoon soon after, when I was out playing (luckily I wasn't carrying bullets anywhere that day), the *co-mandante* came riding by, and he stopped his horse and said, "What have you got? *Tuna* cheese today?"

"Nothing. I was going to look for some *berro* over in the stream."

"Look what I have!" He reached back and took a package covered with paper from behind his saddle. He handed it down to me, saying, "Look."

I undid the paper and it shone sunset-red, shiny and smooth. A violin. Not too big. Just right for me. I touched it, and I laid it under my chin.

The *comandante* handed me down a bow.

"Play it. Make it cry," he told me.

I put the bow on the strings, but I did not pull it. I was afraid. Something made me hold my hand still. If I made it speak to me it would be too hard to give it back. And I *had* to give it back. I knew that.

I held it up toward him.

"It is beautiful," I said.

"Don't you want it?"

"No."

It was hard to get the lie out, so hard that tears popped into my eyes as I said it.

"You are afraid I will ask you to pay me for it. But I know you can't pay. Take it. It is a present."

"No," I said. But I took it.

I was ashamed to show it, for fear Mamá or Señorita Chela or the boys might ask me where I got it. So I had to think where to hide it.

The *comandante* had wheeled his horse and was riding away. When I was sure nobody could see me, I wrapped up the violin in my jacket and hid it by a stone in the tall grass. I hurried home, and was glad to find Mamá busy making *chiles en escabeche*. When she was occupied and didn't have time to look at me, I was all right. She could always tell, by looking into my eyes, if I had done something I shouldn't.

I burrowed around out in our warehouse, and finally I found an old horse blanket, all torn and old. I took it, and folded it as small as I could and put it under my shirt and hurried away back to where I had left the *violincito*. I fixed a place under some rocks and wrapped it in the blanket. I knew I could leave the violin there. Meanwhile, I tried to play.

It was hard to make the music come, and at first it was just rough, scratchy sound, but I found how to put down my fingers to make a scale, and I saw that pretty soon I would be able to coax it to a sing a tune. I was so happy that when darkness fell, and I could no longer see my hands, I was surprised. I wrapped the *violincito* up carefully and laid it under the stones, and rolled them into place. When I got home Mamacita licked me because she was scared that something had happened. It wasn't a bad licking because she had to stop and watch something on the stove. I told her I had gone to sleep out in the fields, and she believed me.

I couldn't go and play it the next day because Señorita Chela sent me with ammunition to a ranch outside Coyotitlán, and it was a long walk in the hot sun—at least ten kilometers, and that many back, of course.

One of the *sardos* passed me, but he did not stop. He just leaned down from his horse and whacked me with a willow whip he had cut while riding along. It hurt, but I did not even look up, and when he saw that he could not tease me, he rode on. Once, when I had been carrying bullets, one of the scouts they had out all the time saw me and asked me

to stop and have a swim in the stream with him, and I
would not. If he had made me undress, he would have seen
what I carried. But he was impatient and went along by
himself.

I found the house I had been sent to . . . a dusty little
chicken farm . . . and left the ammunition there with the
señora. She was good to me, and fried me some sausage
with eggs, and made me hot tortillas.

"Did you see anybody, *niño?*"

"One soldier. He hit me, but he didn't stop me."

"You had better leave the ammunition belts here too. I
will hide them, and send them back to La Coronela somehow."

"I think I have to take them back to her."

"No, *niño*. I have the second sight, and that soldier you
saw, he will find you again this afternoon. But there is a
message you are to take home. Don't forget it. 'Tomorrow
at full dark at the Fourth Cross.'" I said it to remember,
and I left the belts with her, and then I started home.

The country people who fought the *sardos* had made up
names for places where they met, and they called them
crosses. The *sardos* never could figure out where the crosses
were, but all our people knew.

I trudged along, going part of the way in the fields, but
when I came to within about four kilometers of Santa Lala
I came out on the road again. And almost at once I saw a
little round ball of yellow dust coming down the road after
me. I didn't turn, but again I felt a smart blow on my
shoulder, and I almost fell.

It was the soldier who had passed me in the morning, and
there were some others with him, and an officer.

"Take off your shirt, Indito."

I pulled it off. I was not such a fool as to have left the
marks of the crossed ammunition belts on my skin. I had

rubbed out the marks with bunches of grass and had brought up the blood. They couldn't see anything.

"Put it on. Where have you been?"

"To try to buy some honey over at Rincón del Monte."

"Where is it?"

"They had promised their honey elsewhere."

"He is lying, the little Cristero brat."

"Let him go."

"No. Hang onto him. The *comandante* was speaking of him the other day. He has been suspicious. Mixed up with them somehow."

They tied a rope around my neck and made me trot along behind them. I was so tired when we came to Santa Lala. They rode right up to the *comandante's* tent. But he was not there, and so they turned me over to a soldier on guard duty, and told him to watch me. I was to be kept until the *comandante* came back.

I don't know how long I was there. I fell asleep on the floor, and didn't wake up until somebody kicked me. There were hoofbeats and everybody sprang up to attention. I was sleepy and my eyes were sticky, but I saw something awful. The *comandante* had ridden in, and tied by the neck with a rope, being dragged after him, half stumbling and running, was Father Félix. His soutane was all torn and dirty, and his face was pale and drawn. The *comandante* tossed the rope that tied Padre Félix to one of the orderlies, and I saw him jerk Padre Félix along. The *comandante* strode in and looked at me.

"What is this little fiddler here for?" he asked, wearily. I made no answer.

"Speak up," the *commandante* rapped out sharply. "What is it?"

"They found him out on the road. He is always about in the country; they think he carries messages for the Cristeros."

"Do you?"

"No," I answered, sullenly.

The *comandante* stared at me. "Sometimes you say no when you mean yes," he said softly. "Isn't that so?"

But I would not say another word, even when he shook me. Then he let me alone, and passed his hand across his eyes, as if he were too tired to go on.

"Let the child go," ordered the *comandante*. "I plan to catch bigger fish than minnows."

They untied me, and pushed me out. I looked around a little bit for Padre Félix, but I did not see him. As I stumbled home I remembered how he had looked when he gave me the communion, so clean and pure and beautiful.

That night, when Mamá was asleep, I sneaked out and went to the place where I had hidden the *violincito*. I held it under my chin, just to feel it a little while, and then I took a rock and broke the *violincito* into small pieces. I carried them out and left them in a little pile in the road. Soldiers were scouting about all the time. Somebody would be sure to find them and take them to the *comandante*.

Mamacita didn't even hear me or wake up when I got back into bed with her again.

III

"Santa María de Guadalupe . . ."

THE CHRONICLE OF BIBIANA

They told me that Mamacita had died when I was not much past two, and people said that babies of two can't remember anything. But that isn't true, for I often dreamed of her, and what are dreams except memories that come to you in sleep, to comfort you? I dreamed of her and I could see her as she lay in bed, with thick, curling, dark-brown hair spread out on the pillow. How could I have imagined what I saw so often in my sleep, as a small child . . . my father kneeling by her bedside, taking a tress of her hair in his hands and bringing it to his lips, and her laying a thin white hand like a *nardo* on his bowed head. I saw that scene so often, and many times as I dreamed, she would turn to me and say, *"Hijita!"* very lovingly, and I saw that her eyes were a wonderful color, golden like topaz, with black lashes around them, pointed from tears; her eyes seemed to me like daisies with leaves of another color, daisies with their golden centers, but with spiky black petals.

I went sometimes to the cemetery with Macaria, our cook, to take flowers, but I could not imagine my lovely mother far beneath, in the earth, under the stone, and so I never cried there. But oh so many times I wept in my bed after seeing her in my sleep; many mornings I woke up with my cheeks and my pillow wet.

Papacito was called "Doctor" by everybody, and in a childish imitation, I too called him "Doctorcito." He did not ask me to change. My birth had taken my mother's strength, and then her life; I believe he did not like any reminders of that, and preferred his only daughter to call him "Doctor" rather than Papacito or Papá.

He was a short, rather squat person, inclined to flesh and a bit bowlegged, and I took after him. I was never a pretty child. I had my father's olive skin and his small, wide nose. But I had my mother's hair, and as I grew older I could see that I had inherited her golden eyes as well. These were my only beauties.

Doctorcito was busy all day long, every day, every night, for he had a pharmacy, and had to go there regularly to watch over the making of medicines and so on. He had a consultation room there in back of the pharmacy, and also at home, where the two big rooms that opened onto the street were equipped as his surgery and his office. Between those rooms, and the rest of our house, there were great wrought-iron doors, which Doctorcito kept locked with chains and padlocks. The rear part of the house consisted of our dining room and kitchen, a bedroom for me and one for Doctorcito, and in back the kitchens, *despensa*, and back patio and stables. Doctorcito kept four horses and a carriage, but most often he went about riding his saddle horse to see sick people in the country. Our cook's father, a little, gnarled old man who had one leg very bowed and much shorter than the other (it had been broken by a fall and never set properly) looked after the horses. His name was Nicolás, I know now. In all my childhood I never heard him called anything but "Colás."

Children, I am convinced, never think of anything about their lives as strange or different. My life was indeed a lonely one. Macaria washed my clothes and combed my hair, and Petra, who mopped and swept and ironed, took me to and from school and walked with me to my catechism classes. Doctorcito trusted to padlocks and barred windows to keep me safe at home when I was not at school, and trusted Petra and Macaria to go with me whenever it was necessary to leave the house. The result was that, until I was a big girl in school, I did not eat with a spoon but with tortillas, and I drank making loud noises, and I played with my puddings, and took up chops in my hand. Doctorcito hardly ever had time to sit at table; Macaria used to take him his food on trays, locking the iron gates behind her as she came and went.

When school began, and catechism at the same time, I saw other children my age. I began to wonder about my clothes, which Petra made (with dresses and aprons for herself and Macaria all off the same bolt of cloth), and I wished for shoes. All my life I had worn only *huaraches*, mere leather soles held on with leather thongs.

Chela Valera was the one who taught me to be a girl, to try to look pretty (I never could), and to make the best of myself.

She was always beautiful, even as a small girl, and that is rare, I now know. Most girls go through an age, roughly from ten to fourteen, when they are frightful, with teeth too big for their mouths, long knobby legs, and sometimes pimples. Chela, from the day I became her best friend in school, was lovely. She was slim and well formed, taller than the rest of us, and she had long, shining, black braids, white skin, and large dark-brown eyes as heavily fringed and as long and almond-shaped as the image of the Virgin in church, where we went after school to our catechism classes.

I was fat and homely, but Chela took me home with her in the afternoons, and her own mother made me dresses just like Chela's, and I felt very happy to be in the company of such a beauty.

She was never easy to get along with. For one thing she learned everything very fast and was impatient with those of us who were slower and for whom the lessons had to be repeated. Whenever I had to stand in the corner to learn my verse or my multiplication table, Chela would pass by me to the blackboard, or back to her seat again, and, brushing close, would pinch me or stick me with her sharp pen. *"Burra!"* she would hiss at me, and then I would cry and couldn't even see the letters of my verse, and everything was much worse.

Our teachers soon learned to set Chela more tasks than the rest of us, to use up her restless energies and keep her mind busy.

Chela's mother took care of many poor families, especially those of ranchers who sold produce to her husband, and she was always going about town with baskets of food and clothing. She begged medicines from my father, though he used to tease her, saying, "But señora, isn't it enough that I spend half my life attending these people for nothing? Must I give medicines too?"

"Oh yes, Doctorcito, you must," she would answer firmly. "At least some quinine, and some turpentine liniment and some oil for the babies. I make soap at home, and I always set aside some for my poor people. But I cannot make quinine, or I would!"

I went with Chela and her mother on some of these daily visits to the poor and sick, but I was of no use; the smell of sick people in their dirty bedclothes, sometimes soiled with vomit and excrement, used to make me sick at my stomach. I don't know how Doña Leonor managed; she used to wash and change old, bedridden people, and clean their little huts, and look after them as tenderly as if they were her own. Chela was never dismayed by anything. She never fainted (as I did when I saw the wounds of the man who had been gored by a maddened bull or at the streams of blood that burst like a fountain from between the legs of the young servant girl trying to have her first baby) and she did as her mother told her to do, though without any love.

Doña Leonor soon asked me not to go about with her, as she had enough to do looking after the people who needed her without having to catch me and revive me every ten minutes. So I was left at home, and Chela went with her on those errands. She did them because they were her duty, she told me haughtily; she despised dirty, sick creatures. She didn't even like the babies very much, though I did. I loved them and gladly would have waited in the street while the dressings were changed and so on if I could but have bathed and held the tiny little ones.

"I don't like them till they can talk to you and say something," Chela used to say to me. "Up until then, they are just lumps, and mostly bawling."

"Well, you will have to have babies some day, when you get married!" I shot at her.

"Ugh! I suppose I will," she said. "But maybe I won't marry. I'd rather be a man, anyhow. Out riding in the country, chasing rabbits and shooting deer! I'd like that much better!"

"Well, you aren't a man, so there!"

"No," she answered sadly. "Maybe I won't marry, just the same." A dreamy look had come into her eyes.

"You'll have to, Chela! You are so beautiful! All the men will ask you!"

She tossed her head. "One can say no," she pointed out.

I was scandalized. "But you wouldn't!" I gasped. "Your parents wouldn't let you!"

"We shall see!" she said, giving me a sidelong look.

From that moment I kept closer than ever to her. Besides mightily admiring her, I was mystified by her. And I had begun to think a lot about boys and serenades and wedding veils, and all such wonderful things.

One evening when Doctorcito wasn't too busy he came and had dinner with me in the dining room. This was exciting, and I set the table with a fine cloth, and put out good plates and lighted a candle.

Afterward my father talked to me, asked me about school and Chela and what I thought about, and what I wanted to do and so on. I would soon finish sixth grade, and that meant the end of school for most of us. After that most young ladies had cooking and sewing lessons, and dancing lessons, and other such things until suitors presented themselves. In Santa Lala girls expected to be married by the time they were fifteen or sixteen. Eighteen at the very latest.

"Stand up. Let me look at you."

I knew what he was seeing. I wasn't as ugly as I had been. I wasn't so fat any more, and now I knew how to bind in my waist with a tight corset, and walk slightly humped over so that my full bosom wasn't so noticeable. My skin was clear and my hair was very pretty.

"I must send to Guadalajara and get you some pretty dresses," he said. "The boys will be tuning up their guitars in the street before long."

"Ay, Doctorcito," I protested. I never thought myself attractive. Always, before my inward eye, hovered the resplendent beauty of Chela, haughty and disdainful and lovely.

"I will write to your Tía Elena in Guadalajara to buy you some pretty things."

"And some new piano music, Doctorcito. Please!"

"That, too. Well, now, play something for me."

Gladly I went to the piano. One of my solitary joys was playing it, and in the last two years my father had arranged for me to have lessons from Señorita Valdivia, who had studied in Guadalajara and who still went every two or three months to take a coaching lesson from Don Refugio Pereda Holtz, a really great teacher who gave concerts all over Mexico.

Señorita Valdivia was a maiden lady who, like so many

women who had not married, remained in her home "keeping her mother company," and abstaining from society in general, it being thought that dances, picnics, and large gatherings were mostly for the purpose of allowing young people to court while under the eyes of experienced and cautious chaperones. She had lost her father a few years before, and her mother was not well, so Señorita Valdivia gave her piano lessons at home, and seldom stirred out except for her three-day trips to Guadalajara.

I remember the first piano lesson I ever had. As a great favor to my father, she came to our house, to try our piano and to get me started. It was a day in early summer, quite warm, but Señorita Valdivia wore a dress of black wool. She was a long-faced woman of almost forty who wore her hair in a braided bun at the back; in her black, and without powder or lipstick, she looked almost nunlike. Her features were long and sharp, her lips colorless, her eyebrows pointed up toward her still dark hair. But I remember that, when she laid her hands on the yellowing keys of my mother's old piano, I was startled with a strong sense of beauty. Her hands were white and muscular, with broad palms and long fingers; they looked to me like my father's hands, like hands that had skill and prescience and life of their own, so different from the stiff horny hands of country workers, or the soft little cushiony hands of well-to-do young ladies who never did more than embroider or polish their nails. Señorita Valdivia's hands moved on the keys and brought forth music; I almost swooned with joy at the sounds, for though our piano needed to be tuned and some of the notes were tinny (she ordered my father to send to Guadalajara for new felts to be laid under the keys), the music she made reached into my sentimental heart.

She played for half an hour, those beautiful hands flying over the keys, stroking them, urging them, demanding them, caressing them. She swayed a good deal and closed her eyes. I suppose all her emotional life had been channeled into music, and though it was not always the best music she played, she gave her whole heart to it. And luckily for me, she had been well trained.

She put my hands on the keys and instructed me about my position, taught me the names of the notes, and arranged with my father that I was to go to her twice a week, in the afternoons.

I was happy to go, especially as Chela made the rounds of sick people with her mother afternoons and I was unable to bear any of that activity. But I, too, wanted to be important, and my piano lessons gave me a special distinction.

I don't suppose, even now, that I am markedly musical, but I am imaginative and responsive, and I am dutiful. I don't know where I got this, this sense that I must do what I have undertaken to do and do it well. The servants in Doctorcito's house never made me stick to my tasks; they spoiled me dreadfully. And Doctorcito could not think of enough ways in which to indulge me, when he had time to give to me. But from the beginning I made myself little routines, and I devised for myself ceremonials that I felt I had to carry out religiously every day. I loved them, and I derived enormous satisfaction, once in bed at night, in reviewing my day and making sure that I had, 1. Said my whole rosary; 2. Practiced two whole hours by the clock, and extra for scales; 3. Knitted six inches on the scarf I was making for my father; and 4. Written in my diary.

To this day I say over something of the same sort of litany of tasks and accomplishments at night, and if I have slighted some I am restless and miserable and try to make them up next day. I suppose this is the sort of artificial framework of life which we cowards need to have to lean upon. I know that I have never been able to improvise, to meet unexpected dangers or troubles with any skill. I break down, and I am useless.

So I worked hard at the piano, and I made my fingers and wrists and arms do as Señorita Valdivia said they should. I learned the notes and the time and the phrasing, and I began to feel that thrill of anticipation which young people know when they glimpse, beyond the drudgery and study, the slowly opening doors of another mansion of the mind.

This evening I played for my father one of the earlier sonatas of Mozart, feeling just beyond the clean and sunlit melodies some almost understood radiance of the spirit.

"*Muy bonita, hijita,*" said my father, who had not been paying much attention, I think.

"Oh, I almost forgot! Señorita Valdivia says that Professor Pereda is coming here and will give a concert in the Casino. Can we go, Doctorcito?"

"Why yes, you can, of course. If I am busy, you could go with the Valeras. I suppose they will all have tickets. Is Señorita Valdivia selling the tickets?"

"Yes, and they are five pesos apiece!"

This was a good deal of money in those days.

"Well, we will take two tickets," said Doctorcito.

"And afterward, he is going to her house, Señorita Valdivia's, to take supper, and all the pupils are invited!"

Doctorcito's tired face broke into a happy smile.

"That will be very nice for you, *mi vida.* When will this concert take place?"

"On the twentieth of April."

"A month and a half away. We will write to Tía Elena at once!"

"A yellow dress, Doctorcito! With black velvet ribbons!"

"You shall have it! You know the saying, 'She who wears yellow is confident of her beauty.'"

That scared me.

"Oh no, then. Chela will probably have a yellow dress. Mine had better be pink."

"As you wish, *preciosa*. Though you are quite as pretty as Chela, and far sweeter."

The days went by. I said my rosaries, knitted inches on the scarf, and practiced steadily. I was to play one of the Bach inventions at Señorita Valdivia's house after the concert. A pink dress arrived, with embroidered ruffles, and with it a pair of new, black, patent-leather slippers. Posters began to appear showing Professor Pereda, with long hair, wearing a red velvet coat and sitting in front of a keyboard, hands on his knees, staring thoughtfully at the keys.

Chela and I stood and looked at one of the posters, and she tossed her head and her lip curled.

"What an old *fifí!*" she said.

For once I defied her.

"Oh, he can't be! He's a great pianist. Señorita Valdivia says he studied with Busoni."

"And who's that?"

"The greatest pianist in the world; and he's Italian."

"Humph."

"Are you going to the concert?"

"I guess we have to," she answered me glumly.

She was as excited as I, however, on the evening of the concert. We took our seats, Chela, her mother and father and I, and rustled our programs with nervous anticipation. Señorita Valdivia was nowhere to be seen; she was rushing about in the room that had been set aside for the artist, bringing him hot water in which to soak his hands, hot soup to drink, and a bottle of brandy. Doctorcito had been shanghaied into remaining in the artist's room with him, in case he needed reviving; in the passion of his own playing he was likely to lose himself and half faint, between numbers, Señorita Valdivia said. She told this to my father solemnly, enlisting his aid the night before, but as he agreed my father smiled, and when she had gone he said to me, with a sly wink, "He knows how to get himself appreciated, that one. Nothing like having everybody scared that you will swoon and be unable to finish the concert. They'll sit up and take notice!"

The Casino was not, of course, a concert hall. It was a ballroom, where all the best families of Santa Lala met for dancing parties and for big festivities, speechmaking, and card playing. A temporary platform had been constructed at one end of the hall, and Señorita Valdivia's own big Bechstein grand had been transported carefully through the streets and placed there, and then tuned again on the afternoon of the concert.

Everyone had done Señorita Valdivia (for whom they came) the honor of dressing in his best. Most of the matrons of Santa Lala wore black, simple good dresses of silk crepe or satin. Many of them had fine *rebozos* around their shoulders, and all wore gloves. All had been to the hairdresser that very afternoon, and they wore their hair piled high in curls or puffs, or in severe figure eights low on their necks. Earrings flashed, and, as the hall filled, quite a few fans came out to flutter laces and gently move the warm air.

Chela indeed had a yellow dress, and she was so slender and tall that as usual she made me feel like a plump little rabbit. She pinched me when we took our seats, and whispered maliciously, "Look at Señorita Valdivia; you would think she was in love with that old *fifi* the way she runs up and down."

She was darting out to dust the piano keys, then to move a fern which had been placed too near the piano; last, to raise the piano bench with several hard cushions.

But at last the lights were dimmed and Don Refugio came out and bowed low to the amiable, courteous applause. He stood with his head hanging halfway to his knees until there was absolute silence. Then he sat down, wrung his hands together for a few minutes, and then pounded on the piano, banging out a series of deafening chords which I fear undid all the careful tuning work of Don Hermilo, who had been in the Casino with his tuning instruments all afternoon.

Then, turning to glare at the audience (because two people had coughed and a few were rattling their programs), he swung about, placed his right foot forward and the left behind, bent at the knee (he used no pedal for this), and began to play the "Appassionata Sonata" of Beethoven.

It is not usual to start with a work of this calibre, but Don Refugio knew his provincial audiences . . . women who were determined to be appreciative and artistic, men who were polite but faintly embarrassed. The thunder and the movement, the raw emotion, the brilliance . . . these jarred the audience into feelings they had not anticipated, and when he finished he had them in his pocket. Then he went on to play a few gentle, evanescent, poetic pieces of Debussy, and when he sensed that the men were thinking about a cigar and a promenade, he flew into the "Revolutionary Etude" of Chopin. Finishing it with a great flourish, he leaped up, and again hung his head low, while our people stamped and clapped and screamed "Bravo!"

There was then a short intermission, and as she hurried about among the groups of ladies still remaining in their seats, and cast bright eyes toward the excited gentlemen promenading on the terrace, Señorita Valdivia was full of triumph, and of a great pride.

The second half of the program was arranged with Don Refugio's skillful psychology, and when the concert came to a close he was rushed by the people who wished to shake his hand and compliment him, and breathe their excitement over him. He would not speak to anyone, held his hands together as if they pained him, occasionally laying one upon his heart as he bowed. He threw back his hair and panted, and then he stumbled off the stage as if he had opened his abdomen and let out all his vital organs.

However, an hour later, holding court in Señorita Valdivia's *sala*, he looked fresh and hearty, and I knew him for a kind of fraud. Not musically, however. Even then, I realized that, once he was at his work, once he had begun to play, he had no peer.

I did not know enough to be frightened of playing for him. Señorita Valdivia was very distraught, however, as she marshaled her pupils together and made ready to effect a small pupils' recital. She dropped her music, her hands shook, and she was pale as a piece of coconut.

I realize we were all pretty bad and that, after his wonderful concert, it was really an imposition to inflict us on that artist. But, despite his posturings and exaggerated gestures, despite the long hair and the flowing tie and the garnet velvet coat, he was helpful, if not always kind.

He sat listening to us with more interest and attention than our parents, and to each one of us he gave a few words of advice. To me he said, "How long have you been studying, little one?"

"Three years."

"You practice hard. You work. Keep it up. You will go further than some of these others. Remember, *chiquita,* music is ninety per cent self-discipline."

After the chocolate and cakes had been disposed of, mouths wiped of wet brown mustaches on her embroidered Madeira napkins, and dirty plates piled up for her to wash in the morning, Señorita Valdivia clapped her hands.

"An announcement, dear children! Once a year, when I go to Guadalajara for my coaching lesson with our great Maestro, I will take one pupil, the one who has made most progress in the previous twelve months! The Maestro will give that pupil a lesson and counsel!"

We all clapped enthusiastically.

I told this to Chela next day, as we sat working on our embroidery at her house. I was making a set of six napkins,

and she was doing scallops around the neck of a white ba-
tista nightgown for her mother.

For once I saw a look of envy on Chela's face. Usually,
she did not honor me with anything but a kind of careless
scorn.

"I guess you will win it, won't you, Bibi? You do work
hard. It would be wonderful to go to Guadalajara. Not with
that old Señorita Valdivia, though."

"She's very nice, really. Just sort of nervous. She says it's
in her family. Do you really think I'll be the one, Chela?"

"Of course," she said calmly, and then she smiled at me.
"I'll pray for you to win it," she offered.

"I'll make novenas to Saint Cecilia," I cried. "As soon as
I finish one I'll begin another. Who will you pray to, Chela?"

She looked startled, and then bent her head over her
embroidery again.

"I'll pray straight to Our Lord," she said.

It did not seem strange to me to see her very often in
church, deep in prayer, and I was sure it was because of
me. I was always a simple child, and did not distrust or
seek motives beyond those that people offered for their ac-
tions.

So Chela and I grew up, and we had our Baile de
Quince together. At this ball, announcing that we were fifteen and ready to begin considering marriage, we both wore
white dresses. They were made of machine-embroidered or-
gandy that had come from Switzerland, and underneath,
showing through the design, were our taffeta silk slips. Mine
was sky blue; Chela's was a very faint pink. I had my hair
dressed and it was arranged in ringlets on my forehead
and curls down my back. Chela wore hers as she always
did, in a thick black braid, but it had been looped under
and caught with mother-of-pearl hairpins. I looked pretty
and young, but Chela looked like royalty. She always did.

It was funny that, despite her manner, all the boys clustered around her like flies on a ripe peach. "No," I heard her say. "Go and dance with Bibiana."

It hurt a little, but not much, for after all, that way I got lots of partners, and I loved to dance. I was content to be Chela's slave and take her orders and her leavings. She knew it, and her parents knew it, and my father knew it. It didn't worry any of us.

Her brother José Luis was older than Chela. You might have thought that I would be in love with him, wouldn't you? It would seem natural. He was one of the few young men I could see with some frequency, and talk to enough to learn a little about his thoughts. Well, perhaps that is why I did not fall in love with him. He was an odd fellow, and Chela was mystified by him, as were her parents.

He didn't like our provincial life, but he was not rebellious and bad-tempered. He was pleasant and agreeable, but he simply wouldn't do what the other young men did. And, though this was queer, one couldn't tag him with any of the usual labels which make it possible to despise the nonconformist. He wouldn't go hunting, and hated to see animals killed, but he was not a sissy or effeminate. And he didn't try to stop the others. He wasn't a fanatic or a reformer. He simply announced that he would not go hunting, he hated it, and he hoped the others would have a good time, and would anybody like to borrow his horse.

Chela told me, one day, that José Luis was as good a shot as her father, too. But he would shoot only at targets, and he despised the men who wore pistols, because he said they did it only to feel stronger and braver than the others.

He had lost his religion, too, and this was of course the worst thing. Chela asked me to pray for him, and I did; we said a whole rosary for him every day. We were about sixteen, at the age when religion and longings for love get all mixed up together. In ordinary people, I mean. We were ordinary girls. At least, I was.

But I dared to stop José Luis and ask him about why he would not go to Mass any more, and why he let his whole family suffer for him.

He looked at me thoughtfully. He was an odd-looking boy, rather heavy and not tall, with sandy hair and freckles and weak blue eyes. Some of his mother's people were blonds; they had a lot of French blood.

"Would it be better if I went to church, not believing?" he asked. "Do you think that would be a lesser sin?"

I was afraid that he had lost his soul, and I was frightened for him. Tears filled my eyes.

"You could say, like the saints, 'Lord, I am not worthy.'"

"Not worthy because I do not believe?"

"Yes."

He looked down, and I saw the sandy line of his eyelashes and the curious tightening of his mouth.

"You may be right, Bibi. And I will go to church again."

You would suppose this might make me feel that I loved him; I was, by all the rules of nature, ready for such a feeling. But some respect bridled those inclinations. I could only say, gravely and sincerely, "Thank you, José Luis."

So he went again to Mass, and the family was happy. And his father arranged for him to go away to Guadalajara to study law.

I remember when he came to tell us goodbye, Doctorcito and me.

It was evening, after supper, and we had lighted the lamps. He had called on Doctorcito in the office, but they came in together to where, by candlelight, I was working at scales in thirds.

"I came to tell you goodbye, Bibi," said José Luis, and he held out his hand. I rose from the piano bench and put mine into his, and I looked into his eyes. I saw something there that troubled me. It was a look of love, of devotion. I felt worried, almost repelled by it, without acknowledging to myself exactly what it was. I felt suddenly immodest; I did not want him to look at me like that. If I had loved him, I would have joyed in it.

"I am going to Guadalajara to study. I will be a lawyer," he said. "I may not come back for a long time, and I wanted . . . I wanted to say goodbye."

"I wish you all success, José Luis. *Feliz viaje*," I answered primly. He watched my face anxiously for a few moments, and then he dropped his eyes and released my hand.

My father saw him to the door, and it was years before I saw him again. Then he came home to visit with a friend, and my life changed completely.

I first saw my husband at the Valera house. "Fernando Leyva y Portugal," they said his name was, and I heard it echo in my heart. Fernando.

He was slim and fair-skinned, with a slight flush in his cheeks. His hair was dark brown, and his eyes were gray; he wore a small, silky moustache, and when he smiled you could see that his teeth were very even and white.

He did not have eyes for me. I could see that Chela had all his attention, and no wonder. She had grown more elegant, more reserved, more beautiful every year. Hers was not a sweet face, but it was one of remarkable delicacy and pride, and every movement she made, every turn of her head, showed a lovelier line of cheek, jaw, and throat. Besides, she was rather hostile to men. There was someone she loved in secret; she had told me so. I had no idea who he was, or where she might have met him. Perhaps she just dreamed him. Anyway, her indifference made her even more attractive to Fernando. Any fool could see that, and certainly I did.

But what good would it have done for me to feign indifference? I would see him perhaps twice or three times before he returned to Guadalajara. He would never want to come to our dusty little Santa Lala again, unless Chela encouraged him.

I hardly remember the glory of those few days. I went to the plaza with them, and we walked around and around beneath the orange trees while the band played. We went to the Casino to dance, and since Chela would not dance with Fernando, he danced with me. He was a good dancer, lithe and graceful, and his arms held me firmly. I loved to dance, and how happy I was, encircled by his arms, smelling the faint cigarette and lavender odors of his clothes, the top of my head just grazing his chin. He was very attentive to me, looking at me brightly and smiling, but he made strange answers to my remarks, and I knew that his mind was away, on Chela, who stood on the balcony in her pale lemon-colored dress, looking out at the stars, talking with José Luis. From where we whirled on the dance floor we saw her cameo profile, and the shining black of her braids.

I could not eat in the days he was in Santa Lala. I bathed twice a day and changed my dress four times. I combed my hair every hour. I cried a lot. I was in love.

I knew that he and José Luis would leave on Saturday. I steeled myself for the farewell dinner, to which Doctorcito and I had been invited. We were to walk over to the Valera house at seven in the evening. At five, I lay in my white muslin slip on the bed in my room, my rosary in my hands, praying that I should be able to control myself, and not burst into childish tears before everybody. It was all I dared ask.

Then Petra came and knocked on my door.

"The young gentleman, the *licenciado* from Guadalajara, has called, and is waiting in the *sala*, señorita."

I thought she meant José Luis, so I slipped on the cotton dress I had been wearing, ran a comb through my hair, and hurried out. There stood Fernando. He was very pale, and there were faint violet shadows under his eyes.

"She has refused him," I thought, and I felt bitterly sorry for him. I could not bear to see the hurt on his face.

"Señorita Bibiana, I have the honor to ask you to marry me," he said.

I stood dumbfounded, and then the light broke upon me. Chela ordered him to ask me. I knew it, and I felt a deep, horrible shame. But I opened my mouth and I heard the words I said.

"I accept, Fernando."

He took my hand and kissed it, and then he hurried out of the room. He had gone to find Doctorcito, I knew. I went back to my room and fell on the bed, kissing my rosary. I had been tossed to him, and he had asked to marry me out of hurt pride. But I didn't care. He had asked me, and I had accepted. He would be mine! And I would cherish him, I would make him love me.

You see, I had no pride. Pride is a kind of courage, I suppose, and I never had any of that, either. I was simply overcome by my good luck, and I could have kissed Chela's shoes for making it possible for me. No doubt you despise me. If so, you may be glad, for all my suffering came later, and I paid in a million tears for my short rapture.

Doctorcito suspected nothing, for he had always thought me wonderful, and it did not even occur to him that Fernando might really have preferred Chela, because he himself did not. Well, God bless him. His steadfast love was a comfort to me.

Fernando meticulously fulfilled all the requirements which provincial manners demanded of him. His mother, a widow, wrote formally requesting my hand in marriage for her son. She excused herself from making the journey to Santa Lala because of ill health, but she explained their situation to Doctorcito. She told him that they had a large house, where I would be mistress, and she would be guest, the moment the wedding ceremony made me Señora de

Leyva. She offered to be a true mother to me, since I had been deprived of mine so young, and since she had no daughter.

This sounds as if I am preparing you for the usual story . . . a timid and uncertain bride, a hostile mother-in-law unwilling to cede her power, a tragedy. Not so. I was never worthy of Doña Paz, never. She was worth a thousand of me in intelligence, resourcefulness, and courage.

Our wedding was really beautiful. How deeply peaceful and good it is to stand up to be married at the very altar where you received your first communion, where you have heard Mass every Sunday all your life!

Around me were my friends who had known me from childhood. To one side my father, so dear, so loyal, and beside me, my bridegroom, pale and handsome, still carrying a thorn in his heart, but a thorn which I would remove so softly, so carefully, so tenderly with my affection and my service that he would never know it had been there. And in front of us, wearing the white and gold robes that the women of Santa Lala had embroidered for him, good Padre Melesio to say the sacred words, and to forge around us that invisible bond that no man can break.

The only flaw in the perfection of that day was the absence of Chela's dear mother, who had died in childbirth (a late pregnancy) not long before, and the fact that Chela could not be my bridesmaid because of her mourning. I saw her smile at me as I walked out of the church on my husband's arm, and in her face was generous love for me, and I knew her good wishes.

I cannot remember much of what followed. The banquet at the Casino. Our first waltz together, while I was still wearing my bridal gown and veil. Then I slipped away to my bedroom at home to stand before my mirror and look with wonder into the eyes, not of Señorita Bibiana Gutiérrez, but of Señora de Leyva. I changed into my traveling suit, put the last toilet articles into my suitcase. Doctorcito was waiting in our *sala* to kiss me goodbye, and then Fernando and I left, traveling by automobile over the roads to Guadalajara.

Fernando thought it would be best if we went straight to his mother's house, since she had not been well enough to come to Santa Lala for the wedding, and rest there awhile before going away on a honeymoon.

He was so gentle and kind with me. Sitting in the car behind the chauffeur he had hired to drive us, he held my hand, and said that he was afraid all the excitement and strangeness of traveling and being married might be too much for me all at once, and besides, he wanted to give his mother the joy of getting acquainted with me.

"We will be the happier on our honeymoon," he promised, "for a few days of rest there with Mamacita first."

It was a long drive in those days, tiring and dusty. Night had fallen when at last we saw, twinkling afar off on the dark plain, the lights of the city.

I was by then very tired and I felt faint; I had not been able to eat a bite at the banquet, and had not wanted the sandwiches we took along on our journey. I dimly remember seeing street lights stream past us, being affected by a sudden roar of city noise, and feeling a wave of loneliness and fear wash over me. Fernando was leaning forward, looking out of the window eagerly, giving directions to the driver, and I suddenly recalled that this was to be my wedding night. I adored Fernando, but at the thought of surrendering all my being to him I became stiff and dry-mouthed.

We drew up to a walled garden with a great wrought-iron gate surmounted with spikes. Two tall lamps throwing out beams into the dark, stood on each side of the gate. Fernando leaped out and pulled at a bronze fish which dangled from a chain protruding from one of the gate posts. I heard a bell tinkling far inside. Then a servant came running out, a key in her hand. She threw open the gates, and as the car nosed into the curving driveway I saw lights flash on above a broad portico. We swept up to it and stopped; as I descended from the car, supported by Fernando's hand, two large glass doors, protected by wrought-iron designs, opened, and in the light that poured out onto the veranda from the house, I saw a slim, straight figure.

"Mamacita!" Fernando crushed his mother to his heart, and then brought me forward.

She was such a little thing. I am small, but she was shorter than I, and painfully thin. I was conscious at first only of her frailty, and of some quality in her which I could not at first name. It was not coquetry, it was not charm of any facile kind. I still do not know how to name it, that something that went out from her eyes and her spirit and made people love her. But she had it, and it affected every living creature that crossed her path. Wherever she was, people came toward her, on the street dogs rushed up to her and kissed her hand or nudged her lovingly, birds flew down to perch near her chair when she sat in the garden. At parties she was always the center of a circle which formed around her; at home nothing could be done without her. I never in my life knew anyone to match her, but I have read about people with this gift . . . great queens, great courtesans, great saints. They have been endowed with some mysterious magnetism to be used by God in His great design.

"*Hijita*," she said, and she reached up to kiss my cheek. Then she slipped her arm around my waist, and said, "Fernando, see to the luggage. Bibi is very tired."

She led me into the great hall, up the stairs, and to a splendid bedroom at the front of the house. There was an enormous, carved, wooden bed in the room, with a canopy of gold brocade above it, and there were a dressing table, chairs, a chest of drawers, and a wardrobe that reached as high as the ceiling and reflected the whole room in its mirrors.

"Sit down," she said softly. "Let me look at you."

She pressed me into a chair, and then she knelt, before I could stop her, and slipped off my shoes, sliding a puffy silk cushion under my feet. I looked into her face, as she looked into mine.

Her face seemed long, but that was because she was so thin. Her eyes seemed dark at first, because they were deep set into hollows, and shadowed with violet, but they were a clear silver-gray, like Fernando's, and shadowed by dark lashes. Her nose was rather long, high-arched, and her mouth full-lipped and small, very grave and sweet. Her cheeks were hollow, and her head was set on a neck as thin and fragile as a little child's. Her hair was black, with two white streaks at the temples.

"Fernando told me that you were very sweet, very gentle," she said then. "I can see it. I shall love you very much, little daughter."

I looked around.

"This room, it was yours . . . I do not like to feel that you left it . . . for us . . ."

"It was my room long ago, when I came here as a bride with my dear husband. But after he died, I moved out to a small room at the rear of the house. I have always kept this room ready for Fernando and his wife. You are not to feel that you have disrupted anything, *preciosa*. This room, all this house, has been waiting for you . . . these many years."

She leaned hard on me, to rise, and coughed a little, swiftly taking a handkerchief out of her sleeve and holding it against her mouth.

"There is hot water for your bath, and afterward I will send up a tray of supper for you both, and you may eat in your dressing gowns," she told me. "Tomorrow, when you are rested, we will get acquainted."

She kissed me again, and then hurried out, a very fragile, tiny figure all in black.

I bathed in the big, tiled bathroom, with its marble and mahogany fixtures and its thick soft rug. I was young and in love, and I made myself fragrant and lovely for my husband. I cannot remember that we even ate. Fernando may have chosen me as second-best, it may have been *despecho,* or slighted love, which made him turn to me and ask for my hand, but that night I went a long way toward winning him for myself. I was thrilled by his strength, joyful in the first moments of pain. I had begged my guardian angel to show me how to receive him with modesty but with an open heart and perfect trust, and that angel did not fail me. In the morning when we woke, he held me close and kissed me often, and pressed back the hair from my brow, and I saw in his face more than protectiveness and masculine pride. I saw the beginnings of a deep tenderness.

"Doña Paz . . ." I began.

"Mamacita. You must call her Mamalinda, as I do."

"Mamalinda said that she had kept this room for you always."

"Yes. I have always known it. She took away only her clothes and toilet articles. And her crucifix and *reclinatorio.*"

"I would like one for us, Fernando. A crucifix and a *prie-dieu* for me."

"You shall have them."

"She is so delicate, Fernando. And she was too ill to come to our wedding. . . . What is the matter with her?"

"She had lung fever after I was born, and has to be careful of her strength."

"I will be strong for her!"

"Mamalinda is very strong," he answered me, and I learned to know the truth of that in days to come.

We settled into a very full and pleasant life. Mamalinda gave me the keys to the house, to the *despensa,* to the linen room and the silver cabinet, and little by little she taught me the running of the household.

It was a more elegant and sophisticated household than the one I had been brought up in, but she seemed to find nothing unusual in my questions, and took me gravely through all the pattern of each day.

She was up every morning at five, and she attended six o'clock Mass daily, receiving communion and saying prayers for everyone she loved. She would not let me come with her, saying that I must stay at home and attend my husband, so I was able to be with her only occasionally when Fernando, too, wanted to rise early to accompany her. She breakfasted, after daily communion, on chocolate and rolls, and then she consulted with Jovita, the cook, and ordered the menus for the day. There were two other servants, Jovita's daughter, Gloria, who was the housemaid, and who served the table, and Encarnación, who did the washing. They were trained well, but Mamalinda took them through their tasks so that I should know her methods.

All the bed clothing, towels, and underwear were washed on Mondays and ironed on Tuesdays. On Wednesdays, in fresh tubs, the tablecloths and napkins, glass and dish towels and all linens having to do with the food were washed, separated, and sunned, and ironed on Thursdays. Under no circumstances would Doña Paz permit any linen that had been put to intimate use in the same wash as table linen. On Fridays and Saturdays the wash girl did her mending, leaving the finest pieces for Doña Paz herself, who was an artist at weaving tiny stitches so cleverly that it was hard to tell where anything had been mended.

The cook was taught to calculate amounts with great care, and Doña Paz made her plans so meticulously that there were seldom leftovers. These, if there were any, were never kept, but sent out as gifts to the cook's family, or the gardener's. On Mondays, Gloria cleaned the silver, besides mopping and dusting the house in general; on Tuesdays she polished furniture downstairs, on Wednesdays she polished bedroom furniture. On Thursdays she took out and dusted books and on Fridays she dusted and washed the fine china. The gardener, Eufemio, had been trained to keep the lawns and flower beds in order, and to see that new blossoms were always coming along as the weeks went by.

In the back of the house, in a great *traspatio* that had once been the stables, Doña Paz had a special garden of her own, dedicated to the Holy Virgin. An image of Our Lady of the Immaculate Conception was placed so that no rain or wind ever reached her. Before that image Mamalinda had a candle that burned permanently in a deep-blue glass. The garden had been laid out in winding paths, lined with shells, and there were stone benches, wrought-iron chairs, and little tables, for here Mamalinda loved to come and do her mending, or read or pray, and here, on all afternoons when the weather was fine, she received her friends. Eufemio worked over this garden constantly, for he knew that it was most dear to Doña Paz, and he kept it full of plants that bloomed in white or blue. There were alcatraz lilies, and tuberoses and white jasmine and white roses, and white carnations, and blue larkspur and squills and phlox. Bees zoomed about in the sunshine, and humming birds hung, vibrating, above the flowers. Besides those soft sounds, there were cooings from the dove cotes, and the wonderful songs of some *jilgueros*, which lived in a very large cage in the open air, almost free, but safe from marauding cats.

It did not take me long to learn the ways of the household, which ran as smoothly as the tall clock in the *sala*, with Doña Paz to give it a turn now and again with a great key.

We ate our *comida,* the large meal of the day, at two, and afterward everyone had a long siesta. At six we attended rosary and at seven we had fruit, sweet buns, and coffee.

Doña Paz never had formal evenings, I learned; she had kept her mourning since her husband's death, wearing only black, and giving no entertainments of any kind. But she was never alone on an evening. She had been a much-beloved young woman in Guadalajara before her marriage, and very popular, and people her age came in constantly, calling her Pacita, or Pacita Portugal, which had been her name.

I sat silent and amazed at those evening gatherings, for it seemed that Doña Paz drew to her side the most brilliant and important people in the city, and she did it without the slightest effort. They simply loved to be near her, to tell her their thoughts, to hear her quiet comments. And I learned that, in her modest way, she had a strong effect on the artistic and intellectual life of the city.

Young poets were brought to her, and she listened gravely to their verses, praising often, sometimes suggesting a slight change in the meter or another rhyme. Musicians came to play for her on the fine big piano she had in her *sala* (this was a great joy to me), and violinists gave her evening concerts.

She had, without any efforts of her own, a salon, and the most remarkable thing about it was that other women were not envious of her but seemed to love her unselfishly.

I was too young to realize it at the time, but besides her quiet magnetism, which made people seek her out, her comments, in their seeming simplicity, were those of a gifted critic, and she had the ability to inspire enthusiasm in the yeasty young people who were trying to express themselves creatively.

There were always some priests at our gatherings in the evening; Doña Paz was on friendly terms with dozens of them, from distinguished monsignors who spoke French with her and brought her books, to shabby little parish priests who called to ask her to take catechism classes, and remained, transfixed with pleasure, in her company.

To my delight, Don Refugio, or Don Cuco, as everybody called him, dropped in regularly too, and when he did there was wonderful music! He was always dressed in his exaggerated way, and people teased him affectionately, and made fun of him lovingly . . . until he sat down to play. Then there was instant silence. He played as the spirit moved him . . . sometimes nothing but the formal patterns and massive dignity of Bach, sometimes the exotic and delicate poetry of Debussy, sometimes the tender musing of Brahms, sometimes the passion and the nostalgia of Chopin.

Since my duties were quickly learned, and since Doña Paz was always near to rescue me from any mistakes, I shyly asked Fernando if I might continue to study the piano.

He was delighted, and so was Doña Paz. Their eyes shone on me with love. And Fernando arranged that I was to have coaching lessons from Don Cuco himself. Later on, I learned why they were so warmly pleased with me. Innocently, I had provided them with something they wanted very much . . . frequent and natural meetings with the pianist.

By mutual consent, Fernando and I put off the honeymoon; I was happy in his home, and he had little reason to want to leave it.

So I lived in my cocoon, bundled in cotton wool, happy as a child, and though I had ears I heard not, and though I had eyes I saw not.

There were murmurs of the Trouble, and occasionally, in evening meetings, someone would speak hysterically or in anger about the repressions being exercised by the government. And one evening nobody came at all, and I was mildly surprised. Doña Paz sat contentedly, stitching at her embroidery, and the big clock in the *recibidor* marked the hours melodiously. At the sound of ten, Doña Paz sat, needle poised above her work, and frowned, looking fixedly at nothing. Her attitude was one of painful listening. I heard a little spatter of sound, far off, as if someone were setting off fireworks, and I rose and pulled the curtain aside to look up into the night sky.

"Bibi, sit down at once, please, you make me nervous," ordered Doña Paz, and I hastily obeyed, startled at her tone and at her words. But her smile was as sweet as ever, and she passed a hand across her forehead. "Forgive me, when I was a child, during the Revolution, we were taught never to pull aside the curtains," she explained. "It upsets me."

"Will Fernando be very late?" I asked her. He had gone out directly after *merienda*, saying that he had something to look up at the office.

"I think it likely he will be very late," she answered me with composure, holding her embroidery out to study the blending of the colors. "Perhaps we ought to go to bed. I am a little tired this evening, and we are not often abandoned by all our friends, who usually keep us up very late. Let us creep up to our rooms and get a long sleep."

I was, of course, ready to agree at once, and we went slowly up the stairs.

Even then, I never suspected anything; it was so easy to manage me. I am sure that I was always a great comfort to her and to Fernando. To add to my ingenuousness and general lack of observation, I was also a sound sleeper. I dimly recall that sometime in the night I turned in bed, to feel my husband's arms around me, but I had no idea when he had arrived.

There were many agitated visitors next morning, as Doña Paz sat in her white garden. She was very pale and had a headache, she said; the sunshine would do her good. As I busied myself in the house, I glanced out at her once or twice. She was having Eufemio change some of the benches about, and she set him to digging a new flower bed a little distance away from her image of Our Lady. But she was always tearing up the plants and setting in new ones, so as to have blooms all year, and this did not arouse my curiosity.

Only when one of Doña Paz's friends wept aloud and had to be supported into the house, on Fernando's arm, did I begin to feel some strange tension in the air.

"What is the matter?" I whispered, when Fernando persuaded Doña Lorenza to lie down for a little. "Can I get something for her?"

"No, *mi vida.* Just let her rest. Her daughter will be coming for her in a little while."

"Ay, ay, ay . . ." moaned Doña Lorenza.

"Is she sick?"

"No." He turned and looked at me, almost with pity. "Her son is dead," he said then.

"Oh, poor lady." Only late in the afternoon, when Doña Paz had gone to church, to rosary, did it occur to me to wonder why Doña Lorenza had not stayed in her own house that morning. But I was too shy to ask, for it might have seemed like criticizing Doña Paz's friends, something I would be horrified to do.

Not long after, I learned that the government had closed all our churches, and expelled our priests. Even the archbishop! This seemed to me an unbearable situation, and I was as indignant as everybody else. Later, much later, I knew Doña Lorenza's son had been shot; he was a priest.

"What can we do?" I wailed to Doña Paz.

"Well, we cannot live without the sacraments, that is clear," she said calmly. "Luckily, a small chapel was built into this house, which is quite old, and was consecrated years ago. Mass can be said here."

"But there will be no priests to say it! They are being sent out of Mexico!"

"Some will stay," she assured me.

At first there was not much change in our lives. Doña Paz and her friends met at each other's houses to say rosary every afternoon, and of course I was always by her side. Fernando worked harder than ever, and sometimes had to make trips away to other cities for days at a time, on business. We quite often had gatherings of friends in our house, as before, though now there was much angry talk and resentment, and I heard some wild words, too.

I remember an evening when Don Cuco came in and played to us, and Chela's brother, José Luis, came calling. I was happy to see him, and asked him a million questions about Santa Lala.

Don Cuco played only a few short pieces, and then struck all the keys on the piano with both hands, a horrid jangling sound. He turned to me, his face a mask of pain.

"Play something, Bibi," he said. "I cannot play tonight."

He rose from the bench, took my hand, and led me to the piano. I sat down and dropped my fingers on the keys. I began to play, softly, and then I became interested, and did my best. I heard an undercurrent of talk, mostly something between Doña Paz and Don Cuco, and it seemed urgent, but then everything they said sounded urgent those days. I kept on playing, and when I stopped there was an immediate spatter of applause, led by Don Cuco.

He came over to me, and said, "I am overworked, Bibi. You will have to help me. I have gained the consent of your husband and of Doña Paz."

"Help you? How?"

"Teaching. I have more pupils than I can handle."

Delight flared in me. I was thrilled that he thought me capable. I looked toward Fernando, who was beaming at me, as if cognizant of the honor Don Cuco was doing me.

"I would be glad to."

"Good. I will drop by tomorrow and instruct you about your first pupils. Little by little, you could take over several of them for me."

"The afternoon might be the best time," I heard Doña Paz's clear voice, saying. "I need Bibi in the mornings."

"I will come tomorrow at about three."

However, he did not come. He sent me a note. I was to go to an address in a poor section of the city, where there were two little seamstresses who had saved up enough money to have their ancient family piano tuned, and who were determined to take lessons. They were creatures dear to Don Cuco's family, and he could not refuse them. But he simply had no time. He had told them—he wrote me—that he was sending a gifted pupil of his to teach them. And, he went on, they may not be able to progress very rapidly. If they need encouragement, do give it, as you think and feel best.

"Oh!" I cried unhappily to Doña Paz. "I must go then, it seems. I was hoping Don Cuco would send the pupils here."

She turned from where she was packing herbs from her garden into small boxes.

"I will accompany you, at least for the first lesson or two, if you wish, Bibi. And by the way, a nephew of mine will be coming to stay with us for a while. I have given him my room, and he is resting. Do not," she said, fixing her big gray eyes on me solemnly, "do not tell anyone that he is here, I beg you. There are reasons why I cannot discuss his visit."

I nodded, feeling fear.

"Is he . . . is he a priest?" I whispered.

"Yes, Bibi. He is here at the risk of his life, to provide us with the sacraments. He will need to have some sun, and so he will work in the garden sometimes with Eufemio. Naturally, you will not speak to him then."

"He is in danger?"

"There is a price on his head. And there will be on mine if it is known that I harbor him," she said calmly.

I was terrified, and though I moved my tongue I could not make a sound.

"You will say nothing," she told me firmly, and I could only nod my head in assent. Doña Paz was very brave, but she had a coward for a daughter-in-law.

From then on I lost a sense of security in our home, and this was more disquieting than you might think. I had never been an adventurous girl. Under Chela's dominance, protected by our servants and my father, I had been dreamy and safe, encircled within their love and their authority, like a child in bed. The idea of risking our lives at home, of living under this anxiety, of having to invent lies and to act out a part when need be . . . quite unhinged me.

Curiously enough, I now felt glad to escape to the house of the little seamstresses, and to give them their lessons, happily prolonging it by playing for them when they asked. And they asked me, shyly but importunately, every time.

They were typical of provincial ladies who have come down in the world, through bad luck or other circumstances beyond their control. Without the means to do so, they continued to conduct themselves as if nothing whatever had happened. They were both thin and old, gray-haired, shy, gentle, and relentlessly ladylike and gracious. They wore dresses of fine silk, much cleaned, turned, and brushed. I am sure their costumes must have been thirty years old. They did fine sewing, and when I arranged to have them make a dress for me, I saw what their manner was to all their clients. They pretended to be disinterested in the price; they fussed over me and clucked and twittered, as if I were a niece, and they were making me a gown just to please me. No, more to please themselves. The price was not mentioned, and Doña Paz informed me later what it was, and I left it for them in a sealed envelope. Pride is wonderful, I suppose. I have never had much of it, and could not appreciate it.

As for their piano lessons, I supposed that these, too, were an expression of their determination to live as ladies of good family live, with certain important graces. Both had studied when they were younger, when they still enjoyed some measure of affluence.

Their old hands, with pin-pricked index fingers, were less stiff than I had supposed; their sewing and their household activities had kept them reasonably flexible. They remembered something of the reading of notes, and of the position of the hands on the keys.

It was arranged that the lessons were to take place daily for a time, and though this was good pedagogy, I was at a loss to understand how the Señoritas de la Torre could pay even my modest fee. I suspected that Don Cuco had fixed it up with Doña Paz in some way, and in this I was right, but not for the reason I thought.

We did scales, slowly and carefully, watching to see that the hand position moved merely forward or back, but did not otherwise change. We went back into some early teaching books, where little tunes, with discreet counterpoint in the left hand, taught simultaneous use of each hand. Don Cuco was furiously against the tune with chorded accompaniments in the beginning.

They tired quickly, and then they would lift their hands from the keys and say, "Ay, Doña Bibi, play a little for us, if you have time! Please do! A little Chopin!"

I thought they were weary of their back-bending sewing, and also, I felt less frightened in their little *sala*, so I would sit and play . . . Beethoven sometimes, Bach, Chopin, Schubert. They preferred romantic music, and yet they asked very often for Bach. In my preoccupation with myself, my husband (who was so often away, and so often distracted), with Doña Paz, and my fears for the priest we hid in the house, I forgot myself for a little in the music. The piano was old and the felts were thin, the notes somewhat sharp and tinny, but it had been a good instrument, and it was in tune. Sometimes I stayed playing for as much as an hour, while the little seamstresses rocked softly and glanced at each other, and smiled happily.

It came to me, one day, as I walked slowly home from the de la Torre house, that the evening soirees that I had enjoyed so innocently were a kind of informal conspiracy. When this thought struck me, I stood still in the street. It was a warm summer day, I remember, and I was wearing a dress of light, flowered cotton voile. But I had a chill that shook me as if I were about to come down with fever. Doña Paz? Yes, I saw it clearly. It was in her character to conspire against the government restrictions, not only in her own home, but insofar as any planning and any wider activities might go. But Fernando? Could it be? To my pervading fears for myself, I felt the added horror of fear for another person. My husband!

And yet, I was too cowardly to demand any explanations of Doña Paz. You would have to know her in order to understand me. She was every inch the educated, charming, affectionate provincial lady, but there was ice-cold steel in her, and a dignity that could resist any emotion from within or from without, when she so desired. I simply could not say a word, but sat that evening at *merienda*, crumbling my roll into my cup of foaming chocolate, and trying to act naturally. My "natural" awkwardness must indeed have been constant and amazing, for nobody seemed to notice anything amiss with me.

The "nephew" of Doña Paz had gone on his way a few days before, and this evening a new young man, "a distant relative," had appeared, and was seated at the table with us. He had asked a blessing, and now sipped his chocolate slowly. He was young and pale, remarkably handsome in the way of our Central Mexican families, in which there has been a fusion of the white-skinned and hairy Spaniards with the coppery-dark, satin-skinned Indians. The young man was pale, with a delicate line of hair and beard that seemed to me to be beautifully harmonious. His features were the gentler, softer ones of our *mestizo* type, his eyes large and meltingly dark, with the thick straight eyelashes that are Indian, and there was in his attitude and smile the strength of Spain and the stubbornness of Mexico.

"Our beloved daughter, Bibi," said Doña Paz, when she introduced us. "This is Father Félix. You may call him Cousin Félix, please."

He looked at me for a longish moment, and then smiled, I thought, with pity. But perhaps I am now self-conscious about all that happened.

Cousin Félix melted away from us like smoke, as soon as meals were over. Every morning, at four, he said Mass in Doña Paz's chapel, as the "nephew" had done, and always there were neighbors and sometimes strangers with us to attend the sacrifice. Don Cuco was there, on his knees in an attitude of theatrical effectiveness; he was always very sensitive to the style or flavor of the occasion, and I remember that I thought him somewhat exaggerated in his piety; he stared more at Doña Paz than at the altar.

I busied myself as best I could about the house, doing whatever Doña Paz required of me. I mended all my husband's underwear and fine shirts myself, I made jellied fruit jams, the ones we call *ates*, and, since almost every garden had a burdened fig tree, I dried figs in the sun on sheets of glass, and cooked others in syrup until they were transparent. Doña Paz was very active in every sort of preservation and conservation of food, and in her *despensa* she had stacks and stacks of dried meat, home-ground chocolate, jams of every sort, dried fruits, and strings of dried chiles.

In the afternoon, after siesta, when I went off to give those curious piano lessons to the Señoritas de la Torre, I experienced a cowardly feeling of release, of being able to walk and breathe without anxiety for a little time. So often they asked me to play the "Moonlight Sonata" of Beethoven or the "Bach Chromatic Fantasy and Fugue." By much repeating, I really learned to play them quite well, I think.

About two weeks after Cousin Félix had come to stay with us, Doña Paz came to my room after siesta and knocked, as she always did.

"Bibi, *preciosa,* I need your help."

"Of course, Mamalinda."

"We must choose a suitable traveling dress from among your things, one that can be let out and let down. Do you have something that would do?"

I got up, slipped on a wrapper, and went to the big wardrobe. Inside hung Fernando's suits, shirts, and bathrobe, and all my pretty summer dresses and my dressing gowns. I took out a brown-linen dress, a new type with a full-length coat over the fitted dress. It was called an "ensemble" and it was very stylish.

"This one? Would it do?" I already knew what she wanted it for.

"How are the seams?" She quickly turned the dress inside out and looked. They were fairly ample. There was a good hem.

"It will need to be made about four inches longer . . . we can face back the hem with some other material and get three inches, and we might open it at the waist, and set in the belt. No. The belt would be too tight." She frowned.

I calculated Cousin Félix's height and weight. He was not tall, and very slender.

"It could easily be adjusted," I said.

"He will want to wear his cassock underneath, he insists," she told me. "We will have to allow for that."

We took out the ensemble and ripped it apart, and devised ways of making it acceptable.

"It seems safest that he should travel as a woman?" I asked, at length.

"He will travel as you," smiled Doña Paz. "With Fernando."

"Oh," I gasped. "Isn't that . . . terribly dangerous?"

The situation in our part of Mexico had worsened steadily with regard to the religious conflict, for our people were determined not to have their sacraments taken from them, and they had, almost to a man and to a woman, agreed that passive resistance would have no effect. They had made up their minds to resist force with force. We had news of people organizing to fight, of bands that were beginning to fight guerrilla wars against the government troops. They called themselves "Cristeros," and their rallying cry was "¡Viva Cristo Rey!"

"Yes," Doña Paz answered me quietly. "But there is no help for it. You know what our Lord said—"

"He said . . . so many things . . ."

"He who is not with me is against me!" she reminded me. "Father Félix will be quite safe, I think, with Fernando. It is known that you were married not long ago, and that you are shy. He can conceal his face, and it will not seem strange that Fernando is taking you to Santa Eulalia."

"To Santa Lala?"

"Yes. The people there have been without the sacraments for several months. While they are gone, Bibi, you must stay hidden here in your room. You will not mind that, will you, linda? I will bring you books, and you can embroider and I will come often to chat with you and to pray."

There was a very slight flush on her cheeks, and her eyes glistened. She was the kind of woman who rose to her full stature when she was called upon to be brave, to undergo a test, to make a sacrifice. As for me, I was literally rigid with fear. My tongue was swollen and clove to the roof of my mouth, and I could not make my fingers move.

At last I could force out a word or two, in a hoarse whisper. Doña Paz looked at me in some consternation.

"When . . . when will they be back?" I asked. I thought that if I could be allowed to count the hours of danger, ticking them off as they dragged by, I might be able to survive.

"With God's grace, Fernando will return in three days' time. Father Félix will remain."

"He . . . he is going to his death, then?"

"Very likely."

Doña Paz was ripping the hem of the brown linen, eyeing it critically. She was very thin and white, her bent head seemed heavy for her fragile neck, her white thin hands on the dark cloth looked like *floripondio* flowers. She glanced up at me, put down the cloth, and hurried out of the room, returning in a few minutes with a glass of water.

"Drink this, *mi bien*," she said, "it is heavily sugared. You have had a shock and we must not have you ill. I was too abrupt. I am sorry."

"I am frightened," I whispered.

"I know. Drink it."

She stood over me. Sugar started the paralyzed liver into activity again.

"We will pray together for them, Bibi."

Silly words came out of my mouth.

"But I can't stay hidden. The Señoritas de la Torre . . ."

"They won't need you any more, my dear. The archbishop has been taken away."

I stared at her stupidly.

"You were a great help, *linda*. He was hidden in a closet inside their house and they were distracted trying to think of ways to divert him. He could not have a light to read by, of course, and they were fearful of letting him out so that anyone could see him. He is so well known, and there might be some traitor willing to tell, for the reward. And then we remembered that he was very fond of music. Don Cuco couldn't go, and so we thought of you. It was a great comfort to him, sitting there for hours in the dark, knowing that he could hear some Bach, some Beethoven, for a while every afternoon."

I looked down at my hands. I should have been proud. I should have felt honored that I had been chosen to do this small errand of mercy for a man sitting in the dark, in danger of his life. But all I could realize was that they had involved me in this quarrel that meant death to anyone caught in it. They had involved me, Doña Paz and my husband. They were making me an active accomplice now, by loaning my dress and my personality to this priest, who was going to defy all the strength of the government armies.

I was terrified, for myself, for my husband, for Doña Paz, and I was obscurely angered, too. They had thrust me into the midst of the Trouble, without so much as "by your leave."

"Of course you are with us, heart and soul, Bibi," said Doña Paz, looking at me with her great gray eyes. How hypnotic they were, those eyes.

"Of course," I answered, lying, feeling all the chill of death in my heart, already.

Doña Paz was looking at me steadily. I know that she saw into my heart and was ashamed.

She leaned forward and took me into her arms, and pressed her cheek against mine.

"Dear Bibi," she said. "It is not what one does that counts; it is not even how one feels, whether brave or strong or weak and hopeless. It is what one manages to do with the strength God has given."

"You are so strong, Mamalinda," I sobbed.

"Our Lord died for us. Is it too much that once in a few centuries a few of us must die for Him?"

I put my head down into my hands and sobbed. I had a fearful presentiment.

"*Mi hijita*," said Doña Paz, "you must not weep. God has given me some clairvoyance, sometimes. Neither you nor I are to die. Be certain. And we will live to see the end of these troubles."

I believed her. . . . I remained in my room, sleeping mostly. A kind of lethargy had come over me, which I could not conquer. I woke, bathed, put on my dressing gown, prayed, ate, and slept again. Once when I was a child, a little dog of Chela's had been cornered and tossed by a bull, and I remember that she told me it slept almost constantly for several days after, though the wound was not bad. The terror it had felt had built up some nervous exhaustion in its body, and it had been limp, half unconscious, for days. So, exactly was I, until Fernando came home again. Then I could only cling to him, but life began to flow back along my veins.

¡Ay de mi!

Perhaps my husband had seen *la pelona*, the bald skull of the death image, had felt her icy breath on him. Anyhow, safely home, he held me close, and was more loving, more tender with me than he had ever been. In bed that night he told me that he had been able to take Father Félix through the lands patrolled by the government battalions straight into Santa Lala, where there were families ready to hide him, and to arrange for him to baptize, to marry, and to confess the Christian souls. He sighed and turned to me, in relief at having carried out his mission. We were united in our love, and that night God sent into my body the spark of a new life, a new soul. I did not deserve this reward, and, of course, I did not know that in His compassion, God had decided to leave me with some part of my beloved husband to cherish.

Quietly, I began to be seen again, and I conducted myself with great discretion. I had been shy and silent; people did not expect me to be a chatterbox. I was able to perform many small errands for Mamalinda, and as the "nephews" came and went in our house, I served as her messenger. It was wiser for her not to be seen about in the streets too much, for she had always been a circumspect widow, encircled within her home like a seed deep within a flower. Everyone came to her, and now some of the army officials came to her evenings too.

I remember one evening when we were seated in our *sala*, and I was playing the piano. (Don Cuco had dropped in, but he had declined to play, saying that he was very weary. He had been on a concert tour to Mexico City, where he had given a series of six concerts . . . all the Beethoven Sonatas.) Gloria came in, quite pale, and announced in an unexpectedly shrill voice, her eyes rolling, "General Escobar, señora, and his aide."

Doña Paz rose quietly, opened the door which led into the dining room and the back stairs, and our "cousin" slipped silently away. She reclosed the doors, sat down, with composure, and said in her clear voice, "Please tell General Escobar to enter, Gloria. I am pleased that he has called."

General Escobar marched in, in uniform, and ran a bright black eye over our company. When he saw Don Cuco, he softened and smiled.

"Ah, my friend! It is pleasant to be able to tell you once more that you are a great artist!"

Don Cuco arose, and they embraced.

"General Feliciano Escobar," he said, presenting the general to the company.

"*Paz Portugal viuda de Leyva,*" she said. "You are welcome in my home, General." She nodded kindly to the general's aide, a stiff young man who remained standing near the door.

"I would not have thought so, señora," he answered, and my heart sank. "This is no social call."

"Indeed? Why not?"

"I understand that you sympathize with the Cristeros."

"I was baptized a Christian, mi General, married in the Church, and I try to live by the rules of my faith," she answered him openly. "May I ask you something?"

"Certainly."

"Were you not also baptized, General?"

He flushed. "It is true."

"And married in the Church?" She indicated the gold wedding band on his left hand.

"My wife insisted upon it."

"And," went on Doña Paz, inexorably, "is it not true that under your tunic you wear a medal of Our Lady of Guadalupe?"

He made an impatient gesture.

"My belief is private. My duty is something else."

"How sad for you, General, that your duty goes against your faith. But come, we must not quarrel. You are my guest. Don Cuco, if you insist that you will not play, let us ask Bibi, my daughter-in-law, to give us some music."

I turned back to the keys, and let them speak for me. The general sat stiffly on a rosewood chair, listening with courtesy. Doña Paz brought in glasses of wine and delicate *polvorones* that melted into buttery crumbs the moment they were in the mouth. The general partook heartily.

Then he stood up abruptly and made a gesture to his aide.

"Señora," he said, bowing to Doña Paz. "I am indebted to you for your hospitality. I presume to warn you, as a friend, that the laws of this republic must be respected, and that I represent the power of enforcement."

Doña Paz stood up. She was so small, so thin, so unbending. She bowed to him.

"I thank you for your frankness," she said. "Come again, come often to pass the evening with us, mi General."

He bowed and left. The roomful of people (we were about ten, I recall) was silent when he left. Doña Paz did not let it stay so. She immediately opened a conversation on Lopez Velarde, and the evening progressed as her evenings always did.

The next day, before lunch, Don Cuco arrived and had a long talk with her in the garden, and though I was not present, I saw her shake her head several times in denial. As he rose to go, she detained him, one small hand on his arm, and said something more, but he lifted her hand and kissed it, and then laid it back on the arm of the garden chair. He left hurriedly, and she sat on in the sunshine, with her hands idle. Then she came upstairs to where I sat in my room, sewing.

"Bibi," she said, "I must make a little journey. Will you come with me?"

"Of course, Mamalinda. Where are we going?"

"North. Toward the border."

"When do we leave?"

"Tomorrow morning, early. Can you be ready? You will need clothes and things for about a week."

But in the morning I had a fever, and she would not let me go.

"No, no, it is impossible," she said. "I will go alone. You must take care of your health, hijita." And she would not hear of my getting out of bed. I heard her giving Fernando and Gloria instructions about how to look after me.

Was it fear that made me develop the fever? I don't know, I am such a coward. For of course I knew that she

124

had decided upon some action in favor of the men who were fighting in the hills and in the countryside with the Cristeros.

Fernando was terribly nervous all that week that she was away, and Don Cuco called often.

I had a caller, too, and was able to receive, for on the fourth day of Doña Paz's absence, I was quite well again. It was José Luis.

I cannot find words to tell how happy I was to see him. He had dropped by occasionally, but usually these were the merest courtesy calls, very short, and there were always other people present. On this afternoon I was in the garden, where Doña Paz liked so much to pass the late morning hours, pinching dead roses off the stalks, and shaking out the seeds of her white *vara de San José*.

"Oh, I am glad to see you, José Luis! Tell me all the news!"

"The news is bad, Bibi. My father is dead."

"Ay! How awful! What happened?"

"He was murdered."

"José Luis!"

"He was fighting with the Cristeros, organizer of a band."

He stood before me, pale, sandy, short, the sunlight glittering on his spectacles. I could not see if there were tears in his eyes.

"What can I say?" I choked. "Poor Chela, and the little boys."

"I don't know what to do, Bibi. I don't know what I ought to do."

"You must go home, I suppose," I said.

"Not to look after them. Chela does that very well, and I have never liked the farms. I can earn more, and send more to them, by practicing law. I am already building up a small practice. No, I mean . . . about this business, the persecution . . ."

"You cannot avenge your father all alone," I pointed out. "Perhaps it is best to be cautious. To pray that everything will be over soon . . ."

"Is that what you do?" He looked at me so tenderly. If I had not known him since childhood, I would have thought that he looked at me in love. I must tell you that, with worry and fear, I had lost much weight, and I was pale and nervous. Of course he noticed that.

"Sweet Bibi," he said. "You don't deserve to be mixed up in all this."

"I am not mixed up!" I cried, horrified.

"I mean, in my troubles."

"I would help you if I could, José Luis."

"Nobody can help me. I have to make a decision, and I shall be hated by somebody no matter what it is."

"Oh, then don't make it. It isn't worthwhile, being hated."

"I agree." He looked at me sadly, leaned forward and kissed my brow. "Goodbye, Bibi. I don't know when I may see you again. I am going to Santa Lala, and I am not sure when I'll be back."

"Come to see us as soon as you return!"

"I'll try."

He went away.

Mamalinda had returned safely from her mysterious errand, and I thanked God for it. Then things became so bad for us all that she did not go away any more, and we had no more distant relatives to visit us, in secrecy and darkness.

I know that she sent out supplies to the Cristeros (for we were practically under siege), but as far as I knew the only things she set into motion in the underground freight system were dried fruits and cheeses, and such things. But I was mercifully innocent, or stupid. What you will. She was negotiating for ammunition for the armies of the Cristeros, and she herself had, on that trip, set up her stations for the smuggling of medicines, ammunition, and food. I did not realize much of what was going on for two reasons. My husband was not gone from the city, but was frequently at home with me. And besides, I was sure now that I was going to have a child, and I could think of little besides my joy.

Mexico had had revolutions before, long periods of violence and uncertainties. But the children had continued to be born, people had lived their lives somehow, though the battles raged around them, and though there were thousands killed in the fights, there were still others who died at home in their beds, and had to be carried to the cemeteries.

Fernando was very proud and happy when I told him that we were to have a child, and Mamalinda petted me and coddled me. I simply narrowed my world, and was content within it.

I noticed that there were no evening soirees now. Everyone was soft-spoken and sad; all were trying so hard not to sin in thought, word, or deed, for there was no one to confess them or give them absolution.

We had lists of people from whom we must not buy anything. Anyone who had anything to do, even remotely, with the forces which had taken away our priests and our sacraments was not to be patronized. Some of the shops had to close, and there were days now when we did not have enough of the essentials to eat.

Don Cuco came to see us often; when he was not seated at the piano, his pretensions and extravagances were beginning to be offensive to me. Having known the character of a young, virile man, my husband, I could see why Don Cuco was more than slightly ridiculous, despite his art. But Doña Paz seemed to appreciate him very much, and, indeed, so did Fernando. They were always getting into subdued but intense conversations with him. That was when I was usually relegated to the piano and to my Beethoven or Chopin.

I remember now a day when Mamalinda, for once, seemed to have no special duties to perform, people to visit, or guests to receive.

"Let us go and buy wool to make my baby some little coats," I suggested, and she agreed. We put on our street dresses . . . full mourning, as all the women in North and Central Mexico were now using, in honor of the dead who had fallen in the rising tide of battle against the government troops, though this was not officially honored with the name of "revolution," but was called merely a "disturbance."

We knew of a little shop which had some stocks of wool, linen, and cotton material, and which had not dealt with any of the suppliers who were against our cause.

We made our modest purchases. It was a windy day, and I was busy trying to keep my skirts down and my mourning veil from becoming entangled. Dimly, from afar, I heard shouting, and the sounds of a crowd. I stopped, there on the sidewalk. Doña Paz had heard it too, and she stood, very pale, with her hand pressed to her heart.

"We must get inside somewhere," I said. "There is a mob coming this way." The sounds were growing louder and there were crashings and sounds of broken glass.

She seemed not to hear me, but ran toward the menacing, the frightening noise. I had no choice but to tag after her.

We were not far from the railway station, and it seemed to me that the roaring rioting sounds came from there. Doña Paz seemed to be making for it with all her strength. As she ran her hairpins flew out and her hair fell down, but she, who was so correct, so immaculate in her dress, paid no attention but tore on, gasping and desperate.

About a block before we got to the station, we reached a moiling crowd, and Doña Paz disappeared into it. I could not find her to follow. I was tossed and pushed and buffeted, and I fell. I was fearful for my little child, and I crawled away to the edge of the rushing mob, struggled to my feet, and ran madly toward some sort of shelter. All the shops and warehouses had run down their corrugated iron fronts, and there was no place. By chance one of the shops had a small display window, in a sort of box in front, and this was now enclosed in corrugated iron too, but it provided something to hide behind. I crouched there, sobbing without tears, stiff with terror.

I heard the bellowing of the crowd, and a voice which I thought must be Fernando's screaming, "*¡Viva!! ¡Viva Cristo Rey!*" But it could not be. He would not be caught up into this sort of street riot. Then I heard the sound of galloping hoofs, and of shots. I did not dare peek out; a few children and a woman had also come somehow to my little shelter and were huddled down beside me.

"*Dios mio,* what has happened?" I asked the woman. She was a simple servant woman, I could tell from her two aprons, and her braided hair, which swung on each side of her face. She was ashy gray with fright, and the children with her hid their faces under her apron.

"*Sardos,*" she whispered. "They have captured two spies. They have taken them away to prison. *¡Ay de mi! Ay Diosito,* when will it all end?"

We waited there until the crowd had streamed past, until all was silent, and the shots and shouting had died away. The serving woman and her children hurried away first. I remained where I was, trembling, unable to move for a long time more. I do not know how long; it may have been hours. At last I heard the heavy iron front of the shop rumbling upward, and the owner came out to open the protective covering around his front display case. He took me under one elbow and helped me to rise.

"It's all right now, señora," he said to me. "*¡Viva Cristo Rey!*"

"*¡Viva!*" I whispered. I could not have said another word.

"Would you like to lie down inside a little while? Can you get home all right?"

"I . . . think . . . I can manage . . . thank you."

I tried to walk, but I fell down at once. My legs were paralyzed from having been folded under me so long. But I got up and stamped them, and started the circulation. I thanked God as I stumbled home, for I had been saved, with my baby. I had no doubt that Doña Paz had been able to take care of herself. She was so clever and resourceful. But she must be worried about me. I hurried.

Our house was very quiet as I pulled the bell on our *zaguán*. No one came to open it for me. At last Eufemio appeared and let me in.

"Ay, señora . . ." He was crying.

"What is the matter? Where is everyone?"

"The señora, Doña Paz, is at the prison, with the young señor. And Gloria has gone there to take her things . . ."

I could not believe what I heard. "The prison?" I screamed.

"They caught Don Fernando and Don Cuco, too . . . they will kill them . . . The señora has gone to wait there . . ."

I fainted. I was lying on the grass in the sunshine, with bird song all around me, and blossoms overhead, and I could have wished that I were dead. When I came to my senses I knew that I must stand up and get myself to the prison too, as fast as I could.

"How . . . how do I go?" I whispered. Eufemio was hovering over me, his old face set in lines of sorrow.

"I will take you, little señora," he said. "As soon as you can stand."

I don't remember how we got there. The prison was on one side of the city, a great yellow-brick building, windowless toward the street, of course. It looked ugly and cruel, and like a thick yellow snake.

It took us a long time to achieve entrance. There were guards to convince, corridors to walk through, officers to beg audiences of, and then passes and papers. Hours after we had entered the stinking place (for it stank of death and of disinfectants) I was led up to an officer who sat behind a desk in a luxurious room.

He stared at me, and did not tell me to sit down.

"Name?"

"Bibiana Gutiérrez de Leyva. I wish to see my husband."

"That is impossible, señora. He is under arrest, and may see no one."

"What is the charge against him?"

"Treason."

"How can that be? Mexico is not at war!"

He looked down at the papers on his desk and made no answer.

"It is fortunate that you came, señora. You have saved me the trouble of sending to arrest you."

"Why? Why? I have done nothing!"

"You are wanted for questioning."

He nodded to two soldiers who stood at the door and they came forward; they took me by an arm, each one, holding me.

"In there," ordered the officer, and they led me, dragged me really, into a small room next door.

I cannot remember much of what followed. I was questioned for hours, until I was a sobbing, exhausted heap. And I never had much strength of character, or any courage, to begin with. But I could say nothing against Fernando. I realized vaguely, in the depths of my misery, how well and truly he had protected me against any knowledge of himself.

I had never worried about his love, but had only been glad and grateful that he had married me. Now, tormented by questions that seemed to incriminate him, I desperately wanted to know that he loved me, as I did him. I cannot explain why this wish, this longing, came on me so suddenly. Perhaps I felt that his time was short, that I would not have days and months and years to come in which to try to win his heart wholly for myself.

I was not allowed to see him. I was finally released and told to go home. Thank God I had known nothing, and therefore could not tell anything—for I am weak; I might have broken, might have told.

It was dark outside, and Eufemio had long since disappeared. I stumbled home, but there was no one there. I sat all night waiting, unable to sleep, unwilling to return to the prison. No one was in the house. Not a soul. I remained on my knees in the dark house, praying. I knew that it was late for any help, but I had to lean on someone, I had to feel that I was in contact with hope.

Early in the morning, I heard a sound at the door, and I flew down the stairs. It was Doña Paz. She was very pale, but perfectly composed. She had drawn back her hair and braided it, and indeed, except for that, she looked as she always had. I threw myself into her arms, weeping.

"They questioned me . . . I couldn't find you . . . where is Fernando?"

"Come," she said, sighing. "We will talk in the garden." Gloria walked behind her, weeping.

"Go and find Jovita," ordered Doña Paz. "We must have food. The house must be made ready."

"Gloria stayed with me, all through the night," said Doña Paz. "But the others have hidden. It is natural. They will come back now."

She led me out into the garden, and found a seat on a bench near her image of Our Lady. So she sat, her hands clasped in her lap, for some time.

Then she shook herself, and seemed to focus on me.

"Fernando is dead, *hijita*. But we can be very proud of

132

him. He did not reveal one name, or tell them a single thing. And neither did Don Cuco."

"Ay, Mamalinda," I babbled. I could not speak. My head seemed to have burst into fragments. I was screaming, but no sound came from my lips. "Ay . . . ay . . ."

She did not try to comfort me. She sat waiting patiently for me to emerge from my pain enough to listen to her. Then she said, "They were tortured. But they resisted. With God's help."

I was sobbing. I did not dare pour out what I was thinking. I was thinking, "Oh God, I wish they had told, if it would have saved them." But she read my mind, as always.

"They would have been shot, anyhow. Do not deceive yourself, Bibi. We have been fighting to preserve our faith, to keep our sacraments, from those who would deny them to us. We knew the risks. My son would have died, in any case. Be grateful to God that He sent him the strength to keep quiet, not to betray his comrades."

She patted me on my heaving shoulders. My eyes were dry, I could not even find the refreshment of tears. All I felt was a horrible bursting swelling within me that gave me no rest and that ached and ached.

"God bless you," whispered Doña Paz, "for you feel no hatred. Only pain and abandonment and loss. I must pray, so much, not to hate. It is almost impossible for me. I pray to be preserved from hatred . . ." I looked up. Her eyes were closed; her face, too, was closed like a book. I could read nothing in it.

"The archbishop blessed this ground for me," she murmured. "When they allow me to go for their bodies, I shall bury them here. I have known for months that this might happen. I took pains to be ready."

Gloria came out to us, and she gently urged us inside the house.

"You must take something, mi señora," she said. "We must eat. We must have strength."

Doña Paz rose to her feet and marched into the house like a soldier. She washed, combed her hair, took her place at the table. Asking the blessing, she determinedly ate a small piece of bread and drank half a cup of chocolate.

"What is the time, Gloria?"

"Almost noon, señora."

"It is almost time. They told me that I could go for them after one. Leave the doors open. Friends will be coming."

One by one, people came, dressed in mourning, and took seats in the *sala*, then in the hall, then in the dining room. More and more chairs were brought. There was perfect silence, except for the clicking of rosary beads. Doña Paz sat like a stone. When the clock whirred and then released the single chime, she stood up and walked steadily toward the door, onto the terrace, down the three steps, out through the *zaguán*. All the guests followed her. I tried to follow, too, but I fell down on the terrace, and was wrenched with sobs again. I could not move. They left me there, all except an elderly woman, a friend of Doña Paz, whom I had met several times. She got me into the house somehow, and settled me on a sofa, and then she, too, stole away.

About two hours later, they all returned, and it seemed to me that the whole city of Guadalajara had joined in the silent procession. They were bearing home our dead. The men had taken simple open coffins of wood to the prison, and they were carrying the bodies of my Fernando and Don Cuco on their shoulders. Doña Paz walked, straight as an arrow, behind them. They came silently into the *sala*, and thence into the dining room. There the coffins were laid, atop the great dining table. Candles were lighted and set at their head and feet. Gloria and Eufemio came in with armloads of white flowers, and these were placed in the coffins beside our dead.

Both had been shot, but terrible things had been done to them first. Fernando's face was twisted in pain, his eyes staring. But Don Cuco looked calm and peaceful.

We were all on our knees, saying the rosary and the litanies, and the prayers for the dead, and so we passed the afternoon, and continued on into the night. Gloria made coffee, and set out things to eat, and sometimes a mourner would slip out into the hall and take a steaming cup, or nibble at some bread or cake.

Before it was quite dark an automobile drew up at our *zaguán,* and an officer strode straight into the house.

"This unseemly display must cease," he shouted, "or I shall have you all arrested."

No one paid the slightest attention to him, and led by Doña Paz's clear voice, the prayers continued.

He stared around, and blustered, but nobody even looked up. He turned on his heels and left, but some fear entered into him, for at the door I saw him draw his pistol and turn hastily, as if someone had threatened him. No one had said a word. I was the only one who looked.

All that night we prayed and kept vigil, and early the next morning several of the men went out into the garden and dug the graves. We laid them there, among the roses, near Doña Paz's image of the Virgin, and there they are still, in unmarked graves, the flowers blooming above them.

I look after Doña Paz, and do what I can for her, but she does not need me. I am the one who needs her. She is well, she is proud, and she is defiant in her icily courteous way. Sometimes officers come, and she receives them with her perfect manners, and treats them with studied and wonderful scorn.

We pray very much every day. I know that she prays for the souls of our beloved and for the triumph of our religion. But I pray that my child may be a girl, a weak and timid little girl like me. Then maybe I can keep her. Maybe I will have something to love that needs me.

If I have a boy, he will belong to Doña Paz, to the Portugals and the Leyvas. He would never love me, because I am weak. Ay, *Diosito*, send me a little girl like me. Not like Doña Paz. I admire her, I love her, she is worth a million of me, but send me a little girl like me, a cowardly little girl they will not want, or need. . . .

IV

"Rogad por nosotros . . ."

THE CHRONICLE OF EL BIZCO

Uf! That one got me!

I guess it wasn't such a bad one. I never got hit before. Don't know what to expect, though. I've seen enough of torn arms and legs and guts ripped out and opened heads, with something sticky spilling out. Uf!

I can't move, but I don't hurt.

Funny, I can remember lots of things that used to make me laugh, and I laugh now, but there isn't any sound. There's Capitán Bravo over there. He got it too. I wonder . . .

They always called me Bizco. That means cross-eyed. Sure I'm cross-eyed, but they are good eyes, just the same. I am the best shot in the state! I could knock the ear off a burro a kilometer away!

I guess I was baptized. Everybody baptizes their kids, and I must have been. My name is Francisco, but nobody ever called me anything but Bizco. I don't know who my father was, but I think maybe he must have been a military man, because I have always loved guns and horses. An old-time revolutionary, maybe. Those were great guys. Men! Afraid of nothing. I am sorry I was born too late to be in that fight. I would have loved it. And I bet I would have ended up as a general. Lots of fellows, not much older than I, did. Poor boys, like me.

But times were calm when I started out to look for a way

137

to live. Mamá went off with a baker from over near To-
matitlan and I couldn't stand him, nor him, me. So I left.

I lit out and went southwest, and before two days had
gone by I had a job on the big Hacienda Animas, where
they raise a lot of cattle and horses. I was a *caballerango,*
and they had me breaking horses. Just think of that! I was
only twelve, but it doesn't take strength. The way to get
the better of a horse is not to beat him or get him scared
of you. It's just that you have to give them something to
think about. Horses like to think, same as everybody.

I remember the first day I went to work at the Hacienda.
They had a mean foreman, old Gordo. They say fat people
are always jolly, but it isn't so. Most fat men are sore
that they aren't scrawny and flexible and they think up lots
of mean tricks. I saw the other men who were working go
and get their mounts; they were going to ride fences that
day. And I saw the horse El Gordo had told them to leave
for me. I'm no fool, and that horse was young and scared
and he was rolling his eyes, and flicking his ears back and
forth, and he was bound nobody was going to get the better
of him, not that day anyhow. Well, I went over to him, and
I managed to get him saddled up. I saw spur marks, still
bloody, along his sides. They had been tough with him. I
felt sorry. I took the horse over past the drinking trough,
and as I went by I scooped up a little bit of water in my
hat, and when nobody was looking, I poured some in his
ear. Well, I swung up aboard, mounted him as soft as satin,
and away we went, with no trouble at all. My horse was
so busy shaking his ear and wondering what was in it, that
I rode him without a bit of back talk.

That night when they ladled out the beans and the eggs
fried with jerky and the tortillas and the sauce, I had
enough to eat for the first time in days, and I stuffed myself. Felt good.

"You aren't so bad, Bizco," said the fat one to me. "You

138

handled that colt pretty well. Nobody else ever wanted to ride him, so I had to, yesterday."

"Yeah," I said. "I noticed."

"You can have him, if you want."

"Okay." I pretended to be respectful, but he could see that I knew what he was up to. But I never had a particle of trouble with that horse, and we got to like each other fine. They began giving me most of the colts to train and I did a good job, if I do say so. There was only one in the two years I was there that wouldn't learn, and was a bad one. See that scar? Oh, I can't move to show you. Well, he caught me there. Only horse ever kicked me. Only one I ever knew that didn't end up knowing I was his friend. Uf! I like horses better than people any day. The mean ones are real mean, but you know it right now. Not like people that go around laughing and patting you and suddenly they sink a piece of steel in your back. Women? Oh, I guess they're all right. Never had much truck with them. I'm ugly and I never had any money. Besides, I was pretty busy, always.

There was a big guy used to come riding around to the ranches, buying up cattle and grain; he had lands, but he also had a warehouse over in Santa Lala. I liked him; he was fair, never cheated, paid cash, and was good to his people. And he could ride! And shoot, too. Valera, his name was. Well, he watched me training a colt one day and then he came over and pointed to it with his cigarette. He pushed his big sombrero (a fine one, with silver embroidery) back on his head. That meant he intended to be easy and friendly with me.

"Boy, you do well at that," he said mildly. "Where are you from?"

I just waved my hand toward the north.

"Whenever you want a job that isn't so hard on a young fellow, come to me," he said. "I need a groom to live in at my house in town. Take care of two or three saddle horses, and ride out with me sometimes."

"*Gracias*," I told him. I never decided anything in a hurry, and so I took time to think it over. It was a long way to Santa Lala, about twenty kilometers, and I didn't own a horse of my own, so I had to figure how I was going to get over there. Old Gordo was always yelling for a man to go with him to town when he drove in for supplies, because he needed somebody that could handle the team to drive him home, since he always got roaring drunk in Santa Lala. Some of the *vaqueros* went with him a time or two, but either they got drunk too, and when they finally got home the *patrón* docked them both, or they hated to put up with Gordo bellowing and vomiting and falling off the wagon all the way back. The horses always raced home, and they were hard to handle on the hilly parts of the road.

Gordo was due to go in for supplies of the stuff we didn't make at the hacienda . . . lye, flour, rope, and cigars for the *patrón*, face powder and stuff for the *patróna*, cotton cloth and blankets and so on. Filiberto, one of the youngest *vaqueros*, was stuck on a girl who lived near Santa Lala, and I saw him shaving and washing his shirt and I figured he meant to go with Gordo. So I sneaked into the *despensa* by the stables where they kept the medicines of the animals, and found the big tin of Epsom salts they kept there for the bloat, and I put a good spoonful of it in Filiberto's tomato *salsa* when the cook wasn't looking, and then I ground up a few more chiles and slipped them in to cover the taste. Filiberto was sick as a cat in the night with the bellyache, and couldn't go in the morning, so my scheme worked fine. I went along with Gordo, and got myself a good free ride in. Gordo bought all his supplies in a big hurry, once we were in Santa Lala, making me carry everything back to the wagon, and then he gave me a peso and told me to go and eat somewhere and meet him, with the

team, about five o'clock over at the Cantina of the Golondri-
nas. And he went hopping off to get drunk, as happy as a
cricket.

I moved the team over to where they could stand in the
shade; the sun was coming around, and I got them some
buckets of water from the fountain in the patio, and then I
tied them up and went to find out where the Valera place
was. It was one of the best houses in the town, not far from
the main square, but with the back patio facing out toward
the country. Stables in the back patio. I liked that. I hate
to feel cooped up. There were three good-looking horses
there, and I saw that there was a place for a fourth one. I
guessed the *patrón* was away, as the beautiful big black
stallion he always rode wasn't there. I decided to try one of
the others, a prancy little mare, and I sneaked her out easy.
There was an old fellow, a pure Indian, asleep on the hay.
Fine *caballerango* he was! No wonder Don Manuel was after me!

I sure liked that little mare; I rode her bareback, and
when I let her out she could eat the wind. Pretty thing,
too. Four white feet, *cuatroalba*, and glistening chestnut,
with a lovely mane. I walked her slowly, about a half kilometer from the stables, and then, slipping in, and taking
her back to her stall, I began to rub her down with my
hands, slapping her and petting her.

The old guy woke up and roared at me, "Hey you! What
in the name of seven thousand devils are you doing here?"

"Rubbing down this mare. I'm the new *caballerango*."

"Then what becomes of me?"

"I guess you go home."

The old stupid silently packed up his stuff and tied it in
a *paliacate* and went out through the back. Didn't even
question me, or go to ask for his wages, or anything. Well,
the world is no place for burros like that. But I thought I
had better go up to the house and get things straight, so I

141

went along through the back patio, past the rabbit hutches and chicken pens, and in and out among the clotheslines, where the wash was hanging. There was a cook sitting out in the sun, wearing her apron; she was stringing chiles on a cord, getting them ready to hang up and dry.

"Where did you come from?" she asked.

"From the north. The *patrón* hired me."

"A kid like you, and cross-eyed besides? What for?"

I didn't like her tone, but she was plump and had the kind of smooth skin that means good food. I hate houses where the cook is scrawny and has a neck full of cords; they are always saving money on lard.

I just stood looking at her, the way I do when I want to bother people. She got nervous and a little bit mad, and then she said, "The *patrón* isn't home yet."

I just looked.

"Well, you can wait." She finished her chiles, and went into her kitchen.

"Want a *taco?*"

"If you please." It always gets them when you are very polite, after they have begun to get mad at you.

She brought me out a plateful of good bean *tacos* with cheese and *salsa*. I ate them slowly, for I saw her watching me from inside. I ate every crumb, and licked my fingers. That pleased her.

"Why don't you wait in here?"

I went in, and she set a cup of coffee, right out of the bubbling *olla* in front of me. Good coffee, cooked with brown sugar and cinnamon.

"What's your name?"

"What do you think they call me?"

"Bizco." She laughed.

"That's right."

"I've got a little boy. It will be nice to have you around. You can help me look after him."

Fat chance, I thought to myself, but I smiled and said, "Sure thing."

I was too smart to ask her anything about the family, so before long she poured herself a cup of coffee and sat down and I could see she was getting ready to tell me all she knew. Some women just can't help it.

"The *patrón* has two little boys. Quiet children. Well brought up. A big son. And a daughter, an older daughter. You'll have a lot to do with her, for she rides a great deal. There's a little mare out in the stable that is hers, and she won't let anybody ride her but herself. Name's Mariposa."

I nodded.

"And the señora?" I asked.

"She never rides unless she has to. She's an *alma de Dios*. A saint. Always in church, or working for the poor, and taking care of them."

"Where's your husband?" I asked.

"Husband? Pah." She spat. So then I knew about everybody, and I went back out to the stables. I got busy rubbing up some harness and I cleaned the place up. Even horses don't like to stand around in their own dung. I had the place looking pretty good when the *patrón* rode in.

I hurried over and took the bridle when he swung down, and led his horse . . . what a beauty! . . . over to his stall and started rubbing him down. The big horse (Cuervo was his name, and he was shining black as a crow) liked me right away, and shouldered me and nuzzled me. But all horses like me. I wasn't surprised, but the *patrón* was.

"When did you turn up?"

"Today. I've come to work for you. Stable boy. *Caballerango*."

"Fine. But where's Macario?"

"Who's that? An old guy, sort of wobbly on his feet? Drinks a lot?"

"Drinks? I don't think he drinks."

"Wasn't the same one, then."

"Well . . ." the *patrón* was looking confused.

"This old guy was lying right here, sound asleep, on the hay, with an empty bottle in his hand. He said he was going home."

The *patrón* shrugged.

"Guess I can find him, and look after him," he muttered.

"What time will you want me to have your horse saddled up in the morning, *patrón?*"

"About nine. And you had better have that gray saddled, too. You will be coming with me."

I hit my forehead with the side of my hand in a salute, and he went out, stiff-legged, like a man who has been riding all day.

That's how I began at the Valeras.

It was an easy job. Nice. The horses were good, and the *patrón* kept order in his house. There was a son off studying in Guadalajara, who didn't come home often, but when he did, I got along all right with him. He wore glasses, and was kind of soft, I thought; but he was no sissy. He could ride and shoot and nobody picked quarrels with him, so I guess he could fight. He had a little pearl-handled pistol with a snub nose that he wore on his right hip when we went out to the ranches, or riding in the country. I tried to get it, but I couldn't. José Luis his name was, and everybody called him by his two names, not *Güero*, or anything else. He was a *güero* though, quite blond and freckled. He wasn't good-looking enough to have the pistol, and besides, I wanted it. So once when he was home, and got all dressed up and was out walking in the *serenata*, I watched my chance and went into his room and took it. Way early, before the sun was up, he came out to the stables and nudged me with his foot. I turned around in my blankets, and at first I was so sleepy that I was stupid.

"Where is it?" he said quietly. "Hand it over."

I had it near me while I slept, and I pulled it out from under my blankets and gave it to him.

"I don't know how it got here," I said.

"Neither do I, but it is not to get here again. It is to remain in my room where I put it down, or I will make it speak, and to the right person," he said.

I wasn't scared, because I could see that he was one of those crazy guys who say exactly what they mean, and, therefore, of course, I couldn't take it again.

"Let me shoot it some day," I begged. "That's all I want."

"Behave yourself and I will let you shoot it a few times before I leave again," he promised.

He kept his promise too. He set up a white paper marker and measured off the paces, and we shot, first one and then the other. That was a sweet pistol; it fitted into my hand like a glove, and I hit the bull's eye every time. José Luis did too, glasses and all. But that was a bad afternoon, after all. We used up his bullets for the pistol, and on the way home a rattler reared up and struck his horse in the forefoot. I had to run like hell for home to bring medicine and poultices, and we had to let the snake get away. It took us hours to get the horse so we dared let him limp home, and I was busy with him night and day for a week. But I saved him. By then José Luis had gone back to Guadalajara. When I was sure our gray was going to be fine, I asked the *patrón* for a pistol, and for a couple of days off, and I hunted out that snake. By God, I hate those snakes. I found snake tracks and followed them, and I flushed it out from under some rocks at last. I let him wind himself up and rattle, and then I shot his head off. He had seven rattles, too. I put them in my hat band.

Porfiria, the cook, she had a little nutty kid that was always trying to make music. Not that he sang. He never did. And he couldn't even whistle. But he hit sticks together, and rocks, and scraped gourds, and he even had a whole set of gourds about the same size, each one with a different measure of water inside. These made different sounds when he struck them with a little wand. I guess he was sort of innocent. You know, almost crazy. Though he seemed to be normal enough. I tried to get him to wait on me, do errands for me, help around the stables, but he pretended not to understand. Maybe he wasn't so dumb. I couldn't give him a lick, because his Mamá was the cook. You have to keep in good with the cook.

Uf! I'd like to get out of the sun, but I can't seem to get started. Maybe Capitán Bravo . . . he is moving. Seems as if they got him in the chest. He's crawling over toward me.

Where was I? Oh yes, Tranquilino. Poor little kid, he was born on the day of San Tranquilino. Tough to carry around a name that long. Still nobody ever called him anything but Chato. Snub-nose.

He kept out of everybody's way, most of the time. His Mamá used to get a bottle of tequila once in awhile, and really hit it. It never made her mean, but she used to cry a lot, and want to hug Chato all the time. He usually came out to the stable to sleep, and hid himself somewhere when she was drunk. She couldn't find him in the dark and I never would light the lamp for her; I pretended it was lost. She never remembered anything the next day anyhow.

The Señorita Chela, that Chela. Now there was a girl for you! She was the catch of the country, I can tell you. Beautiful as a flying bird, and meaner than a scorpion. She found out once that I had been out on Mariposa, and she took a whip and gave me a licking I won't soon forget. I tried not to cry, but she was strong, and she was so mad her eyes blazed like a rifle in the night. I tried to grab the whip, but she was too fast for me, and the marks she made on my back lasted a week. Well, you know, I hated her, but I respected her. You don't try many tricks with a girl like that.

More like a man, she was, though there were suitors from all over the place mooning around after her.

"Next time I catch you riding my Mariposa, I'll have your hide off you!" she hissed at me, and for a real long time I didn't sneak the little mare out, either. A bit later on, I could ride her any time I wanted to. After the Señorita Chela got the bullet with her name on it.

Yeah, we got into the fighting. I was glad of it. Just grooming the horses and riding around is all right for old people, but I like excitement. And there are more opportunities. *¿Comprende?*

The old lady was very religious, and when she found out I hadn't made my first communion, she carried on until I went to the classes over in the church and made it, lined up with all the others. After that, I was supposed to go to confession and communion once a month, at least. Well, I did. What did it cost me? Nothing. No reason to buck it. And I liked the old priest, Father Melesio. He certainly knew what he was talking about, and you couldn't fool him. When all the troubles began, and the *patrón* and the other men in our town began to line up against the *sardos*, I went with our town, of course. Some of them were really religious, I guess, and felt that the Federals had to be given a few good lickings to make them behave. Others went just like I did, for the adventure of it. Also, I could see with half an eye, when the fighting got tough, that there were going to be some chances to get myself a really good horse. In battles, people get killed, right? And cavalry units ride horses, right? Well, you see what I mean.

We didn't fight battles, at first. I remember the first time we rode out. The *patrón* had called together a lot of the ranchers who sold him animals and grain, and they had had a big meeting in the grain house of one of them, Don Jacinto, the old goat that was after Señorita Chela. (She stood him up, in church, too! I almost died laughing, off by myself. She cooled him down, all right.)

I had been out with the *patrón,* and he didn't tell me not to, so I hung around and listened. The *patrón* stood up in front, and it was the funniest thing; he looked sad, all the time he was telling them they would have to make secret plans and try to fight the *sardos.* Planning some fun like that, and he was about to burst out crying! Matter of fact, every single man looked solemn, and one of them got up and said, Was everybody sure that they ought to fight? Didn't Jesus say if a man compel you to walk a mile, walk with him two, and so on. A few of them worried awhile about this, but after they had talked it all over, they decided they would vote. They put out the lanterns while everybody voted in the dark, and then they turned up the lamps again. Everybody seemed to jump up the walls when the lights came up, but it was just their shadows. They counted up the votes, and everybody was for making a fight of it, but one, and that must have been the one who spoke, so everybody knew who had voted and how, anyway.

"What would you do, Bizco?" one of the men hollered at me, turning around, and laughing. But I had an answer for him.

"I would ambush the sons o' guns," I answered, "and I'd pick 'em off from behind rocks and trees, so they'd never know what hit 'em."

"It's the right answer, by God," one of the men said.

The upshot was, they picked Don Manuel to be head of their group, and they all swore to follow him and take orders from him. They knelt down, too, and prayed, just as if they were in church. That tickled me, in the barn, and with the horse smells all around. They all hollered *"¡Viva Cristo Rey!"*

The first night we rode out, it wasn't to fight at all. Don Manuel deployed us around, and we set out in groups of

two or three. I was with him, of course. All we did was take
old Don Melesio to a railway station some distance to the
north, and stand on guard while he got on. But a man got
off the train there, and came back part way with the *patrón*
and me. He said, "*Ave María Purísima,*" and it turned out
he was a man from Santa Lala originally. He and the *patrón* buzzed together a long while. I went to sleep in the
saddle as we jogged along. Later on, I knew what they had
cooked up. The train man was to keep on traveling back
and forth, bringing information about when troops were to
move in, and he was to get ammunition for us. I pricked up
my ears at that. It sounded as if maybe we would have a
little fun later on. And I was right. At regular intervals, ammunition would be thrown off the caboose on certain runs,
and some of our men would be there to pick it up, distribute
it, and hide it.

I often got in on the distributing end, though I was never
allowed to go and pick it up. The *patrón* was clever, and
we didn't get ammunition on regular days, nor was it
thrown out for us at any regular spot. All plans were
changed every week.

Things began to get more lively soon, and the Señorita
Chela began riding out with us when the *patrón* had special
business. Nobody said anything; we all pretended she was
one of us, but we all knew she was there, on Mariposa,
wearing her brother's old clothes, and with her hair tucked
into a hat. She was good, I'll say that for her, and I'll never
take it back. She could ride and shoot like a man, and there
wasn't any fainting or vomiting or carrying on. She was a
very religious girl too, really. She was always teaching
catechism to the little kids, and after the señora died, she
visited all the sick and old people, and took them things,
just as her mother had always done. We had an old aunt in
the house then, Tía Rita, to look after things, and oversee
the cooking and so on. She was deaf as a gravestone, al-

ways making the wrong answers to everything. But she was loyal as a dog, and I wondered if she didn't pretend to be deafer than she was, especially when the *sardos* sent inspectors to the house and tried to get information. I guess they were onto us very soon. Nothing funny about that, the whole town was Cristero. But they caught on that we were leaders.

Well, on the whole I didn't do so badly. Long ago I found out something interesting that I never told anybody. I found it out from studying horses. Even the best horse will spook if you put him up against the kind of thing that spooks him. I had a wonderful horse once that shied and fought the bit every time we saw a bush with clothes drying on it. And even a bad horse, that nobody can ride, and that is good for nothing but crow meat, can be taught to pull a plow. Depends where you put the burr and how you handle him. So, I figured it works for people too. That's why I made a good thing out of the Cristero fight. I worked both sides. Well, you have to get along in this world, and you can always buy and sell. I don't see anything wrong with it. Though once when the Señorita Chela caught me selling some of our hay to the *sardo* sergeant for his horses, she tried to lick me. They called her "La Despiadada" because she was so pitiless . . . once a *sardo* got on his knees to her, when he found out he was ambushed, and prayed for her to let him go, said he had two kids, and wanted to go home to them. "My father had four children," she said, "and you killed him and unmanned him. Go straight to hell, where you belong!" And she shot him right in the face.

"String him up," she ordered me, "and let him hang where the others can see him when they ride this way."

She used to pray sometimes. At home I found her on her knees, moaning and swaying and saying the words, and sometimes even in the country, of all places. I never did make her out, exactly. Some days I thought she was just plain crazy, but not always, because she was awfully clever, and she had all the men completely hypnotized. Nobody dared to disobey her or say a word back to her.

Once she smiled at me though, and dropped her hand on my shoulder for a minute. It was when we had been out for several weeks, and were all dirty and full of lice we had picked up in a barn where we slept on some old blankets the *caballerangos* there had been using. We were eager to disband, and get home for baths and fresh clothes. I've had lice often and they didn't bother me so much, but some of those fellows that rode with La Despiadada were softies, and they were almost wild. She had been keeping a lookout for us, and releasing us to get on home by two's and three's . . . we never traveled in a bunch anyhow, though we often fought in groups of twenty or even fifty men. Well, when she got to me, and gave me my permission, I started out alone. I was just a kid . . . still am . . . and it seemed safer for me to wander through the countryside alone. If anybody stopped me I could always pretend to be lost.

I lit out along a little stream, and followed it, walking, because Señorita Chela needed a new mount. She took mine, as hers had been hurt in the last fight, and Padre Pistolas shot him. Padre Pistolas was a priest that fought along with us there, for a while. Well, he said he didn't fight, and I never really watched him when there was a real battle, but if he didn't use his guns, why did he wear them? Not that I gave a curse what he did. When we were in a mix-up, it was everybody for himself.

The reason I wanted to go along by the stream was that I hoped to find some horses watering along the way. I did, too. Got me a nice bay. Of course I had to ride him home with just a noose around his nose, bareback, but he was gentle, and fast. I was sure lucky. On the way I spotted some *sardos* and they seemed to be making for a farm where there were some gringos. These gringos were always afraid not to deal with the *sardos* and I suspected that the *sardos* were going to try to buy some oats for their mounts, because the last time I got into their warehouse to steal some, they were getting pretty low.

I hid my horse, tied him up with a short line where he wouldn't be easily seen, and sneaked over to get nearer and hear or see something that would give me an idea of what they were up to. While the *sardos* knocked at the front, and roused the owners, I went around to where they had their grains stored in bins and hid in the loft. Sure enough the *sardos* bargained for the oats, and for some hay and Egyptian corn as well. It was all settled that they would send for it with a wagon in two days' time.

I waited till they were gone, then I took a hatful of oats for my horse and went back to where I had left him. With a good horse under me, it wasn't hard to get back to Santa Lala that day, and as good luck was with me, I saw Gordo coming into town with his team about ten o'clock the next morning. I had stolen a *sardo* coat and cap, because sometimes I gave false bugle calls for the Federals, and got them all mixed up (we won a couple of skirmishes that way), so I went and hung around until Gordo was so far gone in his cups he wouldn't know what was happening to his team, and then I took it, and started out to where the Federals had made their bargain. When I got there I put on my cap and coat and saluted, and I gave the gringos a rigamarole in fast Spanish with a bunch of Yaqui words mixed in, and they couldn't wait to load up the oats on my wagon.

It was getting dark when I drove into Santa Lala again, and I soon made sure that Gordo hadn't even moved from the Cantina. Fact is, he was on the floor snoring like a bull, and I knew he wouldn't be in the mood to notice much when they threw him out at midnight. So I hid the *sardo* cap and coat and drove right up to the commissary of the Federals.

"Oats and hay!" I hollered, and a couple of fellows came rushing over. They knew me, and one of them was very suspicious.

"I'll get the sergeant," he said.

They brought him out. He was picking his teeth with a whittled stick, and he took a good look at me.

"I've seen you around," he said.

"Why not? I live out on one of the ranches and I'm often in here."

"Are you a Cristero?"

"Who wants to know?"

"I do."

"I go along with my *patrón*," I said. "He's a gringo, and doesn't believe in this stuff. He's a Lutheran."

"I thought I saw you working around the Valera place."

"I've got a lot of cousins."

"Well . . . could be . . ."

"I've got some oats and hay here for sale, and if you want some, you better speak up. I want to sell this, and unload and get home before midnight."

"Wait a minute . . ."

The upshot was they paid me for the stuff, and I took the team back and left them where Gordo could find them when he wanted to start home. And I had made myself a tidy little sum. I knew Señorita Chela would catch me in this trick (I had to leave too many tracks), so I told her about it, and gave her some of the money. That's when she smiled at me.

The easiest was picking things off the dead. Lots of times, right after a fight, if the Federals ran away, or if there was a lot of confusion, I could get rings off their fingers before they got stiff, and even if they were two or three days dead, sometimes they had medals on them . . . even those *sardos*, who were fighting our side for being Christians, can you imagine! . . . Even *they* wore the holy medals. It was always easy to catch one of those Federals on a country road and sell him a medal; they were scared to death of us, or rather of La Despiadada, and they wore every medal they could get ahold of.

What I really wanted was a watch, and once I got a pretty good one, or at least it was pretty. Gold, I think, and it had a picture of a girl inside, and a lock of hair, soft like a baby's. But it wouldn't run. I took it all apart once, but the pieces were so small I couldn't put it together again.

It's getting dark. Maybe it's going to rain.

When it rained we had our troubles. But less than the *sardos*. We knew every haystack, and the ones that had pitchforks buried in them. Ha! They didn't always know! Lot of 'em got stuck!

Once we fought back and forth for days around a village called San Anselmo. Wasn't anything there much but a warehouse, and a place where they sold sausage and cheese, a few houses, and a church with a tall steeple. We had cut down that patrol of *sardos* to only about ten when they managed to slip into the town, and they all got into that church and hid in the steeple. We lost two men before it was clear what they were up to. They were picking us off from way up there. Señorita Chela wasn't with us then; she had been shot, and was home in bed pretending to have typhoid so the *sardos* wouldn't search the house.

We were about twenty, but nobody seemed to know what to do. I got an inspiration when I reconnoitered around. In that warehouse there were several sacks of dry chile. I couldn't do anything with it until I got hold of a burro somewhere, so I had to scout around to find one and steal it. By night I had one, and I broke into the warehouse and got those sacks of chile. Then, hiding behind the burro, I pushed him along in the dark until I was close enough to make a break for it. With darkness all around, and the burro smacked on the hindquarters to make him run, I diverted whatever sentry they had on duty. I hauled my chiles into the church and over to the bottom of the stairs leading up to the steeple. Then I lay down on the chiles to sleep till morning, because I didn't want to flush those bastards out till it was full light. I woke up just before dawn, and spread out my chiles, with just enough air between them so they would keep burning a long time, and then I set fire to them. They would smoulder away for some time before they really started burning, I knew, and I waited, with my face all tied up in my shirt until they were going good, and the bitter, pepper-hot smoke was rising in a thick cloud. Then I got out and ran down the street where I could hide. I had my rifle ready, and when the *sardos* started coming out, blind, with their arms up, yelling "Surrender," I picked them off like birds asleep on a wire. They had some first-rate pistols, too. I kept a good one, and sold the others. That was a fine time. After that a lot of fellows never called me Bizco again. They called me Chile Smoke.

Capitán Bravo has got closer to me. He is badly hurt, I think. There's blood all over his chest.

I'm sorry now that I stole his watch. Especially as he stole it back from me. It was like this. We were bivouacking, in two's and three's, and he and I were alone together. We slept in a haystack, one of those they put up in the crotches of trees so the hungry cattle can't get at them and eat them. We were cuddled into one, safe and cozy, and the *sardos* were riding past us down on the road, and never even stopped to search for our horses, which I had hidden well among some willow trees a kilometer away. Capitán Bravo was young and full of fun; he was always in the middle of a fight, and he was everybody's friend. Somebody told me that an uncle of his was a bishop, and that's why he never used his real name. He joined up with us after Señorita Chela was shot. Anyhow, I got his watch that night in the haystack, and the next morning when I slipped down, and scouted around to make sure we were safe, I had it inside my *vibora*, that woven snake of fine thread we wind around our waists and use to keep our valuables safe.

"Pssst!" He was looking down at me from out of the straw, smiling. He was always smiling. Those big square white teeth under the black moustache were always out in the air.

"Cold tooth," I called him.

"Chile Smoke!"

"Diente frio!"

"Is it safe?"

"If it wasn't, would I even answer you, burro?"

"Here I come!"

He fell almost on top of me, knocking me down for a minute. I thought nothing of it, I'm not quick to make something of any little accident. Only walking along toward where I had hidden our mounts, I noticed the tail of my *vibora* was loose. I felt, and I didn't have to look. There stood Cold Tooth laughing fit to burst himself. So I smiled. Let him think it was a joke! Well, it wasn't, and before the week was out, I stole his watch again. He had put it on the ground while he washed in a horse trough when we stopped at a ranch where the people were with us.

It got to be kind of a game, because every now and then I would get it from him, and somehow or other . . . I guess he was just as clever as I was . . . he would get it back. I tried hiding it, but he never let me get very far from him, and I didn't have many chances. Once when I was going out behind the bushes, I buried it and marked it with a rock, but I guess old Cold Tooth had spied on me, because when I went back there and dug it up, there was a rock where the watch had been, so I knew he had found it once more.

I can't remember exactly about this last battle. He had his watch then, I know that. And I kept close to him in the fighting, because he could always get hit, you see, and then I would be able to take his watch and keep it. To remember him by. He was really a good guy. But we both got hit.

Something . . . there's something in my hand. Feels like the watch. Can't be. Yes! . . . he's so near me, it must be the watch! But I can't turn my head, and I can't look at it just yet. I love that watch. Round and heavy in the hand, thick, and real gold. Mostly it kept time, too, if you wound it. I can't seem to . . .

Uf! There's a smell . . . the smell of death. Poor Capitán Bravo. I guess he died just now. I would like to . . . but I can't. I'm too sleepy. I'll just . . .

V

Well, call me Juan. Everybody does; every foot soldier in the army is called Juan. I don't mind, although my real name is Inocencio. Mi General always called me Juan, and anything he did was all right with me. He was only a major, really, but I called him "mi General," and he never contradicted me, though sometimes he would smile. He never let anybody else call him that; he always corrected them very coldly.

I will tell you how I happened to join the army. It was this way. I was working in the fields for the *patrón*, Don Felipe, and I had my month's pay in my pocket. So I went over to the village, to the cantina, and found some friends there. I wasn't married, and I didn't have a girl; what else could I do? We drank and sang and we were happy until a certain stranger threw open the door and stood there looking at all of us. The air was sour with the smell of dirty glasses and the breath of the drinkers, and thick with smoke from shuck cigarettes. This man was in uniform. Right away he arrested all of us and took us away, but not to jail. He took us to the major, the one I always called mi General, because there could be no higher title. That was how I first saw him—sitting at a desk in a campaign tent—the handsomest man I ever laid eyes on. He was one of us, I could see, pure Indian, with a dark brown skin and black hair and eyes. He had the face of an eagle, and his eyes were brilliant and wild, like a captive bird's. His uniform fitted like another skin, and in his left ear he wore a golden hoop. It had been his mother's, and he wore it till the day he died.

He looked at us, as we stood there before him, hiccuping and weaving about.

"You are a pack of drunken fools," he said. "But now you will be my men, in my company, and if I catch any of you drunk, I will devise suitable punishments for you."

One of us, I forget his name, came to enough to call out, "What is this, a *leva?* Are we being impressed?"

"You are, and a good thing too," answered mi General. (His real name and rank were Major Angel Torres Mina.) "Furthermore, it is against regulations to take recruits this way, and I know it. You had better agree and say that you came of your own free will to join up, or, after I release you, something peculiarly unpleasant will happen to you before you stumble your way back to the cantina."

So we all enlisted.

Mi General wanted extra men because they were ordering him to the north, where the Cristeros were roaming around causing all kinds of trouble. They issued us uniforms. Very smart, they seemed to us, with a nice cap. Though I missed my big wide-brimmed straw sombrero, and the new shoes hurt. It was rather painful, getting used to the shoes.

We learned to use our arms and to obey orders, and it seemed a good enough life. Mi General ate with his men, and therefore the food was good. He was always appearing unexpectedly among us, and I guess that's why we became one of the best companies in the regulars. Some of the other officers, I heard, locked themselves away, and had special food and drink, and some of them even had women in at night. Not mi General. He ate sparingly and never drank, not even beer. And he punished the soldiers found consorting with women. You know, come to think of it, he was a good deal like a monk in his personal life. Though of course he despised "the blackbirds"—the priests—as we all did. Many a time I saw him spit as he mentioned them. "Womanish creatures, sitting around on their fat backsides, like wives, letting hard-working men support them, and toil to buy trinkets for their churches."

Oh, he was a man, all right. All of a piece. Disciplined, tough, severe. Hard to all but his own men. With us he was quiet, firm, and unyielding, but he looked after us well. He was like a father, I suppose, or an older brother. Like the head of the family, that's it. He had authority over us, but he was interested in us too, and proud of us when we had maneuvered well. Later, when we were in the fighting, he helped bandage and dose us, working side by side with the doctors and orderlies after a battle.

We were in some bad fighting. Because they were not bound by any rules, you know, those Cristero fellows. They fought a guerrilla war—ambushing, attacking at night in terrain they knew like the palms of their hands, fighting to kill, and not just to frighten, or to gain an advantage from which to bargain. You'd think we had burned their homes, broken their families, spoiled their daughters, the way they hated us! Taught to do so by the blackbirds, of course. When all we were doing was carrying out government orders to shut up their churches and deport the priests that were sucking the life out of them. Later, of course, we were ordered to execute any priests we found still carrying on their mumbo-jumbo. Mi General carried out all his orders meticulously, though he never tortured his prisoners as some of the other officers did. Of course, one shouldn't criticize; they had provocation enough. Those people in the Altos of Jalisco, where the soil is dark red when the plow turns it, they were the most stiff-necked, the most unyielding, the most hypocritical. Can' you believe it, time and again we would pass a man peacefully plowing in his field, but before we had marched half a kilometer he would grab up a rifle he had hidden in a furrow and give a yell, and fifty to a hundred men would seem to spring up from the earth and take shape from behind rocks and trees, and they would come after us before we could wheel and get into fighting position. And they took their toll of us, too.

We were quartered near a town they called Santa Lala (their usual stubbornness, the town's right name was Aguacatitlán de Juarez) and mi General had posted the usual notices about church services, baptism, confession and so on being forbidden, and about persons conducting these rites being summarily shot, when we suffered a severe setback. How it happened I don't know, some traitor in our ranks no doubt; they were capable of everything, those Cristeros . . . but they stampeded and stole most of our horses. And on top of that, a kid of twelve or so, an ugly cross-eyed boy they called Bizco, offered to sell them back to us! And for gold! He wouldn't accept Federal notes! I don't know who put him up to it. How could he have thought of it all by himself? Mi General of course would have nothing to do with him, and sent him smartly about his business. We should have strung him up. He was a Cristero all right, young as he was, and did us plenty of harm. I saw him in the fighting not many days later, and mounted on one of our own horses! And once he blew false signals on a *clarín,* and got our men all in confusion. Devil's brat!

But I was going to tell you about mi General. He was a merciful man. There was the incident of the captive priest, for instance.

Can you imagine? Despite the penalties, notwithstanding the law and the notices, and the punishments that were meted out promptly, one day we caught this priest hearing confessions. And wearing the soutane, too. I tell you, I was really struck senseless when I saw it, the foolishness of the man! You couldn't call it courage, it was too foolhardy.

I had suspected something when I saw so many women wandering toward Don Epifanio's warehouse, among them that Valera girl. Those Valeras were undoubtedly Cristeros, every one of them, from the old man down to that stuck-up daughter, who always carried her nose so high in the air, as if she smelled something bad when she passed us. She was the one who put all the women up to wearing mourning, they had told me. There wasn't a woman or girl in the town but wore ugly black, and they would have nothing to do with us . . . they were in mourning, they all said.

Well, I had had my eye on that warehouse, and I was pretty sure there was something going on there. Suddenly I rushed in, and burst through the back door into the part where they had the grain bins. And sure enough, there they were . . . about twenty women, and that priest. He was sitting on an overturned empty barrel, wearing that soutane, with a strip of embroidered cloth around his neck that was supposed to make him equal with God, able to forgive sins. There was a woman kneeling in front of him, confessing, with her *rebozo* pulled out at the sides to hide her face, and the others were all lined up, some distance away, waiting their turn.

I arrested him at once. The women came at me like furies, and one of them threw herself on me and scratched me . . . see the scar, there? . . . till the blood ran down my neck, but the priest held up his hand, and they all quieted down.

"Go along home quietly, all of you," he said. "No violence. God bless you."

He was only a young fellow, not more than twenty-five, I think, and they were mostly middle-aged women, only one or two young girls. But they all obeyed him at once. He had the same kind of quiet, soft-spoken authority as mi General. Some of the women sobbed, and one of them cried, "Ay, Padre Félix!" in a desperately sad voice. They knew he would be shot at once. But I was obligated to take him to mi General.

I could have arrested the lot of the women, too. It was as much a crime to take part in those so-called sacraments as to administer them, but I would have had to go for rein-forcements, and they might have got away. Besides, the priest was the prize.

"Where are your clothes?" I asked him, for I wanted to know how he had got into Aguacatitlán. But he would not answer. Of course, he must have changed somewhere. In the warehouse, perhaps. I decided to march him to headquar-ters in the soutane, anyway, and send some men back to search for what his disguise had been.

The women went out, sniffling and crying some of them, others flashing their eyes defiantly at me, and one or two, you wouldn't believe it of those women from good families, calling me obscene names. I paid no attention.

Then I saw that Valera girl among the women, the one who pretended to be so pious. "Dirty pig!" and "Murderer!" she spat at me. I arrested her, too.

I made them march ahead of me to where mi General was working at his desk. He looked up as I snapped my heels together and saluted.

"I caught this blackbird hearing confessions. This woman was there; they were all in the warehouse that belongs to Epifanio Montes."

Mi General looked at her and she stared back at him de-fiantly.

"Let the woman go," he said.

I could have laughed, for this made her swell up with fury. She started to speak, but mi General waved his hand at her as if he were shooing off a chicken.

"Run along," he said. "Get out of here."

She panted with temper, and then swung around and ran out, and I had to laugh.

"Quiet!" said mi General. "Do you think I would arrest her just for confessing? I have something else in mind for that one, when I have sprung my trap." And he smiled. He seemed to have forgotten the priest. But then he looked up and studied the face of the priest carefully.

I looked too, and it was surprising, but he looked just like some of those pictures I used to see of St. Anthony. Dark-haired and slight, with a porcelain-fair skin through which the faint bluish line of the beard showed. His eyes were dark and deep-set, and when he spoke, his upper lip lifted a bit to show perfect, white, even teeth. Well, that is the Guadalajara type, men and women both are dark-haired and fair-skinned, with beautiful faces. And his accent was from there.

"Your name?" asked mi General.

"Félix Artigas Esperón."

The little priest showed no fear at all. He was courteous and distant.

"The penalty for persisting in unlawful activities is death," said mi General flatly. "You know that?"

"I know it. I am ready."

Mi General stared at him.

"Are you a woman?" he asked scornfully. "You wear skirts! I find it hard to execute a woman."

The priest stood quietly, the beginning of a smile curving his lips.

"I have some dirty clothes," said mi General thoughtfully, "and my orderly here [with a nod at me] is not the best of washermen. The women in this town will do nothing for us, they send our clothes back dirtier than when we gave them, and I am constitutionally unable to have them whipped. So, before I shoot you, you will do my washing."

The priest bowed his head.

"Requisition some tubs and soap," ordered mi General. "Put him to work."

Well, the priest washed all night. Everything.

Mi General could then have shot him, of course, or hung him up. But he thought of something that was really very clever. It was to make an example of that womanish little priest who had defied the law. He tied a rope around Félix's waist, and took him everywhere with him, like a dog. He tied the rope to his desk when he was working, and to his saddle horn when riding about. Félix had to lope along beside the horse, and when they stopped, he would flop down with weariness, just like a dog. It was terribly comic; we all laughed a lot at the sight. Though after a few days we got used to it, and hardly noticed.

"Down, dog!" mi General would shout at him, and he threw food to him, bones and scraps from the table, as if he were a dog in truth. Sometimes mi General would snap his fingers at the priest and then pull him nearer, with the rope, and pat his head, and pull his ears.

The priest never said one word, or made one complaint. He did ask for water sometimes, and mi General directed that it be brought him in a pan, and he made him lap it, holding his hands behind his back.

One day, when he had made a fast march on horseback, mi General had let Félix run along until he fell, and then he took him up behind him on the horse. "I treat my dogs well," he said laughing.

When we came to a railway line, where there were the bodies of some Cristeros hanging, stiffening, and turning in the air like bags of meal on pulleys, he said, "Take a look, there. Now, be sensible. Come over to our side. I will pardon you, and you can become my orderly, instead of Juan here. Otherwise . . ." and mi General glanced at those blackening faces. Already it was wise not to ride to windward of them.

But Félix would not answer. He only closed his eyes and

his lips moved slightly. I suppose he was praying for those wretches.

Mi General was a superb shot, and he was also a merciful man. He did not often leave those creatures hanging and rotting. He would shoot through the ropes, and detail some of us to dig graves for them. Not the ones we hung, but those we came upon that had been left by others. We couldn't cut down our own at once; it would have been bad for discipline. But mi General never allowed our men to disfigure them. A quick, clean hanging, and it was over.

For a long time I never heard Padre Félix answer one word. But then, after some weeks had gone by, when we were being moved to another town, we were ambushed at night, and there was a real battle. Dozens of those devils, mounted, came down on us from a ravine, brandishing their rifles, and yelling *"¡Viva Cristo Rey!"* until the hills echoed. They rushed through us and past, and away again, and then came back, regrouped, from another direction. There was little we could do, except fire blindly. It was night, and we did not know the country as they did. By morning they had all disappeared, except the dead they left behind. We had many dead and many wounded, among them mi General, who had been shot in the arm. Padre Félix, who could have got away, hadn't done so. Our company surgeon had been shot, and Félix took over his canteen and equipment. It seemed he had studied medicine before he went to the seminary, and he knew what to do. He extracted the bullet from the arm of mi General and bound and bandaged it, and took care of all the wounded who needed first aid. I suppose it was funny, really; mi General made me hold the leash around the priest's waist, and there he stood, in his filthy and torn soutane, with the sleeves rolled up, swabbing with alcohol, painting with iodine, and bandaging. Mi General stood by, unable to do anything, restless, enduring the bitter pain of his shattered arm. Once in a while he would shout "Bark, dog!" at the priest, and Félix, without lifting his eyes from what he was doing, or pausing in one instant in his medical tasks, would obediently go "Woof!"

When mi General went to lie down (he would not take any pain killer, for he knew there wasn't much, and he left it for the men), Padre Félix wanted to move among the men who were dying, and, well, I let him. I guess it was wrong, but I went with him, and hung onto his leash. He begged the men to confess, to whisper "Creo," "I believe." A few seemed comforted; one or two whispered in his ear. I pretended not to hear any of the mumbling or to see when Félix made the sign of the cross over them.

That night mi General was feverish and irritable. He ordered the priest tied to the leg of his campaign cot, and in the night I heard him begin to rail at Félix.

"Your God," he taunted Padre Félix, "is a great one for getting money from the poor and for long prayers over the dying. How does it happen he cannot alleviate pain?"

Then Félix spoke his first words to mi General.

"But He can, when He will," he answered softly.

"Order him to alleviate mine."

"My God does not take orders. But we can pray to Him."

"I must crawl and beg, is that it?"

"God loves a tender and obedient heart, one that accepts His will."

There was a long silence.

Then mi General began again.

"I am a Seri, from the hills. I began in the ranks, as a common soldier, twenty years ago. I have heard many men pray to that Crucified you venerate, but never once did He answer. There was one, a friend of mine, who fell with a bullet in his belly; his intestines lay beside him on the ground like a tangle of wool. 'Christ,' he called, for hours. 'Christ, take me!' But your Christ would not. There he lay dying for hours, until his voice was hoarse, until he could only whisper."

"No doubt he is with Christ now, in paradise."

"He is under the ground, rotten."

"His body is dead. But his soul lives. The soul is like a perfume. You know it is there, you sense the fragrance . . . but you cannot touch it or see it."

"I know those romantic ideas of your kind. Womanish talk, to help cowards bear the fear of death."

"Let me teach you the truth!"

"You will stop barking now, dog! I wish to sleep."

"But . . ."

"Dog, if you bark again, I will have you beaten." And mi General then got up from his cot and kicked Félix several times. Then he turned his face away to the wall. And Padre Félix, sighing, curled up and slept on the floor, like a dog, as he was used to doing.

This Félix had some skill, for he set the arm of mi General, and it grew together perfectly. He might have asked for his release, or perhaps he could have tried to escape. Mi General, out of gratitude, would have let him go, for he was always fair.

But Félix did neither. He remained there, tied up, taking the kicks that came his way, eating scraps tossed to him, or gnawing on bones. Sometimes I watched him, when I was on sentry before the tent of mi General, and when there was nothing to do, he merely sat, or crouched, wherever he had been tied, and seemed to sleep. Just like a dog. A dog would not watch his chance, untie the knot, and make a break for it. Neither did Félix. But I think he was not sleeping; he was in one of his trances. I know he went into trances when he was speaking with someone silently. He told me so.

Mi General had gone somewhere to check some supplies,

or to look after something, and had left me to guard his dog.

I marched up and down for a time, but there wasn't any real use in it. What was I guarding? Just a weak creature that never even made a motion toward getting away. I figured he must enjoy his humiliation, because if he had made the slightest effort he could have got himself decently shot at any moment. Cowardly, womanish creature.

I hunched down, keeping my rifle upright, and looked straight at him. He smiled back at me very sweetly, as if I had said something nice.

I spat.

"What do you think about, just sitting around? I should think it would drive you crazy!" I burst out at him.

"Perhaps," he answered, "I am crazy to begin with."

"Major Torres Mina thinks so, I guess."

"Oh no. He doesn't think so. Else he would not trouble to keep me in this position, in this role."

"What do you mean? Be careful what you say now! He is the finest man in the world!"

Félix nodded.

"Yes, he is a fine man."

"I don't understand you! You ought to hate him!" I really wanted to know how his mind worked. I have known innocents, idiotic people who were born without brains, every country child sees a certain number of these harmless creatures. But this fellow had passed the tests that priests take. Bad as they are, part of a conspiracy to bleed the last peso from simple people and send it away to their pope in Rome, I knew that they have to be well educated. They have to have some brains, to start.

"Hate? There's no room for hate in my religion."

"Pah! Maybe you don't, but those Cristeros that fight us, they hate, and plenty! They ambush us and kill us! And in the name of their religion!"

Félix looked up at me, so sadly. His eyes filled with tears.

"I think about that," he said to me. "I pray for you all . . . soldiers and Cristeros . . . for everyone. It is so easy to turn away from Christ's path."

I got up. "Quit preaching at me. I don't want to hear your foolishness."

"As you will."

"But one thing I would like to know!" I shouted at him. "What do you think about sitting around on the floor, treated like a dog? Like the dog you are!"

"Ah, Juan, when you are interested in another person's thoughts, you have some feeling for him. I am honored that you wish to know what I am thinking."

Something about the quiet authority with which he said this infuriated me.

"Well, to hell with it," I spat out. "I don't want to know. To hell with it and to hell with you."

I stood away from him, and paid no more attention to him, and presently a few soldiers came by who wanted to tease him and bait him. I let them for a little while, then I ran them off. They had no right bothering mi General's dog.

"Thank you," said Félix. "I am a dog, I know, and I was about to bite one of those brutes on the ankle."

I stared at him. His face was without expression, but deep behind his eyes I saw the sparkle of a smile.

"You want to know what I think about? I will tell you," he said, sitting on his heels, as I did, to rest his legs a little. "I am working. I am doing something important, and I work hard at it. All the time."

I showed my disbelief.

"Thinking is work," he told me. "Quite as much as marching, fighting, plowing, anything."

"When you sit there with your eyes closed, doing nothing, you are working? Tied up like a dog, unable to move?"

"Oh yes. I will finish my task before long. With God's help."

"Quit that talk about God."

He just smiled at me.

"My work has something to do with you, Juan."

"I forbid it!"

I knew what he was getting at, then. He was trying to pray us into something. I've heard ignorant village women claim that they prayed things to happen and they did. No wonder he wouldn't unknot his leash and make a break for it. He was trying to pray us into untying it for him! The arrogance of it! I hit him a clout with the butt of my rifle, and knocked him down. That kept him quiet for a while. I hadn't hit him hard, I didn't really want to knock him out, but I caught him just the wrong way, or something. He came to, after a few minutes, and shook his head and tried to focus his eyes at me. He was moving about, swaying.

"Don't you dare to forgive me!" I spat at him. I was glad to see mi General returning. The fellow was driving me crazy.

Mi General saw some blood trickling down from Félix's temple.

"What's the matter here?" he asked me.

"He was giving me some of his lip, and I hit him."

Mi General turned ashy gray, and I could see that he was violently angry.

He called in two soldiers, and they put me under arrest. I had to be in the church tower locked up (that was our temporary prison) for two days on dry tortillas and cold coffee. Can you fathom it? I!

Well, I decided, while I sat there in the semidark, I would have nothing more to do with Félix. I wouldn't speak to him even. He had tried to provoke me, to get me to bash him, that was clear. Clever as they are mean, these

171

priests. But mi General! I couldn't understand why he had got so angry with me.

When I was let out, I had to do laundry duty for a couple of days. And guess who was right beside me, washing, his arms all soap suds up to the elbow? Félix. The dog.

I set my jaw, and I washed with all my might, but each time I had to pick up a wet, heavy load, he was there before me. I let him. Since he was such a fool, why not?

Mi General was studying all the maps he could find, and was very irritable. Once he looked straight at me, and said, "The only way to fight people in a terrain they know, and you do not, is to get to know it as well as they do."

He began sending out scouting parties, three or four at a time, always different men, so that they all began to know the lay of the land pretty well.

Mi General was out at all hours, too, at night especially, learning the look of every place, watching where shadows fell, marking on his maps where there was cover, where there were too many squirrel holes and rocks for a man to run his horse at top speed, everything. That's the way he worked. Not by the books, or by tradition, but by what his own common sense told him was the thing to do, and the way to prepare.

On these excursions he left the priest at camp, tied to his desk, or to the washtubs, with a long rope.

I knew he was getting ready for an engagement when he sent me out on duty to watch the trains, and report to him any changes in their speed or hour of arrival along the track for twenty miles. Each night, for a week, I kept watch at a different point until I had found out what he wanted to know. There was a place where they always slowed down, and went across some rough track at a slow pace. When I told him about that place, and showed him where, and explained the trees, the cover, the shadows, and the type of land, he nodded his head smartly. I could see that he had made a decision.

"Bring me my dog," he ordered, and I went to get the priest away from where he was tied to the doorknob in mi General's quarters, mending some tunics. Mi General made him do all the womanish work there was about.

"Come along, good doggie," I said to him. "We're getting ready for a fight," I exulted, "and I know mi General. He will leave all the excess baggage behind, and well disposed of. He always does. You are going to be strung up."

He put down the tunic, slipped the needle and thread into it, so that whoever picked it up could continue the work, and came along beside me. He was a sorry sight, for of course he had not been allowed to wash or to shave, or to clean his filthy, torn soutane. When we were in the washing room, he had washed his face and hands. But his beard had grown; it was black and curly, and his hair was now long on his neck. He had such a pitying, tender expression on his face that it upset me. He reminded me of somebody. So I pushed him ahead roughly, and I felt like kicking him. But there wasn't time. Mi General had come to find me.

"Get a move on," he barked at me. "And you, dog. Pack up medicines and bandages. We are going out tonight, and there will be a skirmish. Perhaps a real battle. I'll want my wounded looked after. Take him to the dispensary, Juan. When all is in order, bring him back to me, at my offices."

So he was taking Félix with us. Well, I shrugged. I guessed he would hang him up after. Or maybe just shoot him down. But you can't say mi General wasn't intelligent. He always got the last ounce of work out of the men, out of the horses, and out of every villager and rancher where we were quartered.

It was a cloudy night, changeable, and I smelled rain coming. So did the horses, for they had been prancing about, curling their tails into hooks and snorting, the way

173

they always do when there is going to be a storm. Mi General deployed us on different routes, but I could see we were going to converge on that point along the rails where the trains slowed. There had never been trains at night, so I suppose mi General had had some message from our spies. There is no doubt that he expected a train that night.

I was so angry I could hardly see, for he sent me off with three of the silliest foot soldiers in the battalion, and he took Félix up on his horse behind him, and told him to hang on with one arm around his waist. It took me an hour's slogging march to figure it out. Of course. If he needed Félix to help care for the wounded, he couldn't make him lope along beside him; the priest would get to the place we were going exhausted, and be useless. It often did take me a long time and hard thinking to get onto mi General. He was always deep.

We all arrived at the spots designated in good time, and received orders to remain quiet and motionless until further instructions. It was a queer wait, with the storm growling and the clouds scudding to hide the moon. Everything about the land changed every few moments, and for a while you would feel that the storm must pass, and the moon would come out brilliant as silver, and the landscape become familiar again. And then darkness would pass over everything and there would come a moaning and a moving of the leaves, and the grasses all bent down and lay flat.

Over near me was a detachment of men on horses; they were all placed behind some trees, and I heard the animals move and whicker lightly. I looked and saw them all standing with their ears forward, as they do when they know another horse is nearing.

Then it happened. A group of those fanatics emerged from the shadows, mounted, and at the same moment there came a brilliant violet light, and we saw them all, as they leaned, startled, into their saddles, and tried to gain the shadow again.

"Fire!" came our order, and we sent out a volley of shots.

"Alert for the train!" I was ordered, with some others, and mi General wheeled on his horse, and sent some of the mounted men to pursuing the enemy. They were not many, and some of them got away. But we caught about six of them. Then at least fifty others came at us from behind the railroad right of way . . . it was high there, the rails going along at the top of a small ravine, and they had sneaked up on us protected by that small rise. There was a battle, short, but fierce, and this time we lost seven men and two of our best mounts.

The train came puffing along then, and the rain poured down with a roaring of thunder that became almost continuous, with flares and streaks of lightning. In the confusion it was hard to tell which were our own men and which were theirs.

The train had been warned; it raced by, not slackening speed, and nothing was thrown from it. As it passed, it gave those hateful Cristeros a chance to ride along beside on the other side, protected from us, and that's how many of them got away.

When it was clear that the fighting was over for this night, I looked around for mi General, but I saw his horse standing riderless, over near the trees. I got there as fast as I could. He was on the ground, and Félix was with him. He had got mi General's tunic open, and was swabbing iodine into a nasty bubbling wound. I was scared, for in another feeble glow of lightning, I saw the same dark foam bubble on mi General's lips. Hit in the lung.

"Below also," Félix told me. "But it is better not to open the clothes. They will serve as a binder until I get him to cover, or to camp."

With two saplings we made a stretcher of a blanket from

175

under the saddle of mi General, and started back toward the camp. It was a long way, on foot, but I knew how to go, and we went the way we had come, the horse following behind.

The storm had settled down to steady cold rain, and I took off my jacket to cover mi General.

"The rain is good," said Félix. "It will keep off the fever for a while."

There we went, like two companions, that priest in his filthy skirts, and me in my field clothes.

"Hey," I said. "You could have got away! Those were your people who fought us! Sneaky cursed Cristeros! May they all rot in hell!"

He made no answer, and I demanded, "Why didn't you go? You are as big a fool as ever I heard of in my life! A pumpkin head!"

He was murmuring one of their prayers, over and over, and walking along steadily. I had the stretcher at mi General's head, and Félix walked in front. I told him which way to go. We had no trouble. The rats had all gone back into their holes.

"We will shift now, and I'll walk in back," said Félix. He began to set down his saplings, very gently, and, I don't know why, but I obeyed as if he had been an officer. "I want to watch the wounded man, see if I notice any change."

We shifted about. That is how, walking ahead, my back to those two, I heard what they said to each other.

Félix seemed to have grown taller, and he had authority.

"God have mercy," he said, and mi General moved his lips, and then said, whispering, "I am dying."

"Yes," Félix said firmly. "Let me confess you, Major Torres, I beg. Just whisper, '*Creo.*'"

Silence.

We walked slowly and as softly and gently as we could.

176

"You have been a good dog," said mi General, sighing.

"I am, and have been, only what God commanded me. I wish to save you, I am praying for your soul. I beg you, let me baptize you!"

"Set me down."

We put him down, so carefully. I was streaming with tears, I couldn't help myself. Félix, that mountebank, looked calm. Sad, though. I don't think he was happy that mi General was dying.

"'*Creo*, I believe' . . . that is all. Just let me make the sign of the cross on your forehead, and you will go straight to glory, I promise you."

Mi General sighed and seemed to make a great effort. He opened his eyes.

"I will say it, if you wish me to. For you. Because of you."

"Not for me. I want it, I have longed for you to confess! But not for me! For Our Lord Jesus Christ."

"I do not believe. But I will say it for you. I have loved you, dog. Poor dog. My dog." His voice was so soft, less than a whisper.

Padre Félix knelt then, and clasped his hands together and closed his eyes and spoke to heaven.

"Cure him, I beg! Show forth Thy glory in a miracle, my God! So that we may save this soul. So that I may have time . . ."

Well, I could see that he wanted to save mi General, I believed him; I would like to have prayed too, if it would help. Anything.

"For you," whispered mi General. "*Creo* . . . if you want it . . . for you . . ."

"I want you to believe," sobbed Félix.

"Who could not love you?" asked the general. "I believe only in you."

"No . . . no. Our Lord . . . who suffered for us . . ."

"You suffered . . . because of me. . . . Forgive . . ."

"It was nothing. Only believe. Give your soul to God."

"To you . . . to you only . . ."

And I saw that change come then, that change that means death. The face becomes still, the features settle, there is a quietness, something mysterious. He was gone.

Padre Félix remained where he was, on his knees, whispering, moaning.

"We must take him back," I said.

We lifted him up; Padre Félix took one end of our stretcher, and I the other. There was no need to be slow and gentle now. We hurried.

Morning was dawning, as we got into the field camp and turned him over to the next officer, who took over and gave orders to strike, and to get back to our base in Santa Lala. Padre Félix just stood; nobody paid any attention to him. They were all so used to him. He hung his head, and his leash dragged on the ground. No orders were given about him, and I had no idea what to do with him. As I started slogging back toward Santa Lala, he tagged along at my heels. We went along by the railway, it was shorter.

Before we came into the town, we heard clattering hoofs, and a detachment of cavalry rode in, all on fine horses, and in fresh-looking uniforms. There was a colonel with them. He dismounted, and taking up a bit of Félix's tattered soutane in his fingers, he curled his lip.

"Name?" he rapped out.

"Félix Artigas Esperón." Mi General's dog lifted his head. "I am a priest," he said.

"You," the colonel turned to me. "Has this man been arrested?"

"Yes." I saluted smartly.

"Why hasn't he been executed?"

"He was under sentence."

"Why was it not carried out?"

"Our commanding officer . . . he was killed in battle last night . . ."

"String him up now," ordered the colonel. Two soldiers came and took Padre Félix by the arms, and marched him, quick step, over to a post by the railway line. I heard Padre Félix weeping, and I heard what he was saying, over and over.

"Forgive me, my Jesus. I failed, I tried so hard, but I failed. . . . All my work, for nothing . . . for failure. . . . Forgive . . . Forgive . . ."

Then they had noosed him, and they pulled him up. It was over quickly. A very short struggle in the air, and then he hung limp and motionless.

"You! Get back to your headquarters, and report this. Colonel Moreno will take command of your battalion."

I saluted again.

I reported in, and then I went to find someplace to sit down and try to straighten things out in my mind. Mi General? I had known we might lose him some day. But it was hard to know that now I was just another foot soldier, a beast of burden, somebody to take orders. It had had a certain honor to it, with mi General. And I worried about Padre Félix. Mi General would not have hung him. I knew that now. I guess he loved him, maybe even more than me. Maybe almost as much as he loved his horse.

I felt very bad.

We were marched out next morning, and returned to a camp some miles to the south. They were giving up Santa Lala as a bad job, for no garrison at all was left. I heard Colonel Moreno telling one of the men that the ringleaders had been caught and killed in mi General's last skirmish, and they expected no more real trouble there.

It was a long march, and I was tired, so I rested most of the night, but just before dawn I deserted, and went back, alone, toward Santa Lala.

They weren't very hard on deserters if you came back within a reasonable time; quite a few fellows went home to see their wives, or get in a crop of something, and they weren't punished too severely when they came back. I had something I wanted to do.

I found him. Nobody had cut him down. That was what I had been afraid of. So I did, and I carried him over among some trees, where there wasn't so much chance that passing cavalry, or even Cristeros on the prowl, could disturb his grave. I had brought a short-handled shovel with me, and I dug the hole as deep as I could, and before I laid him in it, I went and gathered rocks and stones. I arranged him, crossed his arms on his chest, and straightened him out then. I couldn't do much with the face; it was too late. So I took off my undershirt and wound it around his head. His beard had grown very long. It was pretty. I have never been able to grow a beard. I cut off a little piece of it, and put it in my pocket.

Then I covered him all over with rocks, and on top of them I shoveled in the dirt. Our red earth that looks like blood. Just before I put on the top layer of dirt, I took about twenty small pebbles, and made a little cross with them above his heart. He would have liked that. And then I covered him all over, and mounded the earth slightly, because it was bound to settle, and spread leaves all around. When I got all through, you couldn't see anything.

It was afternoon by then, and I lay down and slept there until dark. Then I started back for my battalion. On the way, it came to me what to do. So when I got to the town nearest our camp, I found a cantina, and went in and got drunk. They found me there late that night, and dragged me back with some others, and all I got was a day in the guardhouse and some heavy duty. I expected that.

VI

"Ten piedad de nosotros . . ."

THE CHRONICLE OF DON CUCO

I have no one to blame but myself. And I have made a mess of my life all the way through. *¡Peste!* I was born to be a fool, I think. I can go back through all the scenes of my life, and each time I had a choice, I made the wrong one, and each time I had an opportunity to select a course that would have been to my benefit, I took the other. It must have been built into me from the start, like the lacing in a gun muzzle that speeds the bullet in a certain direction. Well, God help me. Maybe I couldn't have been different. But I don't know. Sometimes I think . . .

First there was Mutti. You think of a German woman as tall and golden-haired, like Brunhilde in *The Valkyries.* But Mutti was adorably small and round and soft, and brown as a little wren. And on her lips the German language, so vigorous, so tough and harsh and logical, was the softest, the sweetest, the most loving . . . ay, Mutti. But she had German efficiency and German strength of will, and she was determined that I should be a great musician. Determined. She made up her mind. And so I became one. Yes, really. I have no false modesty. I am as good as Busoni. I could have split the world in two and eaten it like an apple. Except that I would not cross the sea again. Saints! Having been seasick, I will need no hell. I have been there!

Mutti was Margaretta Holz. She was the daughter of a German diplomat in Mexico City, and my father, Don

Alejandro Pereda, had gone up to the capital to spend some of his millions. He was a spoiled young man, I have no doubt, but handsome and dashing. I have never been much attracted to women, in general, though I have been capable of love, twice. I have studied women, though, and of course, in my work, in my art, I deal with women all the time. I have observed that if you really want to conquer a woman, the thing to do is simply . . . do it. Women cannot resist a strong will. And Papá decided he must have his Gretchen, and he did. He went to ask permission to court her, as a matter of form, and when Mutti's father denied that permission, Papá simply kidnaped her.

The families got together and arranged the wedding in time, and I was a seven months' baby. So they said! Mutti told me that I weighed ten pounds when I was born, had all my toenails and fingernails, and the beginning of a tooth!

Mutti used to tell me that Papá was fond of saying, when he was more than a bit in his cups, that the first baby often seemed to be premature, but that marriage was good for women, as the subsequent children all came along within the requisite nine months. He was pretty gross, and Mutti often had to put him to bed. She never minded, because he gave in to her right away about the music.

What got me into this last unholy mess, or should I say holy mess? . . . Ha ha! was that damned old psychopath in Guadalajara with his cannon. I couldn't resist making a fool of him. But I am getting ahead of myself.

Mutti always called me Liebling, but I had been baptized Refugio, for my grandfather, and everybody else in the world called me Cuco.

Leibling. Ay Mutti, I would like to hear you say that once more! Just once more!

I spoke German as well as Spanish; can't remember when I didn't, so I guess we went back to Germany when I was quite small. I can't remember the journey. No doubt I was seasick then, too, so miserable that it was blacked out of my memory entirely.

I remember the piano, and the violin, and the music master. He was a funny little man, bald on top, but with long hair down the sides, who spit when he talked. I had tutors, because Mutti hated the stiff discipline and cruelty of the German gymnasiums, but she was a martinet herself about my music, especially as it became apparent that I was going to be quite a pianist. She had known that I was made for music, somehow, she used to tell me, because during the birth pangs she heard music, orchestral music, Wagner mostly, glorious, glorious. She also said that my first cry was on the notes of one of the leitmotifs. Mad, of course, poor darling. But I did love music, and it soon became clear that the piano was my instrument.

At first I loved the noise of it. Later I began to enjoy the skill and power in my fingers. And, of course, I know this now, what I loved best about it was the praise, the cakes and chocolate, the kisses and hugs that I got after I played at Mutti's "afternoons."

Papá died, of apoplexy, when I was about ten. There was a lot of money, but Mutti took wonderful care of it; she moved us at once into simple quarters and did the cooking herself, in order to keep as much of it as possible intact for me. "You will need it, Liebling. It always takes an artist quite a long time to be appreciated."

It was always taken for granted that I was to be famous, and I cannot even remember when it was settled that I was to be a great concert pianist. It was just something that we knew, Mutti and I.

I was completely under her thumb, but I was masculine enough. I ran away twice, and had a shot at learning, in a week, what it took most of the boys my age to figure out over a matter of years. Having assured myself that I knew what life was about, I was content to dig in for strong, steady work, and let it go on about me. I had had my training with the greats, and even a few years with Busoni, before I fell in love.

I married her too. Mutti had been dead for more than a year then, and I was wild with some kind of longing, some hunger that couldn't be assuaged. I had gone to Milan to give three concerts, and I met Lina at a Bohemian party after the stylish reception following my concert. She was studying singing, but I could tell at a glance that she would never be successful, though her voice was sweet and clear as a little silver bell. She was too thin, her chest too narrow. Even then she had bright pink spots on her cheeks and her eyes gleamed too brilliantly. I had not been able to hold Mutti back from the clutch of death, but I tried to save Lina. I couldn't. I know now that my love for her was compassion, and perhaps a transference of the encompassing love I had felt for Mutti, still bruised and vengeful, because I hadn't been able to keep her near me. I quit my concerts and devoted myself to Lina, and loved her and fought for her, but I could not win. Was that the first wrong step in my life? I can't think so. Poor child. She was very sweet, and very grateful, and full of tender little ways. ¡Ay de mí!

It was a romantic age, and I fear that I strutted and played out my part of the bereaved young husband. I wore black velvet coats and wide, flowing ties, and a broad-brimmed black hat, and a black overcoat. All black, even my gloves. And I got some kind of satisfaction from it. There was something of the mountebank in me, maybe. And it is not to be denied that this role focused every feminine eye on me.

But, like Liszt before me, I found that having a certain attraction for the ladies was good for business. And pleasant, as well. In a way, it was the romantic in me which whis-

pered, "You will never love again, she is gone, she is dead
. . . so what does it matter if you take mistresses, or dally
with lights of love?" I became a somewhat well-known lady
killer, and, like so many of us who do, I thought I knew all
about women, and could "manage" them to my will. This
was true, to a certain degree, for music and sex are somehow tied together with strong bonds, as are sex and religion. In the first combination, they are tied to each other in
perfect trust and cooperation—one helps the other. In the
second coupling, there is eternal war. But it is exciting, just
the same.

I got myself a series of concerts in Austria, and after concerts I would never go to receptions or parties, or even take
coffee with anybody, but would stride out into the night in
my black overcoat, alone. If it was fine, I went away in a
carriage. Alone. If it was raining or snowing, I struck out
into the storm on foot. It wasn't long before I achieved a
top reputation. People talked about me, I was an appealing
romantic figure, and my piano playing was good.

I practiced all the time, and I had enormous power. They
thought a lot of that in my time. Nicety of phrasing, delicate colors, people began to think more about those things
later. But meanwhile, I had made my first mistake and returned to Mexico.

I was offered a very good tour in Russia, the Scandinavian
countries, and Germany, but I thought of the winter and the
cold, and I thought of my lonely role (I didn't know how
to get out of it exactly) and I began to brood about Mexico. My native land. I had been billed everywhere in Europe as R. Holtz, or just Holtz . . . but, after all, my name
was Refugio Pereda and I began to work up a longing for
sunshine, for the wide spaces and adobe villages, the Spanish austerity and the Mexican spices of home. I canceled my
tour and took a ship from Naples bound for Veracruz.

Oh God! I became ill almost at once, utterly and horribly

ill. The boat was scheduled to be a month on the water, but we were almost two months, passing through storms, and going miles out of our way to avoid others. Lashed to my bunk half the time, and the rest of the time unable to lift my head from it; anyhow, I prayed for death. I was so miserable that when we landed at last . . . after an eternity! . . . in Veracruz, I had to be taken to a hospital on a stretcher, and I was sick there, in the heat, tormented by mosquitos, and absolutely desperate for another month. By the time I was able to get up and totter about, the Revolution had begun. It was 1910.

Before another month had gone by, I was in the middle of it. Saints, what a time that was! I was carried away by the drama of it, the violence, the fury. And I felt joy to be in the middle of the fighting, because it was so mixed up, so riddled with personalities, with ideals, with treachery, with turncoats. What did I do? I was a spy. And a damn good one, if I do say so. I was a Madero man from the start, but later I had to change my horses in midstream and take a million chances. It was a labor of Hercules eventually to reach Carranza and join him. I covered everything by exaggerating my natural flamboyance. I was a great pianist, a musician, and here and there when there was a break in the clouds, or a momentary cessation of gunfire, I gave a concert, or showed myself about among the right people. That was when I began wearing a red velvet coat. Almost against my will, I had to become a ladies' man again. It was a good cover. It offered my countrymen a chance to hate me for something more normal and natural than negotiating secretly with foreign powers. I don't suppose anyone knows, even today, what I really did in those years, or I'd be as full of holes as a sieve.

Bueno, pues. Or as Mutti would have sighed, *Ach, so.* I managed. When things settled down at last I was called in and formally thanked, and asked what I wanted. A secretaryship? Would I like to have something to do with foreign relations? Education?

Was I a fool? I think so. Because I said I didn't want anything. I had decided to go back to music.

But after I had returned to Guadalajara, after I had started thinking things out, it came to me that I would have to give my concerts only in Mexico, or perhaps in the United States and Canada. Nowhere else. Not Europe! For I would never again get aboard a boat. Never.

Well, I had to sit and eat my pride then, bite by bite, and it was most indigestible. Demons! I might have had the wit to let the government reward me with something. For I was almost penniless by then. Still, having refused once, I couldn't go crawling back. Nothing to do but get to work, and be glad to pick up a few pesos with occasional concerts. I could teach, I supposed. I would damn well have to teach!

I put on my red velvet coat and my broad-brimmed black hat and went to call on the mayor, and I hired the Teatro Degollado and gave a concert. I was rusty. Only I knew how rusty. But I put on a good show, and I am a musician. I made enough money to buy a good piano, and to find a house where I could have a really impressive salon. This I decorated well and pompously, living on an army cot in my bedroom, and eating beans in the kitchen.

I began to get pupils. I gave a few more concerts around, I worked like a dog. I began to be happy. And then what did I do but fall in love with a woman who would never be mine. A most unsuitable woman. A woman who was to keep my heart and spirit enslaved for the rest of my life. A woman who might allow me to kiss her hand, but who would accept my fervent kiss as she did a falling petal from her favorite rose. Paz, her name was. Is. Doña Paz.

She was a widow, and had means. It might have been a good match for me, even apart from the fact that I loved her from the first moment I saw her. But there was around her an invisible shell of virtue and of chastity. I don't know how to explain it. She was not cold, and she was not stupid. No, she was one of the most passionate women I have ever known, but all that passion was for heaven. I suppose she had made mistakes, just like me. Probably she should have been a nun, should never have married. But she had, and she was a widow with one son. God had exacted a human condition from her, and she had done her part. Widowed, she turned her thoughts away from men, but she was generous in many plans for struggling young artists.

I remember when I first saw her. Typically, it was at church. I had not been brought up to be very pious. Mutti had consented to rear me in my father's faith when he and she were married, but she had been perfunctory about it. Yet, somehow, after the uncertainties of the Revolution, and the struggles of my life, I was glad to do what everybody else in Guadalajara did as a matter of course . . . go to Mass, and say my prayers. Tapatíos have always been pious.

I had walked halfway across the city one warm spring day, to give a lesson to a young woman who was lame and couldn't come to me. Walking back, I was tired. The cathedral was near and I went in more for a chance to sit down, and to cool myself off, than to reach out toward the sacrament. I sat quietly in back, and I saw pass me a slender, graceful figure, all in black. She turned her face slightly and I observed her profile, as if cut from mother-of-pearl. So pure, so shining! She had a round, high forehead, black hair, silver-streaked, rising upward from it, her nose was high-arched and delicate, with sensitive nostrils, the lips pure beauty, deep-cornered, full, and tender. A perfect line of chin and throat. She felt my eyes on her and turned, and I looked into hers. They were gray, clear as water, between thick dark lashes under arched brows. I caught my breath. Everyone has his own private image of beauty, made up of memories, pictures, sculptures, imagination. . . . Here was mine, in the flesh. And in her face I saw qualities to love . . . purity, intelligence, courage, self-control.

I lost no time in finding out who she was. "Doña Paz," I was told. "Everybody knows about her. Indefatigable in charities, profoundly pious, and so generous to young artists. She has a kind of salon in her home. There are never any invitations; you must arrange to have somebody take you and introduce you to her. If you go, she will ask you to to help some of her young struggling ones. Doña Paz. Paz Portugal de Leyva. She has been a widow for fifteen years." Like a fool, I hoped.

It wasn't hard to get someone to take me to one of her evenings. After all, I had become something of a favorite son in Guadalajara. Hers was a typical Guadalajara house, old-style, easy, gracious, rich. There was a large front garden, with a curving carriage drive from one great gate in the high wall up to and past the *pérgola,* and back out through another gate. The house was spacious, with an enormous entrance hall, and two *salas,* one on each side of it. A curving stairway led from the hall into the rooms upstairs. I never ascended that stairway, and I never saw Doña Paz's room, but I heard that it was like a nun's cell, small, plain, and white, with a narrow bed and a crucifix, and a *reclinatorio,* where she knelt to say her prayers.

But the salons, the *salas,* were ample, and furnished with the comfortable good taste and luxury of the rich *hacendados.* (Her father had owned large tracts in the state, and even after the Revolution there was still much scattered property, and there was wealth.) The carpets were thick, the Victorian carved chairs were deeply upholstered in velvet, and heavy velvet curtains were caught back from delicate white lace. Best of all, she had a fine old Bechstein piano, and she kept it in perfect condition.

It was a lovely summer evening, the first time I stepped

inside her house. Roses were blooming in the garden, and there was a strong scent of jasmine and *huele de noche*. The heavy glass door, backed with intricately wrought iron, stood open, and light flowed out onto the *pérgola* and the driveway. A number of people were arriving. There was no one to receive us. People went, as a matter of course, into the *sala* on the right, and took seats, and chatted quietly. It was the mayor, Don Leonardo Urueta, who brought me, and when we entered a number of the well-brought-up young people rose to their feet respectfully. We were presented, and I found a seat not too far from the piano. I was happy to see that it stood there in its splendor, unadorned. In Doña Paz's house the piano was to be played; it wore no *mantón de Manila,* no vase of flowers, no bronze statuary. I had barely settled myself and crossed my knees when she came in.

She was always so erect and so slim that one supposed her to be tall. Actually, she was a small woman, not more than five-feet-two. She was wearing black, a very simple dress, unadorned, but earrings of jet and brilliants hung in her ears. Later, I came to know that she put these on for her evenings; they were all she ever did to add splendor to her dress. She came straight to me, so swiftly that it was almost impossible to rise in time. But I managed. She looked up and smiled at me.

"I am so honored that you have come, Don Refugio," she said. "I am humble before your art, having heard you play."

"My art?" I echoed. And, because she drew truth from people, as the sun draws moisture from lakes, I added, "I hope to play better than anything you may have heard from me up to now. I am not in good practice."

"But you will be," she said. "You will continue to work, and to realize your gifts."

Now that was an odd thing to say to me. Most women

acted as if I had nothing to learn, and might have treated my words as courteous deprecation. Not Doña Paz.

Was she hypnotic, with those great clear gray eyes? She seemed to exercise a peculiar power over everyone. I don't know. She cast a spell, that is certain. Perhaps she was a saint. I would say she was a sorceress, except that she was interested only in the good in people, and in what they could make of themselves. I didn't know this at first, and I made the mistake of trying to impress her.

That evening at her house consisted in recitations of poetry, some of them original verses, and later, some piano playing by myself. The recitations bored me; the whole thing seemed very childish, and I could not understand why Doña Paz looked at the awkward young woman, with her stereotyped gestures, so fixedly, so lovingly.

"Preciosa," she said to the girl, when she had finished her recitation, "you have improved so much! Your breathing is much better! But the gestures. Do you not feel that if you kept your hands very still, moving them only in that last line, in those words of supplication, that it would be more effective?"

The girl agreed, and taking her place once more she repeated the somewhat commonplace verses. And a miracle had occurred! Somehow, now they had become truly moving, as she pronounced the simple words, her arms hanging motionless at her sides, and when, toward the end, her voice broke with emotion, and she brought up her thin young arms in a gesture of importuning, she rose to a moment of art.

I could see then the magnet which Doña Paz must be for these young ones, yearning toward some self-expression, unguided as they were, in the main.

The poet who spoke his own verses was helped too, and happily agreed to a few minor changes in his work.

I was asked to play, and, fool that I was, I made another

mistake. I wanted to fire up the evening, give it some excitement. I roared into "Mazeppa." There was a great deal of furious clapping from the young folk, but Doña Paz said nothing. And while I was playing "Variations on a Theme" by Paganini, she quietly rose and left the room. I was offended, and I stopped in mid-phrase, looking after her.

The young girl who had recited poetry hurried over to me, and said, in a quick whisper, "But Doña Paz always goes upstairs at eleven, Don Refugio. You are not to stop. It is just her way. She has her ways."

I continued, and I forgot myself. It was a fine piano, a joy to play on it. But just the same, I was let down and a bit hurt, as the mayor and I strolled home afterward.

"Doña Paz lives a very much regimented life," he explained to me, "but she is never lacking in the will to help. You must accept her as she is. We all know her and appreciate her here."

I was much mollified the next morning when a note, marked "By hand" was left in my mailbox. It said:

> Thank you for your music last night. Please feel free to come and play on my piano anytime you wish, it would be better for it. I am always in my back garden at 11 every morning, should you wish to talk to me some time. It would be a pleasure for me.
>
> Paz Portugal de Leyva.

I wasted no time getting over to her house, and at the stroke of eleven I rang the bell on her gate. A gardener came and opened it to me, and wordlessly conducted me around the house and into the back patio. This was a long and deep garden, sun-flooded, and as beautiful as any I have ever seen. It was set out to white flowers of every kind, white-painted benches were placed among the beds, and there was a lovely fountain singing. To one side there was an image, in dazzling white marble, of Our Lady. The only note of color, aside from the prevailing green and white, was the black figure of Doña Paz, on her knees before a patch of freshly turned earth, setting out small plants. The sun shone down on her black hair, with its silver streaks, and on the slender column of her neck. She looked up as I came toward her and bowed, but she did not get up, or give me her little earth-stained fingers. She wore no gardening gloves.

"I will finish here in a moment," she said, "and then perhaps we can talk and make some plans." I realized then that she had summoned me to do something for her. One of her "ways."

When she had finished her task, she rose as swiftly and gracefully as a girl and went to the fountain, where she washed her hands in the sparkling water, shaking them in the sunlit air to dry them.

"Let us sit here," she said, leading me to a bench shaded by a large orange tree. "I am very happy that you have come."

In that brilliant sunlight, I saw that she showed her age. She must have been past forty then, as I was. Her skin was ever so delicately wrinkled on the forehead and around the eyes, and there was a look of fragility at the temples and by the ears. There was no coquetry in her, and her beauty was, for me, overwhelming all the same.

"I come here to pray," she said. "And this is hallowed ground. I have had it blessed."

"Why did you do that?" I asked her curiously.

"Don Refugio, I have a peculiar gift," she said. "I can feel the future."

She looked at me closely, to see if I thought her mad or silly.

"We will be at war before long," she said, evidently emboldened to go on. "A war between the forces of the angels and the forces of the devil. There must be hallowed ground where we can bury our dead, those of us who will fight on the side of the angels."

I looked around. "That is why all your blossoms are white," I murmured.

"Oh yes. This is a cemetery," she told me. "A *campo-santo.*"

And in time I came to know other ways in which she prepared for the battle in which she expected to fight. But it was not her own life she was to lose. It was her son's.

She enlisted me, of course. And it is true that she foresaw much of what happened to us later. At that time I did not realize that the Revolution I had been so happy to serve might be taken into atheistic hands, might attempt to impose on a pious people a life entirely without the sacraments they revered. But Doña Paz knew that this would happen.

I came completely under her influence. I almost never missed one of her evenings; I often sought her in her white garden. I was profoundly in love, but I could not get up the courage to tell her so.

But I did tell her that I had been with the Revolution; and (perhaps another mistake) once, in lieu of confessing my love to her, which I knew she would turn aside completely, I offered her a special part of myself, my secret self. I told her that I had been a spy. This she received with complete equanimity. We were sitting in her *camposanto* I remember, and she held a rosary in her small, work-hardened hands.

"You worked for the Revolution?" she asked at last.

"Yes."

Silence, and I could see that she had closed her eyes and her lips moved slightly. She turned to me suddenly.

"Will you work for me?"

I looked stupid, I am sure.

"You have told me a secret of yours, one pertaining to your past life," she said. "I will tell you my secret, but it is

194

a living secret, and belongs to my life today. I work for those who intend to be prepared against the forces of evil when they are unleashed. We are known to each other, but we work under cover. We are tied together by solemn vows to God and to each other. Will you join us, Refugio?"

"I want to be with you, in whatever you do, in whatever is important to you."

"Then you will become my right-hand man, the strong arm on which I can lean," she told me. And for once she gave me a spontaneous caress. She laid her hand on my wrist and pressed it. I took that hand and kissed it. I hoped to make her realize that my devotion was to her, more than to her cause. I think she knew it. But she was practical enough to use whatever she needed when it came her way, no matter how or under what pressure.

Nothing happened further for some weeks, and then one day, when I went to find her there by her marble Virgin, there was another man with her. He was a simple fellow, in cheap clothes, with the look and bearing of our Indian people. A bronze and hairless face, obsidian black eyes, the lightest possible line of beard on the skin, thick straight black hair, and long, perfectly straight, black eyelashes. His features were soft and heavy, but there was much strength in his face, and a certain nobility. As Doña Paz introduced us, he gave me his broad hand in a limp, passionless gesture.

"You must know each other, since we are to work together," she said. "I am Paz to you both. Don Cuco, this is Don Carmelo."

We looked at each other. I hoped he liked what he saw. I did not appreciate him at the time, I admit it. But he was a great soul, and he was destined for martyrdom.

"I am a writer," he told me. "You are a musician."

"I teach also."

"We will need you to give concerts, to raise money for our cause. We have to do some printing, some proselytizing."

"Count on me."

That was all that happened. Don Carmelo bowed and took his leave, and Doña Paz returned to her mending. She had a great basket of linen by her side. We spoke a little while together.

"He is our leader," she told me. "He pleads for preparation, and for peace. But I know . . . oh, alas, I *know!* . . . that there will be fighting and bloodshed. I know it!"

"And this printing that is to be done . . . ?"

"Pamphlets. To alert the country people. To prepare them."

In a shorter time than I had supposed, I received word that I was to give concerts in Mexico City, in Morelia, León, Guanajuato, Aguascalientes, Zacatecas, and San Luis Potosí. Dates and theaters had been arranged. Programs and tickets were being printed. I began to get the impression that powerful people were in the movement. And if that were so, there must be equally powerful people ranged against us.

I sat down and considered my position.

First, of course, I was a musician, and it would be good for me to prepare concerts, even to enjoy the response of audiences once more. It would enhance my position as a coach and teacher, and enable me to choose my pupils and to charge higher fees. And, of course, I saw that it gave me perfect cover for a stint of spying.

I had to decide whether I would accept those concerts *and the spying*, or turn them down. Or, there was another attitude: I might accept them and betray my sponsors, refusing to do their work undercover.

To my credit, I never really considered the latter. I may be a fool, I may have made countless errors of judgment in my life, but I have never refused to pay my debts.

No, the problem for me was whether I really wanted to spy for the archconservatives, the people who had hated the

Revolution, the ones who were now gathering their powers to engage the government that had emerged from the Revolution.

But this was not easy to sort out, for the reason that many of the men (not so much the women) I met who were heart and soul with the underground movement to defy the government and preserve religion, had fought as bravely for the Revolution as I had. More so.

And I took another good long look at my part in the struggle. I had been a spy, an informer. Thrilling and dangerous, but the spy has long been known to be a good deal of a merchant, merely selling his specialized services for high pay. I hadn't collected, that's all. And I had not been one hundred per cent raving in favor of rule by some of the half-civilized peasants I had observed in powerful positions, or entirely for the exile of some of Mexico's most brilliantly trained administrators.

Perhaps I was getting old inside, as well as in my very bones and blood. When you are young, you feel that it is grand to destroy in order to rebuild, to start over, to begin anew. But when you have been shaken in battle, in danger of your life more than once, cold and hungry and lousy, you begin to think maybe the old horrible ways can still be endured with just a little dosing and bandaging and patching. Why offer up your life for something brand new, when the new thing, too, is bound to grow old, and to exhibit decay? It is all a matter of time.

The question was, in the end, was I really in favor of the clean-sweep liberal stand to get rid of religion once and for all. Knock down the churches, or turn them into schools, throw out the priests with their paraphernalia, or, if they resisted, shoot them down. Refuse to allow the people to cosset their beliefs, none of which could be proved with figures, slide rules, or computers.

In short, I tried to find my place in the coming struggle,

apart from my infatuation with Doña Paz. I wanted to be sure that I was not, again, in my advancing years, merely being useful to a lovely woman.

It was General Gerónimo Castro Bejar (and his absurd cannon) who made up my mind.

This man was in charge of the military zone of which Guadalajara was the hub. He was a man of the old school, trained at the military college, and, no doubt, an excellent soldier and campaigner. But somewhere along the line he had become fearful of his life . . . not that he might lose it in battle, but that he would be a victim of treachery. A full-flowering persecution complex. Wherever he went he was accompanied by his orderly, who dragged with him a small cannon on wheels. It was loaded, I was assured, and the orderly had a pocketful of fuses. The first time I saw it was at one of my concerts in "The Pearl of the West." I came out on stage, arrayed, as was usual with me then, in full evening clothes, but with a wine-colored velvet coat. As I bowed, and glanced busily about to see how many seats were filled, I looked into the open mouth of a cannon! The general sat by its side, his chest covered with medals, and behind him stood the orderly, at attention.

I played my concert with some trepidation, but the general had been well educated in the Porfirian tradition, and he loved and appreciated music. He sat forward in his seat, and was always ready to start the clapping, and at the right moment, too; he knew the real endings of the works I played, and never made a mistake. The enthusiastic ignoramus who starts applauding and shouting "Bravo" before the last delicate piece of phrasing has been played is the horror of all concert artists.

The cannon at the concert was fantastically amusing, in a way, and yet its appearance at the reception and supper afterward, given in the home of one of my wealthy patrons, was, I felt, insulting. I walked over to General Castro Bejar and tossed my glass of champagne on the cannon. Perhaps I was already a little drunk; I always drink a good deal during concerts—not enough to affect my memory, but enough to warm me up and loosen my muscles. Had I passed the point of safety? I saw the general turn red, then purple. Then, thank God, he laughed. He looked down at his cannon, produced a pocket handkerchief and mopped it slightly, and then said to me, with a bow:

"You have earned the right to name my cannon, Señor Pereda! Ships are baptized with champagne before they slide down the ways, are they not?"

Bowing also (for I was not drunk enough to realize that I had had a narrow escape), I then exclaimed, "I baptize thee, *Defender!*"

"Admirable, admirable," crowed the general. "Have that name . . . *Defender* . . . printed on my cannon!" he trumpeted to the orderly, who, agitated and confused, started to haul the thing away. But the general stopped him.

"Not now, idiot! *Tomorrow*," he proclaimed with great emphasis. (When, no doubt, he would be protected by some other, less dignified cannon, in the interval.)

At any rate, the ice was broken, and the general took pains to be very cordial to me. Indeed, he thought me his bosom friend for a long time.

But that night, after I got home, I did not fall into bed at once, weary and slightly befuddled and stupid, as was my custom. I had in an unexpected way, been waked up by that cannon. There were all those people at the reception —there had been a houseful of people at the concert at the mercy of that psychopath. It came to me suddenly that I could not take a stand with my old friends if their theories inevitably forged forward and intended, by force, to amputate a people from their faith. A revolution, I said to myself, knowing that I was now committed, should achieve justice, fair opportunities, health and well-being for all. It should not be used to enslave men's minds, or cut them off from all they held dear and holy. People should not live in terror of generals with cannons.

Having reached that thought, I pulled off my clothes, got into bed, and summoned before my inward eye the face of my adored Doña Paz. The austerity, the purity of that countenance, the grave intelligence and courage of those gray eyes pursued me into dreams nightly.

Do you know what I did the next day? I went to confession. To prepare myself for what I was going to agree to do.

We had not yet reached the point to which we came later, when priests were all expelled, and Catholics had recourse for the sacraments to only a few brave, fanatical souls who remained in the country under sentence of death. I found a pleasant young priest, round-faced and green-eyed, and tapped him lightly on the shoulder.

"Are you very busy this week, Father?" I asked him, as he hurried along the aisle of the cathedral.

"Why . . . about as always . . . why do you ask?"

"Because I want to confess, and it will take about a week, I think," I told him. "I should like to have your undivided attention."

"Ay, Don Refugio! Are you going to be married?" He was laughing at me, but gently leading me toward one of the confessionals the while.

"No. You are to prepare me for my winding sheet," I told him, "not the scented sheets of the wedding bed."

"We will prepare you for whatever is at hand," he said, suddenly very serious. "Wait here. I will come at once to confess you."

He returned, wearing the amice and the maniple on his left arm, and we began. It did take quite awhile, actually, and the young man's questions startled me in their perspicacity. I wouldn't have thought he would have known . . . but let that go. I had to recall a good many things that were somewhat pleasant in the rethinking, and a great many others that were not. It turned out that the young priest had more fear for my pride of spirit than for the sins of the flesh. I said so.

"The flesh is weak," he answered me, "and must be pardoned. But the spirit must grow strong. We must permit it no hypocrisy, no lies."

We wrestled through a good many points of view that I had not known I harbored, and when at last I heaved myself up off my knees and stumbled to a bench to begin saying my penance, I was, I truly think, a new man, in the ways that count.

It was a stiff penance, and not one that was to be purged by fifteen minutes of prayer. I had to promise to repeat my prayers and promises daily for a month before I would be accorded absolution.

And yet, after that first day of penitence, I felt lighter, somehow . . . as if some part of my wretched flesh had been turned into light and energy. I believe now that when I die all of me will undergo that transformation. I believe, my God! ¡Creo!

Curiously enough, I did not rush to Doña Paz. I spent that day quietly, practicing, working my scales in solitude. (I always dismissed all my lessons for the day following a concert.) It was a good day, and when I went to bed that night, after the light meal I had prepared for myself, I felt both safe and sad in some strange mixture, and yet unburdened and strong. I felt, yes . . . it was the way I had felt after Mutti died, when I had dominated my first grief. Then I had resolved to live to be famous and acclaimed, as she would have wished. Now my firm desire was to be useful, as long as I could.

I planned to go to find Doña Paz in her garden that next morning, but she arrived at my house herself, quite early.

"Have you breakfasted?" she asked, standing there in the sunshine outside on my veranda.

"Only coffee."

"Come and breakfast with me, at my house, and then we will go to hear a young man who makes wonderful talks! And by the way, the concert last night was magnificent!"

"There will be others, Doña Paz. Many. In other parts of the Republic."

A glow came into her face, which always showed pale, faintly lined, in bright sunlight. She put her hand on my wrist and pressed slightly.

"Don Cuco! Are you with us?"

"Yes. I am with you."

The young man who made such beautiful speeches was a country teacher who foresaw the violence of the coming months, and who was already pleading for peace, for non-resistance, for prayer and fidelity, but not for fighting.

He was remarkably eloquent, and I myself was quite carried away, but I saw Doña Paz's face set in lines of stubborn resistance. As we walked back toward her house, she said, "What did you think of our Teacher, Don Cuco?"

"I admire him. He is a man of courage."

"Oh yes, but impractical. Poor darling."

"His is the best way, though," I ventured to say.

"Perhaps St. Francis could calm the beast that came toward him with bared teeth, and slavering, but most of us sinful human beings cannot," she sighed. "No, Don Cuco. We will have to fight."

"You are Mohammedan, my dear, rather than Catholic," I told her.

She stopped stock still in the street.

"What do you mean?"

"They believe that the soldier killed fighting for the true faith goes straight to heaven when he dies."

She threw up her head.

"Yes. Then I am perhaps a Muslim." She smiled. "I believe in martyrs."

I pondered this, and came to the conclusion that she did indeed, and that she had chosen me to be one. A thought to cool my ardor. Well, perhaps it would not come to that.

But the ensuing months taught me that my beloved Doña Paz was right. One cannot be lukewarm about matters of the soul. As Jesus himself said, "He who is not with me, is against me," and I found it to be literally so, as I went about my concert-giving and information-gathering.

A little protective coloring was necessry, but all I had to do was permit my natural flamboyance to increase slightly. I was everywhere welcomed as a great pianist and a great artist, and I must insist that I tried to give my very best to this part of my life. I practiced incessantly, I read and memorized my scores, I worked at my music as I had not done in the years when it was my whole life. Now it was my protection, but some kernel of integrity in me forced me to give the very best of myself to my music, since I was using it for an ulterior purpose. I felt happy about many things, but this false front, for what should have been art as pure as even I could present it, worried me most.

It was not at all difficult to gather information as I proceeded on my tours. Musicians, especially musicians with long hair and velvet coats over whom the ladies swoon, are not often considered intellectually dangerous, and I overheard, and was carelessly tossed, much information that I could use to alert my fanatical beloved.

I played in many Mexican cities, but no city where there were regularly stationed battalions was overlooked in my tour. And there were always officials at the receptions.

I have, as all musicians must have, an excellent memory. It is astounding how most people permit this gift of the mind to rust away, for want of use. In memorizing pages of music, I developed the ability to roll down before my inward eye whatever page I had need of, and simply read the notes. In keeping track of information I had only to envision it mentally, in white letters on a black background, and whenever I needed to recall it I merely summoned it. Certainly I was never such a fool as to write down anything whatsoever, and no doubt that is why I was able to be useful for as long as I was.

My first tour lasted four months. Then we thought it best for me to remain in Guadalajara, teaching and making occasional sallies to coach and play concerts nearby, for a year. Too much touring might be suspicious. I was to become one of those hardy perennials of the concert world, of which every country has several examples.

"Don Cuco, the pianist? Ah yes, he comes to give a concert once a year. About this time. Yes, indeed, he will be here next month."

My concerts, whenever possible, coincided with the usual spring maneuvers of troops. And, of course, I always traveled by train. You learn a lot on trains . . . especially if you keep your eyes peeled at sidings, and watch the kind of trains that go by on the other track.

Things grew steadily worse. By the time Doña Paz's son had married and brought his rabbity little bride home to Guadalajara, we were at war. In every sense, except that the Catholics, fighting for their priests and their churches, were known as *insurgentes* or "rebels."

Fernando's wife was a gifted girl, really, as far as music goes. I could not tell her what I soon found out about her . . . that she would never be a great musician because she lacked the character. Art requires thirty per cent talent, thirty per cent very hard work, and forty per cent character, I believe. This is why so many quite talented people never get anywhere in the world of art. The kind of character I mean is the kind you cannot permanently discourage. Bibiana was born discouraged, I think. Still, she helped us very much, because she was so much wrapped up in herself and in her husband that she never saw anything else. She was profoundly in love, very much in awe of Doña Paz, and terrified lest she do something to estrange her young husband. I understood that he had married her more or less in pique, having been infatuated with some other girl in Bibiana's town. Well . . . poor young things. So much of their lives is lived out in confusion of one kind or another.

Bibiana was useful to us, especially when Doña Paz and I had to decide where to hide the archbishop. Our decision was good . . . he was never found . . . but he had to endure a miserable prison, cramped into a stuffy closet without much air, and with no light at all. There was no way to amuse him, to break the awful tedium, until I hit on the plan of sending Bibiana to give piano lessons to the little seamstresses who were hiding his reverence.

But that is the way. I soon learned that I was expected not only to gather information and pass it on to our side, but also to help in some smuggling. I had not bargained for this, but having started, how could I stop? It is always hard to draw a line at what you will do after you have entered into a conspiracy of any kind. I began to carry ammunition to Doña Paz. It was Fernando who achieved miracles finding it, and buying it for us. He made quiet trips around, and through some of the old family connections he learned how certain officials of the other side could be approached, which ones were careless, where an orderly would take a bribe. He patiently compiled all these statistics in a small red-leather notebook, taking precautions, and acting throughout with enormous circumspection and intelligence. But I wonder if it was worthwhile, all the care and prudence? It might have done just as well to gather a group of twenty horsemen, put on masks, ride up to a warehouse where there were guns and ammunition, yell and fight, and make off with the booty. For that careful little notebook, with its records of where we could worm ourselves in with the enemy, to outwit him and steal from him, is what brought us to this pass. Better to have died of a bullet, on a good horse, in the thick of the fight than wait here in prison, captive, knowing what will happen to us.

I must not forget, though, that we were able to be useful and effective for more than a year. Long after the young Teacher who had counseled peace and nonviolence and patience had been tortured to death.

And I will remember, now that I must remember something good before they begin on me again . . . I will remember Doña Paz.

She has the gift of prophecy, but it is a harrowing one. She smells death coming; she is no stranger to that pale angel, for she has felt his wings brush icily against her as he goes to fetch someone away. I suppose she knew that Fernando and I were marked, for on that last visit I made to her in her garden she sat in the thin winter sunlight, her hands idle for once. Tears were dripping down her cheeks, though her features were not contorted in pain. She was like a statue in the rain, her expression unchanging.

"I will come here to pray for you," she said. "I will be near you both, here in my garden. The earth has been blessed; it will be doubly sanctified."

Another time I might have tried to change her mood.

But maybe I have the gift of prophecy too; I knew that our time would not be long. Instead, I blurted out what was in my heart.

"I have loved you," I told her. "Whatever use I may have been to the cause is due to that."

"No, Refugio. We are all one in this struggle. We are part of each other. The bodies are separate, but the soul is one. Do you believe me? Do you know this?"

She turned those beautiful gray eyes on me, and I saw love shining in them, a love beyond flesh or pain or wounds or fear.

"We are one, Refugio."

This was my marriage, when she told me that we were one. I know that she meant that she and I were one with all who held firm to Christ, and to His promise. All unworthy as my motives had been, I had achieved that measure of union with her, and it was reward enough.

It sustains me.

I know that she is praying for me now. . . .

They are coming for me again. . . .

¡Jesús!

VII

"¡Viva Cristo Rey! . . ."

THE CHRONICLE OF JOSE LUIS

I was always something of a disappointment to my father,
I fear. I did not want to be; I adored him, and would have
given anything to be first in his affections. I wanted him
to be proud of me. I learned to be a good shot (despite my
poor eyes, or perhaps because of them, for I had good
enough sight at a distance) and to ride well. But I hated
to hunt, I despised killing anything, and bullfights seemed
to me not spectacles in which one admired manly courage
(they are that), but exhibitions of man's inhumanity to the
dumb beasts. Why should they have to fight and give up
their lives, and the horses be terrified and sacrificed in order to prove to the mob that men are brave? I could never
stomach it.

You might wonder how a country boy brought up in the
heart of the *charro* country, whose father dealt in horse-
flesh and cattle and pork and grains, could reach these con-
clusions, suspect anywhere in Mexico, but most especially
so in that heartland of the *macho* concept. I don't know. I
was just born that way.

Why did I not study medicine then, take the accepted
route for a young man who turned away from death and
suffering? I don't know. Except that somewhere along the
way, while I was in school and reading everything I could
get my hands on (despite the headaches that ceased only
after I was fitted with glasses), I began to feel an enormous
love for the achievements of man in an effort to control

and discipline his bestial instincts. I began to love the law, and the whole concept of justice.

My father was the typical country gentleman of the Altos of Jalisco. He was brave, courteous, protective, and honorable, and devoted to all the traditional sports that proved virility and manliness. I can still see him, the handsomest man in the country, so straight and flexible on his beautiful black stallion Cuervo, broad shoulders fitted into a short leather jacket, slim, muscled legs in striped homespun curving around the barrel belly of his steed, a pistol at his waist, a wide-brimmed gray-felt sombrero held on with leather thongs that tied just under the square chin.

Father, you must have prayed on your knees many a night, asking God to teach you to love your oldest son, that somewhat short, blond, uneasy, unhappy boy who hated all the things you stood for. Though not you, Papá; never you. I loved you always, and was mightily proud of you.

Well, Carlos and Eduardo have turned out to be your kind of man. . . . Eduardo is your reincarnation, in looks and temperament . . . so they will carry on your name and the traditions you loved and fought for. Because of them, I have taken my decision, for I know that I am not needed in Santa Lala by anybody now.

Mamacita was the sweetness in my life, and so her memory shall be with me always, like incense. Bibi was sweetness to me too, but I must forget her now. Before I surrender her image to those parts of my life that I leave behind forever, I will think about her a little.

I see her first as she was when Chela, my cruel and beautiful sister, brought her home to Mamacita. Our town was small and we all knew the lives and miracles of everyone there. So we had all known about Dr. Gutiérrez's motherless little girl who was being brought up by the servants in his house. Good women they were, loving and decent and protective, but it took my mother to teach Bibiana the manners of our class, and the hopes and aspirations of a young girl whose father was a practicing physician, and one of the elders of the town.

Bibi was fat and short, and she had crooked teeth, and a funny shy smile, and she bobbed her head as servants do. But she was like some thorny little fruit; I knew from the first moment what delicacies and honey were inside.

My mother taught Bibi to eat with a knife and fork, instead of a spoon and a tortilla; she taught her the combinations of colors considered acceptable by our Spanish-descended families (though the Indian-preferred tones of orange and pink, purple and scarlet, bright green and yellow, which were the shades her *nana* dressed her in, looked sweet and touching on Bibi, somehow. They made her into the little humming bird she was in fact.).

But Mamacita couldn't teach Bibi her own arts of nursing and caring for the sick. Like me, Bibi fainted at the sight of blood, and her eyes rolled up and she turned white as wax whenever she looked, inadvertently, at any violence.

I remember now one Saturday evening, about seven, when it was still light, and we were all kneeling with Mamacita in the *sala,* saying our rosary. Bibi was near the window, and it was she who saw, out in the street, a drunken *charro* come pounding along our street in pursuit of a poor hungry dog that was out nosing along the gutters, hunting for any scrap of food. With a yell, the *charro* (who still kept his wonderful seat on the curvetting horse) dropped a rope over the terrified dog and hauled him up, hanging him and dragging him. With that glee in any rough cruelty which seems still to be part of our race when under the influence of alcohol, the *charro* then thundered back along the street, the dog bumping and squealing at the end of the rope. Bibi simply fainted. However, my mother, when she looked, put down her rosary quietly and went out. Picking up her skirts, she ran, and when the *charro* turned and prepared to dash back down the street, she stood in front of him and made him pull up his horse, rearing and pawing the air, so as not to run her down.

"Cut that rope with your knife," ordered my mother, "and stop this unseemly exhibition before the homes of decent people."

Muttering, "I was just a little fun, Señora Leonor," the *charro* (mother had recognized him as one of our men, from a ranch to the north) did as he was told, and Mamacita picked up the beaten and bruised and yelping animal and covered him with her *rebozo*, so that he would not see any more of his tormentor. She brought the creature home, poured a little tequila down its throat, and then gave both Bibi and me a couple of spoonsful. The dog, relegated to the kitchen, was given a bowl of warm milk and a bed. But Mamacita, having revived Bibi and me, went determinedly on with the rosary.

"The third sorrowful mystery. The Scourging of Our Lord at the Pillar . . . Our Father . . ."

The sight of Bibi keeling over quietly onto the carpet remained with me, and I knew that my fainting, too, was womanly, and repulsive to my father. I made myself learn to stop that nausea when it took me, and I devised all sorts of exercises for myself to prove that I could stand pain, even if I could not bear to inflict it. I walked on pebbles barefoot until I could do it unflinchingly. I slept without covers on cold nights (Mamacita not knowing), or on the floor of my room instead of my bed, until night air and a board-hard couch were nothing to me. I learned to go without water all day, and I learned to fast all day too. Such exercises, when she noticed them, were permitted by my mother, even admired, for she thought they were due to religious longing for chastity and austerity, and she began to dream that I might become a priest.

Dear Mamacita, you would have liked that.

But my motives were rooted in an earthly love. I wanted my father to be proud of me. I longed to hear him say, "This is my oldest son, José Luis. He is a real man, *muy hombre! Muy mucho!*"

Yet, I never managed to evoke paternal pride in him, except for my prowess as a rider. Even there, Chela was better than I, for she never worried about her horse, and would lash her mare into a run even where there were gopher holes in the earth and small rocks that could make her stumble and even fall. Luckily, Mariposa never broke a leg. But I adored my old Polo, and would not force him, and feared to hurt him in any way.

Chela had all the qualities I should have had, as oldest son, as head of the house, after my father. She was fearless, she had the Valera good looks (whereas I took after a short, sandy-haired, and bow-legged grandfather), and she had a kind of arrogance and temper that would have set well on a man. They brought her low, poor thing. But I suppose that was her destiny. God generally manages to bring down all the high and the mighty; only He can command, only He can dominate the earth and the air and all that walk thereon or fly therein.

But I was going to allow myself to think of Bibi. Her tenderness, though it drew me to her, made me avoid her, too, when we were younger, because I was trying so hard to make myself into a tough, manly boy, for my father's sake. But by the time I had grown past the first years of adolescence, and knew what I wanted to do, her gentleness appealed deeply to me. And I remember now the very day I fell in love with her.

I had been away at law school. Perhaps my father was secretly rather pleased with my decision to study law. It is always good to have a *licenciado* in the family. I was home on short vacation because I had a chance to start as a *pasante*, or undergraduate assistant, in a good law office in

Guadalajara, and was to get a good start during the long school vacation.

Chela was then about sixteen, and Bibi slightly younger. I was already past twenty. Bibi had had typhoid, they told me, and Dr. Gutiérrez had almost despaired of her. They had cut off her long beautiful golden hair, and had worked over her for days trying to keep down the fever. But at last she was better, and she and the doctor were invited to dinner with us next day. That slender, pale young woman, with the short ringlets of bronze-gold hair all over her shapely head . . . was that my darling, plump, round-faced Bibi? It was indeed, and she was very lovely. But she had the same shy ingenuous smile, the same beautiful, innocent hazel eyes, with their starry dark lashes.

It amused me to see how Chela managed her. In every relationship of two people, lover and sweetheart, friend and friend, even mother and child . . . there is one who demands and manages and exerts his will, and one who accedes. My sweet Bibi would always be an acceder. And I wanted her for myself. But it was too early to speak, too early for anything, though I managed to walk beside her in the *serenata,* and I talked to her at length about my plans and hopes.

"Do you think you might like to live in Guadalajara?" I asked, just once. But she recoiled. "Oh no! How could I ever leave Doctorcito and home?"

But, of course, she did. And almost without a second thought, too. That was later, when I cursed myself for a fool for not having spoken before, for not having made an effort to win her. Because, when I took Fernando Leyva y Portugal home with me, I hadn't the faintest thought that he might fix his eyes on Bibi.

I had begun to practice law then, by myself, and with many very blank and disappointing days, though I was better off than most because my father sent me some money every month to help me cover expenses, and, also, he was able to direct a certain amount of business my way.

Fernando was well established; some years older than I, he was of an old and wealthy Guadalajara family, and his remarkable mother, who was very much the queen of Guadalajara, despite her being a widow and most modest in her ways, got him all kinds of connections in the businesses of the established and known members of society there. Not in the government, of course. The Leyvas and Portugals were known to be completely reactionary, and the most rigid kind of Catholics.

I had lost my faith in those student years. Or so I thought. What is faith? I believed in God, and in His Holy Mother. But I suppose what I must say is, that I had lost the *fear* of God. That is another thing. I couldn't believe in a philosophy of life based on simply waiting to find out what God's will is, and then obeying. No, in spite of my spectacles, and my dislike of blood and violence, I was a tenacious fighter, and my creed was that justice must be done, and that one must never give up. And, to me, it was terribly obvious that God's plan did not include justice here on earth. Everywhere, in the deaths of children and of innocent people, in the bad fortune and deformity and trouble that were inflicted on good and decent souls, I found no justice, but only that constant appeal for submission . . . acceptance. . . . I could agree that these things seemed to be the will of God, but they did not endear Him to me, and I shook away and demanded justice. A man-made idea, justice, but one that man can make a stab at achieving.

I was all aflame with my ideas, and not too sympathetic with my family's strong Catholicism, or their mounting rage against the government, which was simply carrying out the provisions of the Constitution.

With youthful idealism, rooted in a love of the law, and

in the hope that through law and order we might see a great era of true justice arising in the caste-ridden Mexican provinces, I tended to side with the Federal position in the whole matter, or at least to insist that everything could be settled by talks around a conference table.

I had said as much to Fernando, as we traveled toward Santa Lala to take a vacation at my home.

"*!Ujule!* Pepe Luis," he said. "I wish you were right! Some of Mamalinda's friends still think that way. But she and I . . . I am afraid I smell the blood already. I have a nose for it."

His nose was a high-arched aristocratic one, the lips beneath it sensitive and fastidious. He was a remarkably handsome young man, and there was a steely core to him which I respected but could not understand too well, my own temperament being inclined to compromise. I never did understand why he liked me, or consented to come home with me for a visit. Could he have seen a picture of Chela somewhere? Maybe, though I don't know how or when. But, certainly, the moment he set eyes on her, he was lost.

I hadn't dreamed that he would be so taken with a simple provincial girl. Guadalajara is full of beautiful women, cultured, artistic, sophisticated, charming. My sister Chela was neither cultured nor artistic nor sophisticated. Nor charming. She was an arrogant and opinionated young female boor. Ah, but she was beautiful, superbly beautiful, healthy, strong, and full of vitality. To the somewhat pale young man, used to much delicacy, Chela was as tough and astringent as a drink of tequila. And there's no getting around it, after a surfeit of sweet, thin wines, there is nothing like tequila. Fernando fell helplessly in love.

It was natural that Bibi would melt in admiration and awe of the polished city lawyer, Fernando. When I saw him so smitten, I hoped that Chela might also feel his special qualities. For he was a very fine gentleman, and a man of honor. I got Chela to one side, at Fernando's request, and sounded her out about him. She was wearing pale yellow, I remember, and from the round neck of the yellow cotton frock her high-spirited head was lifted in her customary pride. She wore her long black hair severely drawn back, braided, and formed into a crown; even I, her brother, could see that the lines of brows and eyes, round forehead, slender nose, of lips and chin, were as perfect as those of the famous one-eyed Queen of Egypt, whose beauty still bemuses us, though she has been dust for centuries.

"Fernando is much taken with you," I told her. "Do you like him at all?"

She shrugged. "He's all right."

"I think he would like to court you seriously."

She turned in alarm, her eyes widening.

"Oh no! I don't want that! Tell him no!"

"You might change your mind . . ."

"Never. I am promised to someone else."

"Who?"

"I haven't told anybody yet."

Her long lashes shaded her eyes then, and I couldn't see her expression.

"Well . . ."

"I mean it, Pepe Luis. I won't change."

We were going hunting. Not that I hunted. I hung around camp and held horses, and so on. But Fernando seemed to be enjoying himself, and he was a good shot. My father liked him.

We sneaked home ahead of time, though, and I helped Fernando get the musicians for a midnight serenade. I hoped that might help his cause. Chela adored serenades. She rushed to the window when the music began, and I caught a glimpse of her white dressing gown of ruffled cotton, and of her long black braids. But when Fernando began to sing she slammed the shutters, in her bad-tempered way.

I could see that he was hurt, and hard put to it to finish the song. But he did, and paid off the musicians handsomely too.

I gave that business up and went to see Bibi. I had it in mind to ask her to wait for me, but there was an aura of some kind around her, a sort of suspended excitement. I thought it better to wait. I don't know, now, if it would have done me any good to speak. Perhaps not, because my strange sister had sent Fernando to Bibi, as if to say, "Peddle your charms where they may be appreciated," and Fernando, cut and desperate, was fool enough to obey her and lay siege to Bibi. When he saw how foolishly and promptly little Bibi fell in love, with all her heart, he was too honorable to retreat. They were married the next year.

I went through a rather bad time then. Naturally I did not want to visit them more than was absolutely necessary for appearance's sake. I did not want to betray myself to Bibi. Though I suppose she would not have seen anything; she was absolutely bewitched by Fernando and by Doña Paz.

But Doña Paz was another reason why I kept away, and to myself. She was an unconscious hypnotist, I am sure. Something in those wide, pale gray eyes, when she fixed them upon you, sucked up your soul, and every time she looked at me deeply, in her grave concentrated way, I felt myself losing my grip on reality, as I do in an opera house or a theater when I concentrate on the lighted stage. In no time at all I go to sleep, and the drowsiness is very hard to fight. But I fought the feeling with Doña Paz, because I did not want to be drawn into her conspiracy. She was a determined Cristera, and she kept the little coterie (no, it wasn't little, it was large, and it extended, in links, all over the city) which surrounded her on the *qui vive*. "*¡Viva Cristo Rey!* they used to say to each other when they met, on the street, or in shops, or in private homes. And her motto was, "He who is not with me, is against me."

At that time I had made special friends with a man who was a teacher from a small country town much like Santa Lala. He was a Cristero too, or rather he opposed the government policies and heartily disliked the government troops which were set to closing churches and running the priests and nuns out of the country. But he was everywhere, preaching, attending meetings, and exhorting the more fiery of the young people and the women to keep the peace. "Pray, pray and work!" he begged, "but do not take up arms! It will be disastrous for us all if we fire even one shot! I beg you, my dear brothers and sisters in Christ! Let us endure, in His way!"

But he was like that other one, a voice crying in the wilderness. For tempers were growing hotter, and the men of our state, brave and jealous of their virility, were greatly moved by their wives' tears and desperation, and deeply offended that thousands of people had been deprived of the sacraments by a handful of agnostic politicians.

It was coming, I knew it. There would be fighting.

And before I had made up my mind how I would try to keep my footing between the two extremes (for I disapproved of the closing of churches, but even more I disapproved of any violent revolt against the government), I learned that my father was dead. The telegram said only, "Father dead come at once, Chela."

But on the dusty trip home by train and stage, hearing my fellow travelers muttering, talking together, sullen and full of resentment, I realized in advance a part of the truth. Not all of it, though. Chela told it to me in unvarnished, cold words.

I had then to make a decision, and it was a hard one. Should I stay on, take my father's place, lead the men in rebellion against the law? This would have been to deny all my beliefs. If the law was against the public will and the public good, it must be changed, and would be changed, but not by bloodshed and killing. So I reasoned. But blood calls to blood, too, and I wanted to avenge my father and to justify him. Which course to take? I decided to stand by my convictions and let time justify my father. And let God avenge him. When I faced up to the choice that was mine I spent an awful night, a kind of layman's Gethsemane. Perhaps it is blasphemy to say that. I do not wish to blaspheme. But I suffered, and it was like walking about with a thorn in my heart, to let my family know that I would not stay and take Father's place. I meant to return to Guadalajara and to the law.

It was the wrong decision, I know now, though my reasons were sound. I should never have left Chela to do what I was expected to do. God knows I rue it, in spite of all.

For Chela, full of hate and coldly vengeful, took over and led the men. She was equipped to be a fine leader, knowing the countryside as she did, and all the ranchers thereabouts. And she was a phenomenal rider and a good shot. She had another quality I have never had, except that I now know I may have had it in a more hidden, more sophisticated form. Cruelty. For who is more cruel, the primitive person who tortures and kills like a cat, to whom it is the law of his being, or the person who guards his mental honor and his inner self-appreciation, and lets a woman ride out to expose her life for the things he ought to defend? *Mea culpa.*

My punishment is that she never reproached me, or in any way gave me to understand that she took on a man's duties, and became known far and near as the Pitiless One because I had scurried back to my safe little rat hole in the city.

One might have thought that her beauty would have been a deterrent to her in pursuing the road my father had taken. But she saw to that. She whacked off her braids and wore old clothes of mine. She became sunburned and thin and wiry in her constant riding and raiding, but as she was, naturally, in mourning for my father, in the intervals when she allowed herself to be seen about Santa Lala, nobody thought it strange that she was losing her looks. Women in Santa Lala take a melancholy pride in letting go all the vanities of this life when they are keeping a year-long vigil for beloved dead.

I think I have a right to say for myself (the habit of the lawyer is not easily broken entirely) that I did not know she was planning to take over the leadership of my father's *guerrilleros*. But (again the lawyer), I should have known it. It was very much within her character, which had always been forthright and tempestuous, and of all people in the world, she most took to heart that dictum "Better to die fighting than live as a slave." I should have known she would launch herself into the danger with all her and my father's courage, flying like an invisible pennant from her flat felt hat and her cropped head.

When Don Jacinto sent me the news that she was seriously ill, I realized at once what had happened, and I knew then what I must do. I closed my law office, went to say goodbye to Bibi (who was beginning to learn what she would have to endure in weeks and years to come), found a place where I could buy (clandestinely . . . there was no point in trying to be honorable and law-abiding any more, considering what I must do) two good pistols and plenty of ammunition. There were rifles at home, I knew, but I took care to provide myself with all the ammunition I could. For them, too. I had boots and riding clothes, sombreros, ponchos, *reatas* . . . everything else . . . at home. And now, poor Chela would not be using them any more.

She was unconscious when I arrived home late one night. I had gone by a round-about way, and had entered the city after nightfall. The town was alive with Federal soldiers, a well-disciplined lot, too, as far as I could ascertain. Their commander must be one of the men who took the army very seriously. . . . Let's be fair. They all did, when there was fighting to be done. But many of them, out of a kind of false appreciation of their men, let them live most undisciplined lives when not on active campaign . . . drinking and women, and even fairly extended leaves of absence, too. But the *sardos* then in Santa Lala were clean, smart, alert. I was glad that I had provided myself with an army manual. It would be necessary to know the rules, and also to apply them.

I stood by her bed and looked down at Chela. Her clipped hair was rough and spiky, her face wan and hollow. Under the closed lids I could feel her dark eyes searching, restless. But she lay in a gray shadow, for she was paralyzed. Dr. Gutiérrez had given it out that she had typhoid. Nobody should wonder at this; typhoid causes at least a third of the deaths in our part of the world. He had her under sedatives, but I wondered about them. The patient seemed to be free of pain, lying like a felled log, but what of those moans just under the breath, the moments when the eyelids flew open and the eyes searched blindly in the room for something, those desperate weary sighs?

Tía Rita stood by, weeping, but she was a good nurse, for all her emotionalism. Nothing fazed her, none of the ugly and evil-smelling duties that fell to her, caring for a helpless and unknowing patient, not even the sorrow she felt, and her constant fear that Chela might die. It is a sin, I know, but I prayed for her death. It would be such a torment to her, when at last they could keep her unconscious no longer, and she had to know what she had now become.

Don Jacinto led me away after I had spent a little time near Chela's bed. My two little brothers, thin and spindly adolescents, clung to my hands. Again I felt myself a selfish and inhuman brother, not to have stayed home and played the father to them; they were too young. They needed a man. Well, I have paid for my selfishness, God knows, and will continue to pay for it, as I think one always does, one way or another.

"You have come home, José Luis. Will you take over now? I have tried, but I am not good enough."

"I will do what I can. I should have come before."

"I thought," he began shyly, "that perhaps you were not with us. Oh," he added quickly, "I give you the right to act as you think best. You are, after all, an educated man, a lawyer."

"If the men want me, I will lead them. But I will need you, Don Jacinto, and the others. You must advise me well."

He stuck out his hand, clasped mine, and then pulled me into his embrace, patting me on the back. I had not received such an *abrazo*, full of absolute confidence and affection, for many months, and it moved me.

So I became the leader of the Cristero troops of the red earth around my native town. They called me just Pepe Luis, most of them, at first, but before too long I was known as *"El Nueve,"* because, after our second battle, I hung nine prisoners to the very posts along the railway where my father had been sacrificed. I gave stern orders, though, that there was to be no disfiguring of the enemy. Ever.

And the fighting, the bloodshed? It nauseated me, as it always had. I planned our campaigns . . . most of them were raids, to get arms and horses, or to blow up a bridge or an army warehouse . . . with as much care as if I were writing a thesis, and I tried to avoid direct engagements whenever I could. But there were some, and in the first two or three I had to drink heavily to get through the awfulness. Horses shot and squealing, men on the ground with their intestines out like a tangle of sausages, the pitiful dead. The smells and the sounds were almost as bad as what the eye was forced to register, and I could not get away from my senses, anyhow, anywhere. These things had to be looked at, smelled, heard. By the time of the third battle, I was beginning to develop a callus over my senses, but my brain continued to insist, "It is horrible . . . it should never be . . . it can result in no good . . ."

But these were my own people, my father's friends, the sons of ranchers he had known all his life. They were defending what they believed in, and what they felt they had an inalienable right to. I could not any longer be one of those who stood aside to let the others bear the heat of the day and the fear and violence of the fighting, the stinks and the screams of the dying.

Chela began to fight to move a little. Brave girl, poor brave girl. Patiently, and with the insistence and the stubbornness of which she was capable, she worked at it, finger by finger, as the long fly-buzzing hours of summer crept by, as we came into the soft sweetness of autumn, and the frosty nights of winter. Don Jacinto spent many hours devising ways of giving her a little help. He fastened wheels to a padded armchair; he cut and sewed the straps that held her upright. And Tía Rita, just because she couldn't hear, was a comfort to her, because her conversation always sprang from within, and from what she, Tía Rita, had been thinking about. She expected and required no answers. Her words were as inconsequential, and therefore, to Chela, as pleasant as the sound of the fountain in the patio.

I took over my little brothers in the hours when I could be home. They needed discipline, and they needed attention. Tía Rita was quite incapable of teaching them anything, and Don Jacinto, though he had all the best will in the world, had an uneducated accent, and was mostly wise in country ways, the ways of the rancher. Good ways, but Eduardito and Carlitos needed more.

They had learned to ride, of course, and clamored to go out with me, but I peremptorily forbade it. I made them get at their French, their history, their geography and mathematics. I was determined that they must go to the university and learn a profession. They were sullen and rebellious at first, but admiring of me, too, for all young ones need the strength and security of a strong disciplinarian in the home. It gives them something to lean against, something which is fixed and immobile, and unshakable in their lives. And, I thought, with so much rebellion and disorder all around us, a firm law at home must be something they can count on. So I made my laws for them and for the house; I posted my rules, and I thrashed the boys when they broke them. I didn't have to do it more than a couple of times, thank God, for I hated it. But I am certain that it was good for them. They will be strong, stern, self-reliant men.

Except for Don Jacinto, I was alone in my work with the men. We had lost Bizco before I came home. They told me he had died thieving; they found a watch clasped in his dead hand. He was a thief and a liar, but a brave little devil. I had always found him amusing, and it used to be fun for me to keep ahead of that agile, scheming mind of his. If he had stolen the watch, then he died happy. That is something.

Among my men were two railroad workers who had managed to jump clear when we blew up the *calabozo* on the end of a train, to get the money and ammunition they were carrying there. It was some months before I could trust them, because they might well have been spies, sent to betray us all. And yet, when they came crawling to us after the explosion, singed and blackened, and whispered, "*Ave María Purísima . . .*" I could not stop myself. "*Sin pecado concebida . . .*" We took them in. I never learned their names. I would not let any of my men tell each other their names, if they had not known them before joining up. I was Capitán Nueve, and both train men were known to us as Tizne. Both leaped to answer whenever anybody yelled

"Tizne," and this was a camp joke, for *tizne* can be the beginning of a horrid curse.

There were many ugly encounters. . . . On the whole, I was a successful commander. I lost a minimum of men, and we took a maximum of booty. For one thing, I was careful never to repeat one of my coups, either in location or in the manner of planning. And I kept strict order.

Bizco had annoyed the *sardos* by hiding and giving confusing orders on the bugle. But this would not be repeated. They were alerted to most of those tricks, which had been inspired mostly in boyish horseplay with its undercurrent of contempt, which had worried and deceived them at first. Besides, they now fought our way, guerrilla fashion, and of course they had the advantage of reserves and of authority. But we had the sly and wily countryside with us to a man, and we knew the land.

But once I miscalculated, and we were caught in a cross fire. It was toward evening, we had been reconnoitering, expecting to be joined by some men from the group that had been working under orders of the commander we called El Coyote. We were riding along in the shadow cast by some foothills. There was sparse cover of tuna cactus, when suddenly we were fired on from the hills above, and from below, where there was a shallow canyon. . . . It was my mistake not to have made certain of that canyon. It was deep enough to hide a mounted man. There was nothing to do but make a rush to get out, firing all the way, and most of us managed to fight free, but I lost eight men, the most I had lost for months. I was tired and depressed, eaten alive by lice, and I think if I had tried to pull off my boots I would have pulled off my feet inside them. When I got us fairly away and we reformed and I counted up, I broke into tears. It was suddenly too much. The fighting was getting us nowhere, the people were without their sacraments still, the boycott we had all been observing seemed to hurt nobody but ourselves, and I felt, in that moment, that we had a lost cause. I was ready to give up, and after I had dispersed the men and sent them to their homes until further orders, and began to find my own way back, by devious zigzagging paths, I tried to decide if I could retire without being a coward and a traitor.

But think as I would, I could find no way that would provide an honorable escape from the footless, dreary bloodshed and dying. I had to go on. I was like a man in the first minutes of malaria, when he knows that no matter what is done for him, he will have to go through the wrenching tooth-shaking chill and the awful hallucinatory fever before there will be even a temporary break in his misery.

There was a ranch about six kilometers from home where I could turn my horse in with the rancher's mounts, change my clothes, and go in a simple disguise over to Santa Lala on foot. The rancher's wife knew me; she hurried me into the warehouse where they stored some grain, and handed me a bottle of kerosene. I stripped and rubbed myself down with my undershirt, soaked in kerosene, and soaked my hair in it. How wonderful the purplish smelly stuff seemed to me, for it meant an end to the filthy lice that somehow we never got rid of on campaign; some fellow always had them in his hair or in his clothes, or in his saddle blankets. Then I poured out the rest of the bottle into a feeding pan I found there and put my clothes into it. The rancher's wife, good soul, would have my things washed and boiled later, and ready for me when I came back.

And my disguise? I dressed as an Indian charcoal burner, and I lugged a great sack of it on my back into Santa Lala. A few homes burned kerosene, but most of them used charcoal, and housewives were always on the lookout for some from the foothills, where Indians had pits to char the *huisache* . . . a stout wood that burned perfectly with a dry hot flame. I wore huaraches and a big, semitattered straw sombrero, very dirty white-cotton trousers and shirt, and a poncho, for it was cold. Everything dirty and worn, but free of vermin. With my sandy hair and light eyes, you might think I couldn't manage the role, but defecting Irish and French soldiers, from the time of the Reform under Juárez, had left their mark on many an Indian village in the north, and men with ruddy skins and light eyes were not uncommon among them. Besides, there had been cactus juice for me to stain myself with, and it was easy enough to rub charcoal dust into my hair.

I shouldered my load and began to trudge along the way home. Toward Santa Lala I met patrols now and then. One smart young officer made me turn out my whole load of charcoal, and he stood over me very sternly until he had convinced himself that I was not carrying arms. Of me, he had no breath of suspicion. Wearing the disguise of an Indian has a special advantage beyond many others . . . one never has to talk much. Our Indians are taciturn and can put more insolence, or more affection, into their silence than most of the rest of us can put into ten-page letters.

I made it to our back *zaguán*, knocked, and began the singsong sales ritual of the charcoal seller. I was admitted into the back patio. I hoped and prayed sincerely that no one troubled to notice that the charcoal man never emerged.

Tía Rita hurried me into my room, and at once brought two big washtubs and filled them with water. There was good homemade soap made with lye and ashes, and weary and longing for sleep though I was, I scrubbed until I felt clean again, at last, and, with sheer joy, shaved, scraping off the whiskers and filth. Most of the stain remained, it had to wear off, but I didn't care about that. I was always hidden, if I was at home when one of the soldiers came pounding on our *zaguán*. We had good hiding places, as all ranchers and country people in my part of the world do . . . we have come through too many upheavals not to take adequate care of our silver and our arms, and there was a chest in my bedroom with a false bottom and a little trap door that let me down into a small cellar. There were always coverlids and pillow cases and such stuff in the chest, and even though I lifted the door, they fell back into place. The contraption had been well made, and if you did not know the secret of it you would never have dreamed that it was not exactly what it appeared to be.

While I was in my bath there came that devilish pounding at the door. Quick as a wink, Carlitos rushed in, stripped, and got into my dirty bath water, and I, scarcely toweled, got into my hole beneath the chest. Tía Rita spirited my clothes away somewhere, and so I waited out that crisis, which, luckily, did not last long, or I would have died of pneumonia, mother-naked in my hole.

I shivered and gritted my teeth to keep them from chattering, but though I was determined to endure a long wait, I did not have to. Some officer was always dropping in to make sure of Chela; they suspected her, but they never dared to lay a hand on her, and she always stared them out of countenance. She could sit up for some hours by then, strapped to the chair only around the waist. One twitch of her shawl, and they would have known everything about her, but not one ever dared draw that near. Such is the power of a strong spirit. Chela somehow both drew all the suspicion to herself and thrust it off, at the same time.

She froze the intruder, and they got me out in time to save my life, though I trembled in bed for an hour before I could sleep.

This time I lay low for weeks, working out in my mind the details of a plot. I, the lawyer, the man who loved constitutions and agreements and fair, reasonable action, had been somehow sucked into this bloody business, and I hated it. Talks, reason, legal means . . . these would not stop the fighting now. Nothing would.

And yet I could. If I, who hated it all, stopped firing at impersonal targets and picked a couple known to us all. If I killed the fountainhead of the orders to the Federal troops, the very pinnacle of the Federal opposition. Yes, that very one. The President.

You can determine now to what extremes I had brought myself. I was about to do what every cell in my body was against. But I had been coming toward it, step by step.

I was not a believer, and therefore I could not comfort myself by saying, as so many did, "We are martyrs for Christ! We die with Him! ¡Viva Cristo Rey!" Nor could I say that I would not make a desperate plot to slaughter the leaders . . . on the Federal side first . . . but if need be, ours, too . . . on pain of losing my soul. I had come to a point where I was willing to do anything, pay any price, if I could but put a stop to the bloodshed, the whole evil pattern of fight and kill and run and hide, fight and kill and run and hide. . . .

The first thing I did was play sick; I needed absolute quiet to gather my thoughts. For one whole day (except for a short interval in my hole), I resolutely thought of other things. I went over the basic precepts of my training in law. I thought of Bibi. (¡Pobrecita! We had had the news of the death of her husband, and of old Don Cuco, too, who was so in love with Doña Paz and thought nobody knew but himself.) I thought of the past, and when it was safe I sat with Chela, and we talked softly. Though I could not stay with her long, her thoughts disturbed me, for she was feverishly antigovernment. I wanted to clear my mind of everything, and then, somewhat at ease, like a housewife who sits in her newly washed and polished rooms, begin to plot. I would work out my plan like a piece of mathematics. I had always been good at figures, and I played a fair game of chess.

There were three who had to be killed. Yes, but two of

them were very often together. Thoroughly well protected, of course. And yet they had to show courage; they had to move among the crowds sometimes, and occasionally they were forced to travel.

The railroad men! The Tiznes! They could be found. I could arrange for them to be my informers. All I had to do was wait until those three were together on a train. Or even only two of them. Boldness was the answer. Simply move in, get on the train, get close, and shoot them dead. I would myself be dead in the next few instants of course.

There was one thing. Somehow I would have to work my way out of Cristero country, down to the capital, to México and fit myself into the anonymous life of the city.

Can you imagine how it feels to make up your mind that you are about to kill yourself? That is what I was doing, even as I planned to become a murderer, a traitor to the state, a regicide. That is not the word. I meant to kill the President of my country. And even though I knew I had to do it, or the brutal miserable guerrilla war, unending and daily more savage, would never end, I realized all the degradation of my plan. The degradation was for myself; I loved my country, with all its errors, and it was a hateful, primitive thought that I must add chaos now to her other troubles. But ride around the whole thing as I would, look at it from every angle as I did, struggle with my thoughts and my heart and my feelings though I might . . . I saw no other way. It was a personal sacrifice I felt I must make.

The more I thought of it, the more certain I became. I suffered and could not eat, and I vomited several times a day. In the end, still resolute, I decided against implicating anyone else whatsoever in my plan. I would find the railway men only to ask them to help me get to México, where I could hide; I would be my own informer. I would take no one into my confidence.

When I had made up my mind to work entirely alone,

I began to feel a certain respite. My agitated insides returned to their normal rhythms, and again I felt hunger, and I ate.

The next step would be getting to Guadalajara. My illness gave me a flash of inspiration for the way in which I might do this.

Dr. Gutiérrez was attending Chela, and came often to the house. He was known to all the soldiers in the city and to their commander, but he was a doctor, and he had never gone riding out. He was always at his post, mixing up his medicines, making his rounds. Indeed he never refused to cure anyone who was sick no matter what side he was on, and he had even done surgery on some of the *sardos*.

Now I was about the same height as Dr. Gutiérrez, and whereas his hair was sandy gray, mine was sandy. It occurred to me suddenly that it would not be hard to pass for Dr. Gutiérrez at night, if he were willing to lie low at his house and let me assume his clothes and his personality for a few hours.

I waited for him to come; I could not send for him. As I waited, I grew only more calm, more determined.

At last I heard a banging on the *zaguán,* and a little later his deep voice, and Chela's answer. Then I emerged from my room and waited for him in the corridor. He came out, tired, bent, in a hurry, with that quick walk that all doctors seem to have, for there is never enough time for what they have to do.

He stared, but did not say a word. I made a gesture to him, and he followed me at once into my room. I closed the door, and then I wrung his hand. "Doctorcito," was all I could say, at first.

He sat on my bed, smiled, and waited.

"I have been . . ."

He raised his hand to stop me.

"I know. One more who offers a flower of blood to Our Lady. I know."

"Doctorcito . . ."

He drew a deep sigh.

"Will it help, all the fighting and dying?" he asked, in his old, almost timbreless voice.

"I don't know, Doctorcito. God knows I am sick and weary of it."

"My Bibi is a widow because of it. And most of my old friends are under the earth."

"I . . ." I tried to get at what was in my mind. "I must get back to Guadalajara, Doctorcito. I daren't show myself openly. They know me. I am Capitán Nueve."

Doctorcito looked down. His old hands were clasped between his knees, hanging down. They were heavily veined and spotted with those "cemetery blossoms" . . . the brown splotches that the years mark first on our hands, then on our brows.

"You want me to help you," he said, flatly.

"If you would . . ."

"Anything I can do. Don Manuel was my best friend. You are his oldest son. Anything I can do."

"It is hard to ask you, for it would mean keeping you from your work, from your sick."

"For very long?"

"For a night and two days. That would give me time."

"What must I do?"

"Doctorcito, I want to disguise myself as you. I could manage it by night, I think. You would only have to stay inside your house, pretending to be sick, or very fatigued, for two days. Could you?"

He smiled.

"I stayed home, and would not speak to anyone or see anyone for a week, after my wife died," he told me then. "I will stay home and think of her, Pepe Luis. When do you want to come to my house, and how will you manage that?"

"I can manage that between patrols. Tonight. Late."

"I will expect you. Luckily I have an old bag, and I can let you have a few instruments and bottles of pills to fill it with." A sudden, endearing boyish grin touched his mouth. "It will be interesting to see how you get yourself up to pass as the Doctorcito," he commented. He rose, briskly.

"I will expect you," he said again as he left.

I had then to tell Tía Rita and the little brothers and Chela goodbye. This was harder than I thought. Especially difficult, I found it, to leave those young boys, who needed a guiding hand, and who were beginning to look up to me as a father. To try to leave something with them, I took them into my room after *merienda* and we recited the rosary together.

"Let us offer our rosary," I said before I began, "for the protection of Mexico, and for the glory of God."

Those two young, smooth faces looked at me; they held their black-bead rosaries in their boys' hands, the fingernails none too clean; their eyes, with whites shining like porcelain, looked into mine trustingly.

"And I want you to promise me, each one of you, on your honor, that you will not get into the fighting that is going on."

"But . . ." began Carlitos impetuously.

"Promise."

They looked astounded, and protesting. They had been very proud of me, and of Chela. But I could not go unless I felt peaceful in my mind about them. I insisted.

"On your honor!"

I overcame their wills. I made them promise.

"On the cross!"

They promised and they kissed the cross.

233

"The first sorrowful mystery," I began, "the Agony in the Garden. Our Father . . ."

Their voices deepened and strengthened as they said the words with me. Tía Rita came in and joined her voice with ours. And I heard Chela's. Then Porfiria, the cook, came in, and little Tranquilino. I remember the smell of the candle, the soft words, the feeling of unity among us. The rosary was deep in my heart from the time of my childhood. How I longed to believe again! That longing is the beginning of faith. I know it now.

After I had finished leading them, we all breathed amen, and I said, "I must leave again. Tonight."

"Then I must go and fry the beans the way you like them, and get out the pickled chiles and some good sausage," announced Porfiria.

I sent the boys to do lessons before supper, and with Tía Rita I went to my sister, to take my farewell of her. She was sitting strapped into her chair, her hands busy with some knitting. She was gaunt, now, and her great dark eyes were set into deep violet hollows. My lovely Chela. It was my fault. I can never make it up to you.

"Don Jacinto is a good man to rely on," I told her. "If I don't come back."

"I will be praying for you every minute of the day while I am awake, until you return safely," she told me fiercely, the old fires starting in her eyes.

"I believe that our troubles will be resolved before long," I said. "I pray God they may be."

"When we have our sacraments again," said Chela. "I long for confession. I long to be able to receive Our Lord once more before I die."

"No talk of dying," I answered briskly. "There is too much to do. I know that what business is left us you can carry on from here, Chela. And dear Tía Rita is our guardian angel."

I kissed them, and blessed them, and we all cried.

Afterward, we ate a hearty supper, and tried to be natural. There was nothing I wanted to take with me, and so, when the right moment came, I slipped along in the shadowy street to Dr. Gutiérrez, and at my first touch on the knocker the door swung open.

Silently the doctor led me into his bedroom and waved toward a chair, where he had laid out a suit, shirt, tie, hat.

"There's just one thing," he said quietly. "I will stand by you, Pepe Luis, no matter what happens. But if there is an emergency call for me, I cannot deny it."

"Doctorcito, I know that. I will take my chances. And God bless you."

"Take my horse. I usually ride out when I have a call to someplace in the country."

"I should not leave you without your horse."

"I thought of that, and I took care to get myself another one after I left you today. Don't think of anything, my dear boy, but of getting away to safety. One favor."

"Anything I can do."

"Go to see my Bibi, and tell her I miss her. Now that she is a widow, I wish she would come back and live here with me. I know she respects her mother-in-law . . . loves her, really . . . but I am lonely. I want her back."

"I'll tell her, Doctorcito. And I believe she will lose no time in coming."

"Well . . . I am going out for a while. I will come back at half past twelve. You should leave quietly at the back, shortly after."

It was a simple plan, and it worked.

I made my way far to the north and left the doctor's horse with a *ranchero*, a friend, who promised to get it back to him.

I took a train, then, for Guadalajara, found a seat, covered my face with a newspaper, and slept all the way in. I was not bothered, and once in Guadalajara I had friends who would look after me. They took Doctorcito's message to Bibi.

I lay low there for a couple of weeks, and then I got on a train for México. While in Guadalajara, I had prepared the simple kind of disguise I intended to use in the capital, and I had it with me in my suitcase. So, as soon as the train pulled into the station in México, I went to a hotel for down-and-outers who had just a few pesos, and took a room. It was the sort of hotel in which you pay your lodging in advance, which lent itself well to my purpose. In that dreadful little cubicle, smelling of former occupants, of bedbugs and worse, I stripped, attached the curious, not too obvious "hump" I had built for myself to my back, and put on my shoes, one of which had a three-inch lift on the sole.

With the hump and the built-up shoe, in simple clothes that would get dirtier and shabbier daily, as I had no others, it would be hard to recognize the dapper, immaculate Licenciado Valera, I thought. I had let my hair grow and the forelock hung down over my brow; on my head I put a greasy cap. And I had with me the tools of my new trade, which I had practiced in my solitude in Guadalajara until I had all the ease and skill of a professional. I was a bootblack. Limping along, my hump just barely noticeable, my bent back and shoe giving me authenticity, I carried my little wooden shoe rest, with a space for my rag and polishes. And under these was an unsuspected flat drawer where I kept my pistol.

So I began my life, earning a bare living by polishing boots, slipping without any disturbance into the life of the shoeshine boys who hung around the railway station. Most of us slept, in fine weather, wherever we could find a warm spot. The boys knew where there were bakeries, the oven warming the wall we lay against, or where there were factories that worked at night, the heat from their machines sending a fetid warmth up through the open-barred outlets in the sidewalks. I did not shave, but merely clipped my beard with scissors, and to my surprise, I saw one day that there were white hairs in it. It didn't matter of course. Nothing mattered, but what I was doing, and I had begun to be able to lay some tentative plans. When it rained most of us simply stayed in the station, pretending to be awake and eager for customers. We took turns at this, sleeping in the latrines, and we looked after each other. It was touching to me how simply and kindly the boys accepted me as soon as it became apparent that I was really one of them, without a home, with no one to look after me or care if I lived or died. Most of them were in the same case, and there was a gallant camaraderie among them. All for one, and one for all. We even divided our take, and when one of us had a specially good day, we treated the others to the greasy rolled *tacos* or *tortas* with beans that we bought from the vendors who trundled their wares about in the station or on the streets nearby.

I speak of "the boys." It is true most of them were very young, some only eight or so. But there were more than a few of us who were in adult life, though we were all "afflicted" . . . crippled, or deaf mutes, or simple-minded . . . a pitiful crew.

Sometimes generous people tipped us, sometimes drunks turned out their pockets for us. Severe ladies scolded, on occasion, and advised us to get to work like men and stop idling about. Thank God nobody came to gather us up and cart us off to institutions. I heard that this happened sometimes and all of us dreaded it beyond all measure, each for his own reasons.

I began to gather information. The shoeshine boys, in their humble way, learned a lot about the movements of important people by rail, and as I never asked any questions whatsoever, but merely kept my ears open, I heard about my quarry and his protectors in many unexpected ways. It seemed that some of the people in high posts had favorite shoeshine boys, like favorite dogs, and called out for them when they arrived at the station to meet a train, or to take one. Of course they traveled in coveys, accompanied in many cases by soldiers, or armed guards, as well. And yet I could see that, when my moment came, I would be able to do what I felt I must do. What would happen to me afterward did not matter at all. I was prepared to die . . . even to suffer, which is worse. I had made all my goodbyes in my heart, and taken leave of everyone and everything. I was like a leopard on a rock, waiting patiently until my prey passed below so that I could spring on him. And I knew that he would come, sooner or later, to the station.

Then one day, the smell of my fate came nearer. We were idling about, some of us working, others of us standing around, our shoe rests in our hands, late on a rainy afternoon. The train from the border was due at eight-thirty, but it was delayed and would not rumble in until around midnight. This was bad luck for us. Nobody stopped to get a shine at midnight. Then three well-set-up men marched in, very military in bearing, all wearing identical double-breasted suits and wide-brimmed felt hats. On their hips, under the tightly fitted coats, one could see the shapes of pistols; I hunched down in my corner and made myself as inconspicuous as possible. A little waif of fourteen, with no name save Gusano, had been more or less a companion of mine in recent weeks. We looked out for each other as best we could. He had the false energy, the nervous strength of a consumptive; I tried, in whatever ways I could (without leaving my chosen character), to help him, to see that he ate, to watch that he kept warm. Gusano, who had existed on the streets of México and in the station for as many years as he could remember, whispered to me, "Moors on the coastline!" to warn me; I made no response.

The men marched around, bright-eyed. One of them gave me a casual kick. Gusano was up and squared off to him before I could say a word.

"It's Gusano," said one of the others gruffly. "He has been here always. He's all right. Who's this one?" Evidently they pointed at me, for Gusano answered, "He's my old man. Let him alone."

"Harmless," commented the one who had pointed, and they marched on. Gusano followed at a distance, whining, but they never stopped and he got no customer. One of them tossed him a silver peso.

Ages later, it seemed, they left, and Gusano came hurrying back to me.

"*Sabes una cosa,* Jorobado? (They called me 'Hump.') Do you know what, Hump? The President is coming here to entrain for the north tomorrow. We'll see him!" The young eyes shone with delight, and I mustered an enthusiastic smile.

"*¡Caray!*" I grunted. "Will they let us stay?"

"Sure. They know us. But those were the Secret Police, clearing the place out. They don't want any bums hanging around," he answered, in all innocence. "The President will be here tomorrow morning about noon."

I drew a long breath. My chance had come. I had been waiting exactly five months and thirteen days.

I stumbled away when I had the opportunity, to lock myself into a toilet, to clean and oil my pistol again. All in readiness.

There was some work when the Veracruz train came in, and Gusano and I made enough to buy a couple of *tortas* each, and *tacos* besides.

I had another friend who hung around the station in the evenings, especially on cold nights. He had a little steam wagon on wheels, with a contrived oven heated by hot coals, in which he roasted sweet potatoes and long macho bananas. He announced these by blowing on a shrill whistle, and he was known to us all as "Vapor" or "Steamy." He was past middle age, grizzled and bent, with very dirty hands, and he gave the impression of stupidity because he had a severe speech defect. In fact, his Spanish was so strange and muddled that many passed him off as an imbecile, without noticing how well and quickly he made change, how intelligent were the bright black eyes that roved constantly under the thick gray brows. I bought Gusano and me a hot baked banana whenever I could; it warmed our hands and our bellies, and was wonderfully filling, and I got to know something of Steamy.

I wondered idly why he hung about the station sometimes without blowing his whistle, apparently without any wares to sell, and why sometimes on a rainy chilly night when he could expect business he would not appear. I knew he was something false, like me, and on occasion I turned over in my mind the idea that he might be on the same mission. However, I dismissed that idea; he was too peculiarly tender. He could not have the instincts of a murderer, refined and perfected by guerrilla fighting, as I had. He was always carrying around some pup with a splint on its leg, or a sick bird, tied, with a string around one leg, to a perch near the steamy warmth. I learned much later that he was in fact the opposite of a murderer; he had been a doctor, disgraced in some scandal, and had gone down to the gutter in drink and misery. Finally, he had ended up with his steam wagon and his yams. His speech defect was due to a tongue half wrenched from his mouth in revenge, after the scandal . . . but no matter now. He sold his potatoes and bananas, but also he passed dope. I learned that later.

I was determined to sleep somewhere reasonably warm the night before my quarry arrived at the station; I meant to be rested and to have clear eyes and a true aim when my moment came. Gusano and I set out, shortly after eleven, for a bakery, where it was known that a place by the wall near the ovens was to be ours. But it had begun to rain, and there was no protection there, no overhang.

"I know a little culvert, kind of low, but watertight," Gusana told me. "I guess the two of us could get into it. It's here in the yards, though, and maybe . . ."

We stood shivering in the rain, and Steamy came by, blowing on his whistle.

"Know where we can flop?" Gusano asked him.

"I've got a place. You can come along with me," he said, in his awful jargon, which we at least understood. "I'm not going to stay out in the wet tonight."

It seemed a long way, but I was glad when we got there. Steamy had built himself a little den out of straightened cans and bits of old board, and a few signs he had knocked down and carried away, and once we three were inside, his little oven, provided with coal, made the place cozy. It was small and musty, but I had long since ceased paying any attention to either smells or dirt. I thought only of being fairly warm and fairly full of food. That was all.

Steamy hopped about, happy as a cricket to have guests. He gave us each a roasted yam and boiled coffee, and, like three street dogs, we lay down on some old papers and rags in his hut, glad to have shelter, warming each other.

I had my shine kit right beside me, and my arm around it. It held my pistol, ready, and I couldn't risk anything happening to it.

I arranged myself for sleep and, as if I had been bitten by a snake, the pain began. Horrible pain. Stabs of fiery hot pain that throbbed along my whole jaw. Toothache. I turned over, I pressed the place, I groaned. I had never had such pain in my life. The searing misery exploded inside my eardrums, too, it seemed, and before long my whole head was throbbing.

I sat up and saw that Steamy had lighted a stump of candle and was looking at me sympathetically.

"Toothache," he mumbled.

I could only curse. I remember to this day the agony I felt. Steamy tried to feel my jaw, but I struck his hand away. The thing had leaped on me like a scorpion, and, like a scorpion, it was not going to let go.

Steamy turned his back and fumbled among the tattered rags he wore. He got a clay jar and poured a little cold coffee into it, and dropped in a white pill.

He held it out to me.

"Drink up," he said.

"What is it?" asked Gusano, curiously.

"Little painkiller. So he can sleep till morning. Better go have it pulled, first thing."

I drank the coffee, and very soon after the pain subsided. I knew it was still there; for a little time I felt the throbbing, but it hurt less, and I sank into slumber.

When I woke, Steamy and his wagon and Gusano were gone. It was light. I clutched for my shoeshine kit. It was with me, and nothing had been disturbed. I sat up, feeling my head, and my swollen and painful jaw, but the toothache was gone.

I got to my feet, pushed open the make-shift, contrived door, and looked up at the sky. Suddenly I was wild. It was late afternoon. There were long shadows. The President! The train had gone. My long-awaited chance had come and I had lain, drugged, in a miserable hut blocks away. I stumbled out toward the street. There was a fence behind which several huts like Steamy's were clustered, and as I went toward it I saw rise before my eyes the image of Our Lady of Guadalupe, in her rose gown, her hands clasped, her blue robe with its spangling of stars flowing out around the tender young figure.

Our Lady!

It was not a miraculous vision. The image of Our Lady of Guadalupe was on the poster advertising a bullfight; it was old and hanging partially torn away and loose. The bulls had long since been fought and sent to their deaths. There could be no heavenly intercession in such gutter miseries as toothache, a steam wagon, and such a strong painkiller that it must have been one of the heroic drugs. Could such things have been used in God's work, to save a soul from destruction? I was not so credulous as to think so.

But there was another miracle, one in which I could believe, that day. As I walked along the street, bells began to ring, and people started rushing past me, jubilant, waving newspapers.

"Amnesty!" shrieked the headlines.

I could not wait to cadge one, or to pick one up where it had been thrown down and forgotten. I bought one from an urchin who had a dozen of them under one arm and was brandishing another.

"Amnesty!" The government had worked out an agreement with bishops! The Cristeros had promised to lay down their arms. The government would pardon all who had been in the fighting. Concessions would be made. The Troubles, the Terrible Time was over . . .

I could not believe it at first, but as the night came on, it became clear that it was indeed true, and I began to feel an icy terror of what I might have done.

I remember the next few days as a time of utter bewilderment and confusion. I hung about the station, I did what I had been doing. I had to convince myself that there was no trick. Churches were opened again. The amnesty had been granted in good faith; no one was arrested. I think a week must have gone by before I drew a deep breath and dared to believe that I might go home.

I did not relinquish my disguise at once. It would have been unfair, I thought, to Gusano and Steamy and the others. I bought them all *tacos* one night, and then, when they were sleeping, I bought a third-class ticket on a train going west and north.

In Guadalajara I finally took off the shoe with the lift, and the hump, and my filthy clothes. I soaped and disinfected myself; I lay in a hot bath, dressed in clean linen, and wore one of my suits. But I suffered tortures . . . it was harder getting used to being straight, to walking on equal shoes, unbent, than it had been to deform myself. Every muscle screamed, and I paid for my deceits a thousandfold.

But I was able to stand erect and walk into Guadalajara cathedral to hear the bishop say a Mass of Thanksgiving for peace. As I knelt, letting all that the years before had been run swiftly through my mind, I felt a softening and loosening of all my tensions. It was as if the block of ice that had enclosed me had begun to slough away. My blood moved warmly in my veins. I felt strong and free. And in one glorious moment, the moment of the elevation, all my lost faith flowed back into my heart.

¡Deo gratias! I cried with a fervor I had never known as a boy, when I had simply moved through the known rituals.

I went home then, and embraced them all once more. I said farewell to Santa Lala, and to all that I had been.

Now I am on the train, going north. The red earth of my state slips steadily past the train window, loamy red earth, enriched by the blood of thousands who fell in the fighting.

Passing the train window are scenes and images I will never see again . . . my father on Cuervo, Chela, when she was beautiful, in her yellow dress, dear Mamacita, Bibi when I first loved her. And others, too . . . Steamy and Gusano . . . Bizco, long dead . . . Don Cuco and Fernando. . . .

Requiescat in pacem.

I will pray for you all, every day of my life.

I am going to a seminary in Texas.

Help me, Our Lady, to persevere, and to be a good priest.

Mexico needs priests.

My beloved Mexico!

"Requiescat in pacem"

Acordáos, Señor, de vuestros siervos y de vuestras siervas que nos precedieron con la señal de la fé y duermen el sueño de la paz.

A ellos, Señor, y a todos los que descansan en Cristo, os rogamos les concedáis el lugar de refrigerio, de la luz y de la paz. Por el mismo Jesucristo nuestro Señor.

Así sea.

FROM PRAYERS FOR THE DEAD
IN THE SPANISH MISSAL.